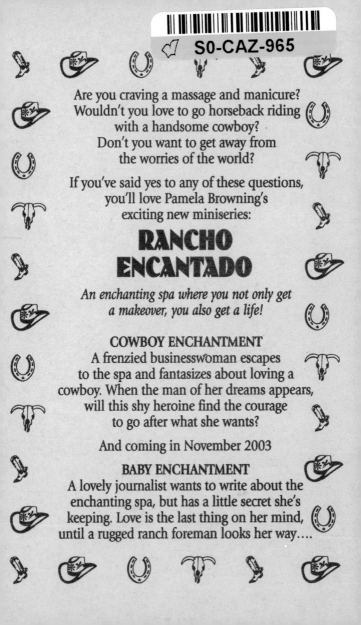

COWBOY ENCHANTMENT
Pamela Browning

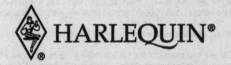

HARLEQUIN®

TORONTO • NEW YORK • LONDON
AMSTERDAM • PARIS • SYDNEY • HAMBURG
STOCKHOLM • ATHENS • TOKYO • MILAN • MADRID
PRAGUE • WARSAW • BUDAPEST • AUCKLAND

Pour mi esposo caro,
who first showed me the delights of the California desert.

ISBN 0-373-16982-5

COWBOY ENCHANTMENT

Copyright © 2003 by Pamela Browning.

Visit us at www.eHarlequin.com

Printed in U.S.A.

ABOUT THE AUTHOR

Pamela Browning grew up near the Atlantic Ocean and saw her first desert only a few years ago. That was when she knew she had to write a book that fit the setting, and thus RANCHO ENCANTADO was born.

She has never met a talking cat, but she knows what her cat Melissa would say if she ever found herself in the middle of a desert.

"Wow, what a great sandbox!"

Pam loves to hear from her readers. You can e-mail her from her Web site at www.pamelabrowning.com.

Books by Pamela Browning

HARLEQUIN AMERICAN ROMANCE

*Ranch Encantado

Don't miss any of our special offers. Write to us at the following address for information on our newest releases.

Harlequin Reader Service
U.S.: 3010 Walden Ave., P.O. Box 1325, Buffalo, NY 14269
Canadian: P.O. Box 609, Fort Erie, Ont. L2A 5X3

FROM THE DESK OF ERICA STRONG
MACNEE, LEVY AND ASHE

THINGS TO DO:

8 a.m. breakfast meeting

Conference call at 11

Prepare for the Gilhooley account

Pick up suits at the dry cleaners

Become a cowboy's sweetheart...

Prologue

Near the California-Nevada-Arizona border, 1910

The dry desert air has preserved the scroll well, though the ink has faded to brown.

"What is it?" asks the young rancher, who cannot read a word of Spanish.

"Ah," answers the elderly priest with a twinkle in his eye. "It contains an old legend telling the reason we call this place Rancho Encantado—the Enchanted Ranch."

The rancher shuffles his feet in the dust. "Well, Padre Luis, we thought it was a pretty name," he replies. His bride waves fondly from the window of the old adobe hacienda, one of several buildings on their newly purchased spread in the desert area known as Seven Springs.

"A pretty name? Yes, I suppose it is. But this place received that name because good things happen here. Unusual things, unexplained things."

"Like what?"

"Just...things. But they are things that touch the soul."

"Oh. Well, it's good of you to tell me. But this legend of yours sounds like so much guff." The rancher is eager to escape the loquacious priest, who arrived unexpectedly to hand over the land deed and the Spanish scroll. He is glad for the school and hospital that Padre Luis founded here, but he and Betsy have no need of the school yet, and he hopes they will never need the hospital.

The priest seems eager to explain. "The legend came about because of what happened at Cedrella Pass. A lot of people died there when the West was being settled. A Shoshone woman took it upon herself to reverse the curse."

"Yeah, that's great. So are you telling me there's something special in the water?"

The priest raises his eyebrows. "*Quizas*. Perhaps." He smiles mysteriously and winks. "But more likely, it's something we always carry with us, something wonderful, something within the human heart."

While the rancher is mulling over this pronouncement, the priest heaves his bulk up onto his mule. "Remember, this is a special place," he says.

The rancher stands watching as the rotund priest rides down the long driveway toward the dusty track that serves as a road. Then, with a shrug, he rolls up the parchment and heads for one of the outbuildings, unused at present except for storage.

He'll toss the parchment scroll into one of the old trunks there. Then he'll forget about it. He has a ranch to run, after all, enchanted or not.

Chapter One

Erica Strong sauntered into the Last Chance Saloon and shimmied onto a bar stool. Her jeans revealed a rounded derriere, and her shirt was unbuttoned to show impressive cleavage. Just for effect, she reached up and unfastened one more button. She wasn't wearing a bra.

The rugged cowboy on the next stool edged a little closer, his interested gaze straying to her throat and lower. He was perfect—strong chin, blade of a nose, sculpted lips—and on his head he wore a battered Stetson hat. She batted long eyelashes, stuck out her chest and waited for the inevitable invitation.

"Can I buy you a drink?" His voice was deep and sexy.

She slid off the stool, her breasts grazing his sleeve. "Yeah, cowboy," she said as her heart started skipping beats. "I'll have a margarita, heavy on the tequila."

A slow smile lit his features, and his eyes held a lurking twinkle.

"I'll have more than that," he said. "What are you doing this evening? Are you up for a little fun?"

Rain pelted the taxi, and the windshield wipers scraped back and forth, back and forth. The cabdriver

hummed tunelessly to himself, adding to the clamor of
the usual New York rush-hour traffic. Unfortunately the
saloon scene was only a daydream—a frequent and wistful daydream. And so was the cowboy.

"You want to get out here? Walk the rest of the way?
The traffic, it cannot move." The driver blinked at Erica
in the rearview mirror and lifted his shoulders in an expressive shrug.

"No," Erica said firmly. "I want you to take me to
my office like I told you."

"Okay, okay." He drummed his fingers on the steer-
ing wheel, bored.

Erica pulled her wet coat closer around her. She'd
been unprepared for rain and was shivering now. She
tried to summon up a repeat of the cowboy-and-saloon
daydream, but it had slid beyond her reach. For a moment she hated reality and that there was no saloon, no
cowboy and no cleavage.

Outside, the city loomed dark and gloomy, another
watery and dank February day during which Erica had
hopped from conference room to boardroom and taken
innumerable calls on her cell phone from people who
didn't know who she was.

Correction. They knew who she was, all right. She
was Erica Strong, a woman on the fast track to make
partner at MacNee, Levy and Ashe, a Wall Street investment firm. She wore power suits and shoes that cost
hundreds of dollars, lived in an expensive apartment
soaring high above Central Park and flew business class,
not coach. She employed a cleaning lady and flitted in
and out of company parties at the Waldorf. Since she
wasn't much of a cook, she often ordered in from Curry

in a Hurry, the Indian restaurant down the street. She should have been on top of the world.

But she was miserably unhappy.

After two cell-phone calls for her, the cab started to inch along. Finally it picked up speed and shortly thereafter swerved to a stop in front of the tall gray building that housed the offices of MacNee, Levy and Ashe, cutting off a limo whose driver opened the window, leaned out and cursed. Erica pressed a bill into the cabbie's hand, told him to keep the change and realized he wasn't listening. Instead, he appeared stupefied by the gorgeous blonde who was striding toward them on seemingly endless legs.

The blonde happened to be Erica's sister, Charmaine, and when she spotted Erica climbing out of the taxi all wet and bedraggled, she waved. Charmaine protected herself with an elegant umbrella and perhaps an invisible waterproof armor. She wore a spiffy new raincoat of a particularly flattering cut, but then, Charmaine always looked wonderful. She was a world-famous model.

"Erica, hon! Haven't seen you in ages!"

"I thought you were still in Hawaii."

"We finished shooting early, and I got back last night."

Erica, who'd twisted her ankle while jumping over the gutter, limped toward the portico. "Don't hug me, Char, you'll get all wet," she warned. A passerby jostled her so that she narrowly avoided toppling into the street.

Charmaine laughed, a sound like little bells. Irritating little bells. But then, why wouldn't she be happy? Charming Charmaine lived a charmed life.

"I'm supposed to get wet, silly. This is a raincoat. But let's hurry inside. I have to tell you something."

The elevator was mirrored all around, which only irked Erica all the more. The mirror unnecessarily reminded her that Charmaine was tall, svelte, lovely. She, Erica, was short, angular and skinny. Besides, her hair was a lank brown, which could easily be fixed, but if she bleached it, the upkeep would take time that she didn't have to spare, and as for a perm...well, she'd never had decent results, no matter what the ads said. Next to her sister, who had a stunning tan, she looked pale and wan. Why, she was paler now than she had been moments ago when they'd stepped into the elevator. She was paling by degrees, and soon she would be transparent.

"You look terrible," said her sister, who had the regrettable tendency to be blunt.

"Thanks. That helps so much," Erica retorted on a wry note. Her throat felt raw and her nose was congested, which could only mean that she was coming down with a cold. Another one.

Charmaine's reply was instant and breezy. "Oh, I'm here to help. Wait'll I tell you why I rushed over to see you."

The elevator disgorged them onto the floor that housed McNee, Levy and Ashe, and on the way to her office, Erica brushed past two assistants and one records clerk without saying hello. She waited until Charmaine had followed her into her inner sanctum before slamming the door harder than she intended.

"Well, Char, you'd better make it quick. I've got an appointment fifteen minutes ago." She shoved her glasses up higher on her nose, more a habit than a necessity.

Charmaine looked nonplussed. "What's eating you, Erica? You seem awfully frazzled."

Erica flung herself on her office chair and dug the bottle of aspirin out of her middle desk drawer. "It's the same old, same old, Charmaine. Too much work, too little time. If I'd known it was going to be like this, I would have told Harvard Business School to take their MBA and shove it."

Charmaine seemed thoughtful as she removed her raincoat and hung it on the coat tree behind the door. "What if I told you I have the solution for everything that's bothering you?"

It was clear to Erica that Charmaine didn't have a clue. Well, no one did—not her friends, not her other sister, Abby, not anyone. Truth was, Erica wanted to shuck her life like a snake sheds its skin. She wanted to stop being Erica Strong, investment banker. And she wanted to start being someone else, someone more exciting, someone soft and sweet and sexy.

In short, strange as the fantasy might seem, she wanted to be a cowboy's sweetheart.

Ha! Fat chance of that in New York City. Fat chance of meeting the perfect cowboy anywhere, come to think of it. She looked like exactly who she was—Erica Strong, investment banker. Straight, mud-colored hair, now drying plastered to her head. Brown eyes behind big glasses. Fingernails bitten to the quick.

"Aren't you interested?" Charmaine asked brightly.

"Okay, what is this marvelous fix-all you've got for me?" She sighed and popped an aspirin out of the bottle.

Charmaine grinned. "My friend Justine Farrell—you know, the former manager of the Razzmatazz Modeling Agency who discovered me all those years ago? Well,

Justine offered me a free makeover at her ranch in California. At Rancho Encantado. Their motto is Where Dreams Come True. And—''

Erica's head shot up. "Wait a minute. Isn't that the dude ranch-health spa that's become so famous? Where people claim they got more than a makeover, they got a life?"

"So I've heard. It's supposed to be the site of a vortex, a place where the earth's energy can be experienced in a soul-empowering way."

Erica groaned. "Sounds too New Age for words."

"Well, I'm not saying I believe in it." Charmaine sounded defensive.

"I didn't suggest that."

"Nor do I believe in the Rancho Encantado ghost."

"Why would you want to go there? It's not like you need a makeover." Charmaine was wasting too much of her time and Erica was becoming impatient.

"I can't go. The agency's sending me to Aruba, and we're going to shoot in two weeks, which is when Justine has an opening. The ranch is booked clear into next year, and…well, Erica, I want you to go in my place."

For an instant, only an instant, Erica considered it. She'd love to get out of the city for a while. She'd like a chance to kick back and enjoy herself as she hadn't in ages. The very words *Rancho Encantado* spilled across her mind like the balm of spring sunshine, magical and soothing and full of promise.

"I went to Jamaica a couple of months ago," Erica said.

"That was no vacation. That was a working conference. You packed your laptop, you took your cell phone and you worked twelve-hour days."

"I can't leave here now," Erica said abruptly. "There's a meeting in Kansas City in a few weeks that I can't miss."

"Blow off the meeting."

"Fat chance. This is the first time we've come up against Rowbotham-Quigley for a lucrative piece of business with Gillooley, a satellite communications company, and R-Q will be sending in their best team. Or at least their best team since their *numero uno* team leader went on a leave of absence." Rowbotham-Quigley was one of the prime investment-banking firms in the city, and MacNee, Levy and Ashe was still building a reputation. If her firm could snare the Gillooley contract, it would be a major coup, not only for MacNee, Levy and Ashe but for Erica herself.

"So?"

"Plus, I've got a stack of work in preparation for the Kansas City presentation." She waved her hand over the papers on her desk.

"Erica, Erica," Charmaine chided, sitting on the edge of the desk. "There's focused, and then there's over-focused. You, my dear, are the latter."

"This job requires a lot of hours."

"Can't you think it over? Must you turn down every opportunity to enjoy yourself? It's almost like this job is a punishment. I can't for the life of me understand why you think you deserve to be unhappy."

Charmaine would never understand. There was no use trying to explain the constant day-to-day pressure, the need to keep on proving herself, the sense of failure if she fell short of expectations.

"Don't you have to pack for Aruba?" Erica said uncharitably. "Isn't there somewhere you're supposed to be?'' She rooted around in her briefcase for an energy bar and ripped off the wrapper.

"Yes. I'm supposed to be right here trying to talk some sense into your head. Rancho Encantado may not change your life, but it could change the next couple of weeks. Why is that bad?''

Erica sighed. "It's not, although a change in my life wouldn't be unwelcome." She finished the energy bar in a couple of munches and tossed the wrapper in the trash can.

Charmaine slid off the desk and stood frowning at her with her arms folded across her chest. "What's this all about, Erica? You've never said *that* before.''

Erica ran a hand through her hair in an attempt to fluff it.

"I think I hate my job. I don't like my hair. And I'm coming down with a cold." She sneezed to prove her point.

"Bless you." Charmaine reached for the box on the credenza and handed her a tissue. She frowned. "Erica, how much vacation have you banked?''

Erica, blowing her nose, tried to think. "Oh, a couple of weeks at least. I stopped thinking about taking time off when it became clear that I'd never be able to get away.''

"Give yourself a week to get over this cold, inform the powers that be that you're going on vacation, and hie thee to Rancho Encantado. You said you don't like your hair. They do makeovers, Erica. They'll pamper you and feed you properly and fix up your wardrobe. Besides, you love to ride. They have horses.''

"Char," Erica began, but the images brought on by her sister's description of Rancho Encantado were too alluring to banish; a new hairdo sounded wonderful, and a wardrobe fix sounded even better. And it was a ranch, after all. It had been ages since she'd been on a horse. She wondered if there were cowboys.

Charmaine slapped a plane ticket down in front of her. It seemed to glow with light from within, and Erica's eyes widened.

"I've already bought your ticket. Now I dare you to tell me you're not going," said Charmaine.

"I don't know, Charmaine. I haven't had time to think about it."

"Don't you ever do anything on impulse? Wouldn't it be fun to have fun? You've given McNee, Levy and Ashe what could have been the best years of your life. If anyone gives you a hard time, tell them to stuff it."

It was the "could have been" that stopped Erica from protesting again. She was thirty-two years old. She'd given up expecting to be married or to have children, and she'd seldom traveled except on business. She had so far fulfilled none of the fantasies that had sustained her through her youth, and maybe she never would. Her life was slipping by, and she was wasting it on meetings and phone calls and reports. She had become a professional success, but her personal life was edging toward failure. The thought was enough to bring tears to her eyes.

She hid them by getting up, walking to the rain-streaked window and blowing her nose again. She had composed herself by the time she turned to face Charmaine, and in the moment her eyes met her sister's, it occurred to her in a lightninglike flash that sometimes ordinary times called for extraordinary action.

"What…what time does that flight leave?" she asked unsteadily, eyeing the ticket on her desk.

Her sister let out a giant whoop and ran to wrap Erica in an impetuous hug.

"I never thought you'd go!" Charmaine said. "I didn't think I'd be able to persuade you."

Erica smiled thinly and returned the embrace. But already she was planning ahead to the one thing she wanted out of this vacation: to meet the perfect cowboy and indulge herself in a madcap fling.

Of her life fantasies, that one was the most precious of all, and Rancho Encantado might be her last chance to make it happen.

Chapter Two

The cowboy, this perfect cowboy, was dark-haired and powerfully built. His hair hung slightly too long at the nape, and his jeans were streaked with dust. He wore a white T-shirt that showed off his tanned, sinewy arms, and his torso tapered into muscular legs that looked as if they'd be equally at home straddling a horse or a woman. The jeans were tucked into boots, tooled leather ones. Dusty boots, which he planted firmly in the dirt as he led the horse toward the stable.

This cowboy was no daydream. He was real. As this realization dawned on her, the air seemed to wrinkle, and Erica felt herself tilt toward him as if pulled by gravity. She gripped the edge of the Rancho Encantado check-in desk, feeling weak in the knees. Well, she had flown into Las Vegas more than two hours ago and had eaten no food on the plane, so no wonder she was shaky on her feet.

Her eyes were still on the cowboy. "Who is *that?*" Erica said, her voice a mere murmur.

Justine, standing beneath a sign that read NO CELL PHONES PLEASE, glanced up from Erica's registration card. "Oh, that's Hank. My brother. He'll be your riding instructor if you choose to take lessons." She tossed her one thick silver-blond braid behind a shoulder and returned to her task.

Erica's mouth had gone as dry as dust; her mind skittered over the possibilities. She had arrived at Rancho Encantado only minutes ago, and already she'd seen the man of her dreams. It would be counterproductive, she figured, to mention that she'd known how to ride since she was ten.

"You might as well sign me up for those riding lessons," she said as nonchalantly as possible, considering the fact that her entire body was vibrating at a new and higher frequency.

"Group lessons or private?"

"Private, please."

Justine checked a box on the card and dropped it into a folder.

Erica cleared her throat. "I suppose a handsome guy like Hank is already taken, right?"

"Women ask me about him all the time," Justine said, her mouth twitching with amusement. "As it happens, no, he's not."

"I see," Erica said.

"But he's not interested in getting to know people in a more personal way, either," Justine added.

"Mmm," Erica murmured, but Justine's caution didn't worry her. She didn't have to get to know him well; all she wanted was a fling.

Justine handed her a printed schedule. "Okay, Erica," she said. "You're all set. Your wardrobe consultant, that's Sue. Hairdresser and makeup artist, Tico. Yoga with Ananda, riding with Hank and…oops, our physical fitness instructor is all booked."

"That's okay. There's enough going on to keep me busy. Say, I hope I haven't created a problem for you by arriving in the middle of the week. I had some things I had to clear up at work before I could leave."

"Most guests arrive over the weekend, but sometimes we have people like you whose job responsibilities make it impossible for them to arrive until midweek. We always accommodate." Justine slid a room key across the counter. "I'll let you get settled in your room, and then you can join me for dinner."

"Oh, I don't want to be a bother. Shouldn't I be eating in the communal dining hall with the other guests?"

"I thought it would be fun for me to have company at the Big House for dinner and for us to get better acquainted. Plus, I'm being selfish. I'm hoping you can distract me from the many trials and tribulations of running a place like this."

"It's a deal! I'll look forward to letting you fill me in on the lost legend of Rancho Encantado."

"If only. The thing is, the legend *is* lost. What's left of it has been handed down by word of mouth through the years, and I know only enough to say that it has something to do with unexpected transformations. Since we specialize in makeovers, the legend fits in with what we do. That's all we need to know."

"I suppose there's no ghost, either?" Erica couldn't help asking.

Justine smiled. "Some people claim to have seen him, but he's certainly never shown himself to me. If he had, I would have put him to work."

"It's a man?"

"They say it's Padre Luis, a priest who was instrumental in building a school and hospital here. I understand he was much revered by the miners and their families. I'd like to see Padre Luis, but oh, well. I have my fill of personnel problems without adding a priestly ghost to my list." She called toward the employee lounge, "Tony, will you please show Erica to her suite? Unless Padre Luis wants to do it, that is."

"Sure thing, and as for that priest, I've never seen him either. It's a rare person who has, I think." Tony, the withered little old man who had picked her up at the airport earlier, emerged from the lounge looking as if a strong wind could blow him away. Nevertheless, he insisted on hefting Erica's bag and transporting it to her quarters.

"This tiny bag? It's not a problem for an old cowhand like me," he claimed with a ready grin.

During their ride from Las Vegas, Tony had treated her to a discourse on their surroundings. Now he was eager to fill her in on the geology of the desert, knowledge of which was, according to him, necessary information if she was to enjoy her stay.

"First you got your mountains," Tony said, jerking his head toward the tawny snowcapped peaks as they left the reception building. "Then you got your valleys, like this one. You may notice that it's green here. That's because there are seven springs in the area, some in the mountains, some right here. The water keeps everything well irrigated."

"You'd almost think we weren't surrounded by desert," Erica observed. She'd been surprised to see cattle grazing peacefully as they'd driven through the gates.

"Yeah, I know. That's the beauty of this place. Well, in the desert, after your valleys, there's your basins—they're low places with no outlets, as opposed to a valley, which is a low place *with* outlets. Basins collect white mineral deposits and become salt flats like the ones dotted with pools of brackish water that we passed after we turned off the interstate. At the edges of some of your basins, there's rolling dunes, some of 'em right pretty.''

"Like at the beach," she supplied.

"Except there's no ocean. Now, apart from all the things I've mentioned, scattered around the desert you'll happen upon such oddities as cinder cones and black lava flows from the days of volcano activity. Oh, and not to forget the strange shapes of the eroded rocks. It's not always a welcoming place, this desert."

"I guess that's why there aren't many towns. People didn't want to settle here." Erica recalled vaguely from history lessons that the nearby Cedrella Pass had been one of the main southern routes to California during the gold rush.

"Oh, people settled here. We've got the ghost towns to prove it." Tony cackled with laughter. "Miners came, found gold, silver, minerals. We've got an old abandoned borax mine over on the hill. Shipped a lot of borax out of here in its day." He pointed toward the north, and she saw bits of equipment strewn over a distant hillside.

She lost sight of the hill when they entered a grove of stately date palms surrounding a series of rock-lined pools. OASIS HOT POOL, said a sign near the biggest one, and several people were soaking in it, almost obscured by rising steam. "These are some of the seven springs right here," Tony said. "That big pool stays at a constant temperature of 107 degrees, winter and summer."

Erica took in the rustic benches placed here and there

among the palms and a flock of guests drifting down the path toward the recreation hall wearing blue robes bearing the Rancho Encantado crest. "The weather is pleasant at this time of year," she said. "I don't think I needed to wear wool." She'd traveled in a business suit.

"Oh, the temperature in the desert sometimes gets up to 120 degrees in the summer," Tony told her, "but at this time of year you don't have to worry about heat stroke. Could have some spring storms with rain, of course, later on."

When they emerged from the palm grove, she was immediately struck with the grandeur of the scenery. The snowcapped blue mountains in the west loomed beyond a series of golden hills undulating in gentle folds. On the east side of the valley, jagged peaks rose abruptly to a height of eleven thousand feet, their parched flanks eroded into canyons from which boulders and rocks had emerged over the ages to form huge alluvial grades.

"So what do you think of Rancho Encantado so far?" Tony asked with a grin.

"It's a little overwhelming," she said honestly, at a loss to explain the infusion of energy she'd felt as soon as she stepped out of the van. She could not imagine how this down-to-earth old cowhand would react if she told him that the earth here seemed to throb with a certain energy, that the mountains seemed to be bending toward her in a gesture of inclusion. Amazingly her hair was infused with curve and body from the dry desert air so that it bounced around her ears and rose around her cheeks to frame her face. For the first time, despite her aversion to New Age anything, she began to wonder if there really was anything to that vortex stuff Charmaine had mentioned.

She knew from Rancho Encantado's lavish brochure that the guest quarters were located in a series of low adobe buildings with names like Tumbleweed, Cactus Flower, Sagebrush. Erica's suite was in Desert Rose. As in the other fourplexes, all the suites opened onto a central courtyard, which in the case of Desert Rose was occupied by a rock garden planted with giant cacti.

In one corner, Erica noted, a gnarled Joshua tree shaded a gray cat, which sat washing itself in the waning sunlight. When the cat spotted her, it stared at her for a moment before quickly slipping away toward the line of eucalyptus trees that separated Desert Rose from the stable. Seeing the cat disappear so readily gave Erica an eerie feeling, which she told herself was ridiculous. She was suffering from jet lag, no doubt, and could attribute the strange sensations and thoughts she was experiencing to that.

"Here we are," Tony said cheerfully as he held open the door to her suite.

Erica was pleased to see that her quarters were small but luxurious. A sitting area opened into a bedroom with a large bed, handcrafted in classic Southwestern style. The bathroom was elegant and had a huge tub. Tony pointed out that the minibar was stocked with several varieties of what Charmaine called designer juice— mango-kiwi, strawberry-passion fruit, guava-coconut.

"You'll plug in your computer at the desk. The phone blinks with a blue light instead of ringing, so as not to disturb your peace. If you change your mind about those slot machines, my phone number's next to the phone. I'll be driving a vanload of guests to the Lucky Buck Saloon this evening." Tony winked at her as he went out and closed the door behind him.

Erica's one suitcase had already been delivered to her room, and the clothes hung in the closet. Thus she wasted no time before shucking her wool suit and digging out one of the only two pairs of jeans she owned. They were relics from her years in graduate school, but Charmaine had encouraged her to bring them.

"You can't go to a ranch without jeans," her sister had argued. Erica had bowed to Charmaine's fashion sense, which was usually infallible. What difference did it make what she wore? She was going to get a makeover, wasn't she? But if she wanted to be a cowboy's sweetheart, she'd have to start somewhere. Blue denim seemed as good a place as any.

HANK MILLING swung down from the saddle and whipped out his trusty Bowie knife. The woman was tied to the railroad tracks, a huge locomotive barreling toward her. In two strides he'd reached her. She held out her arms and—

No. Definitely not. Hank settled back in his chair and tried again.

Hank galloped across an arroyo and reined in his horse near an enormous mesquite thicket. He pushed his Stetson hat off his forehead and studied the gal who was backed against a boulder, terror lighting her big blue eyes.

He saw immediately why she was frightened. A huge rattlesnake was coiled in the thicket, its rattle sounding a warning.

"Don't worry," he said, yanking his six-shooter out of the holster at his hip. He fired at the rattlesnake and neatly decapitated it in one shot. He twirled the pistol, showing off.

"I guess you need a ride back to town," he said to
the gal, who was buxom and wore scanty shorts. Her
hair was long and blond, her hands and feet tiny. He
was close enough to detect that she smelled like honeysuckle, his favorite scent ever since the summers he'd
spent in Virginia visiting his grandparents' horse farm.
She looked like someone he'd like to cuddle up to in his
lonesome desert camp out under the stars while coyotes
howled in the hills all around.

"Well, I—"

The gal had barely begun to speak, no doubt planning
to tell him how grateful she was for his help, when his
reverie was interrupted by a baby's fussing. Damn. He'd
just reached the best part of his daydream, the part where
he scooped the gal up onto the back of his saddle and
rode off toward camp.

The baby's fussing turned to crying. Hank sighed and
went into the little kitchen off his quarters adjoining the
Rancho Encantado stable. Mrs. Gray, the stable cat, had
followed him in earlier, which had surprised him, because she had three kittens to tend, but maybe she was
looking for a handout.

"I'll take care of you later," he told her, but she only
stared at him, unblinking.

He twisted the top off a can of chicken-and-rice baby
food and emptied it into a dish. How his daughter could
eat such pap was beyond him, but then, babies had been
a complete mystery to him before he'd taken over her
care, and he freely admitted that he didn't always understand this one. Now Kaylie was seven months old,
full of spunk, brimming with energy, and it was all he
could do to keep up with her. Working full-time didn't
help, but he was lucky that Justine had allowed him to

stay on here, which meant he was provided with a home, a job and a baby-sitter. In turn, he tried to do as much as he could around the ranch to help her out.

He approached the alcove off the bedroom. Kaylie stopped crying when she saw him and began to pedal her legs energetically. When he grinned at her, she grinned back, and Hank's heart went soft and warm with love for her.

He picked Kaylie up, straightening her playsuit as she settled into his arms next to his heart. She gazed up at his face with expectant round eyes.

"How's my girl, huh? Ready for your dinner? And then I've got to get back to work. I've got to go out and teach another city slicker how to ride."

Kaylie snuggled her face into his neck, and he inhaled the sweet talcum-powder smell of her. He hadn't known that it was possible to love a child so much, that was the truth of it. And maybe, if his ex-wife hadn't died so tragically, he never would have. He had certainly never wished for anything bad to happen to Anne-Marie, but his relationship with Kaylie would never have come about while Anne-Marie was alive. She had not only moved here from Chicago, where they had lived when they were married, but had been adamant that she didn't want Hank in their lives. It had been an awkward situation, considering that his sister Justine was Anne-Marie's best friend.

He inserted Kaylie into her high chair and pulled a kitchen chair up in front of her.

"Okay, cutie, open up. Over the teeth, past the gums, look out, tummy, here it comes," he said, spooning up a bit of food. Kaylie opened her mouth wide to accept the spoon, looking like a hungry little bird.

His feelings for Kaylie made all the rest of it worthwhile—his displacement from home, the heavy workload, the lack of someone special in his life.

Oops, correction.

"*You're* someone special in my life," he told Kaylie, speaking past the lump that knotted in his throat whenever he thought about how lonely he was. "You sure are."

At that, Kaylie blew bubbles. The drollness of her action lifted his spirits considerably.

He finished feeding Kaylie and handed her over to Paloma, her baby-sitter, who'd just returned from using the washer and dryer at the Big House. Then he headed back to the riding ring to give his next lesson. He might be down, but he certainly wasn't out. Not by a long shot, and not as long as he could create fantasies in his mind to help ride him over the rough spots.

KEEPING IN MIND that she was going to meet Justine for dinner, Erica added a beige linen blouse to her jeans, which were dismayingly too big. She grasped a clump of the extra fabric around her waist, trying to figure out how many pounds she'd lost since she'd worn them last. Ten? Fifteen? Chalk it up to her hectic lifestyle. Sighing, she released the fabric so that the jeans hung loosely on her hips.

She marveled at the improvement of her hair, which felt not at all like her own now that it sprang upward and outward from her scalp. Still, her reflection in the mirror didn't offer a whole lot of reassurance. She wore no makeup.

Even though she already felt more relaxed, she looked tense and weary, even exhausted. She ditched her clip earrings, which hurt her ears, but decided not to remove the gold disc bearing her initials that she wore on a chain around her neck. It had been a present from Charmaine, who loved jewelry and had brought it back from a job in Italy. She decided that she would take a piece of turquoise-and-silver jewelry back to Charmaine when she returned to New York. Charmaine loved native-made Indian pieces.

Tomorrow she would begin her makeover. Was she expecting a miracle? To look like Charmaine, for instance? No. Definitely not. Anyway, she was aiming for a more voluptuous look than Charmaine's, however that might be accomplished.

Defiantly she shoved her glasses higher on the bridge of her nose and headed for the stable to check out the horses, which would give her something to do before she showed up for dinner. Perhaps she would even run into the cowboy. *Her* cowboy.

Consulting the map of the property that was printed in the back of her schedule, Erica walked along the lane between the two rows of eucalyptus trees until she reached the stable. She'd barely entered the shadowy interior, redolent with the distinctive familiar odors of hay, saddle leather, feed and horse when she heard a curse from one of the stalls at the other end.

"Damn," said a husky male voice. "Don't I have enough to do with Kaylie and a full load of students and refurbishing the buildings, not to mention working with that rapscallion horse of yours?"

"Erica is Char's sister," replied a voice that Erica immediately identified as Justine's. "You can fit her in. And Sebastian is not a rapscallion horse, as you so delicately put it. He's misunderstood, that's all."

Erica shrank into the shadows beside the door to the tack room, unwilling to move for fear her presence would be detected. A gray cat, the same one she'd noticed beneath the Joshua tree outside her suite, materialized from behind a half-filled feed sack and sat staring up at her without blinking. She willed it to go away, but it didn't.

"Sebastian is a handful and the bane of my existence. Even Cord McCall, who knows a lot about horses, has given up on him."

"You have no intention of giving up on Sebastian, Hank. Those years of college vacations spent working on a Texas ranch have served you well. Anyway, let's keep this conversation on point. We were talking about Erica Strong."

"I can fit her into a group lesson, but I told you I couldn't take any more private students," the man said. Erica peeked around a post and saw that the speaker was none other than Hank.

"I consider Erica a personal friend, and she signed up for private lessons. Listen, Hank, you'd better behave yourself. I won't have you being rude to my guests."

"I'm not rude."

"That Ferguson woman from Michigan insisted on leaving because of something you said."

"She came on to me. I told her to back off."

"That's not her story."

"Look, Justine, there are two types of women who come to Rancho Encantado looking to improve their lives. One type hauls in a complete wardrobe in matched Louis Vuitton suitcases. The other kind arrives with a cell phone clamped to her ear and a cigarette in her mouth. Deenie Ferguson was the former, and this Erica person sounds like the latter. It's the type I like the least.''

"I happen to know that Erica doesn't smoke, and there wasn't a cell phone in sight. Not that she'd be allowed to use it, anyway. Not that she'd be able to use it in the valley, either. You're being pigheaded and unreasonable."

"And you're not?"

Justine sounded extremely exasperated. "You know, Hank, I sympathize with what you've been through. It wasn't easy, that whole business about Anne-Marie and now having Kaylie to look after. But I need your cooperation, and besides, it wouldn't hurt you to socialize more. It would be good for you, good for business."

He let out an explosive sigh. "All right, Justine. You win. You call the shots around here." His words held a bitter edge.

"That's right," Justine said levelly.

"I can fit this Strong woman in at five every day. That's the best I can do. Even then the lessons will be cut short because I have to get back to Kaylie before Paloma leaves at suppertime."

"Fine. That works for me."

Erica heard the slam of a stall door. When she peered around the post that screened her from view, she saw Justine's tall figure striding toward the Big House, her braid swinging behind her.

Erica meant to tiptoe out of the stable unnoticed, but her shoulder caught a bridle strap where it was suspended from a hook on the post, and the bridle fell to the floor. Immediately the cowboy swiveled around and peered through the gloom toward the noise. He spotted

Erica right away, frozen as she was in embarrassment at being caught eavesdropping.

"What was that noise? And who the hell are you?" he growled, staring at her across the length of the stable floor.

In one of the stalls a horse nickered, and a couple of others nosed their faces over the tops of their doors. The gray cat said, *Now you've done it.* Before Erica could register her utter incredulity at the phenomenon of a talking cat, it turned and slinked into the tack room.

Never mind the cat's talking; Erica was even more unnerved by the man's anger. "A...a bridle fell off the hook." She jerked her head toward the post where it had hung.

"So why don't you pick it up?"

"I'm going to." She bent and scooped the bridle up from the floor, dropping it again in her haste. The man started toward her, looming tall in the slanting light that fell across his features. As he drew closer, Erica saw that she had been right: he was an incredibly handsome man. His hair was a rich brown, the color of mahogany, and his eyes were a deep cerulean blue, the blue of the deep part of the ocean, the blue of the sky in the hours before dawn. Abs like a washboard, even as seen through his T-shirt. Thighs muscular and outlined perfectly by snug, faded jeans. He radiated a rugged masculinity that put her in mind of Clint Eastwood in his younger days. She drew in her breath sharply as a slow heat radiated through her in recognition of the man's appeal. It was overwhelmingly sexual, that appeal, sexual and vibrating with a kind of slow-simmering energy beneath the surface.

His eyes held hers as he bent with a ripple of toned

muscles to pick up the bridle. "You didn't answer the second part of my question. Who are you?"

She must have inhaled some of the dust stirred up by the falling bridle, because when she tried to speak, the words caught in her throat. "Er—Erica. Erica Strong," she stammered, feeling foolish and out of place. She, who could chair a meeting of financial wizards with aplomb, who could field three phone calls at once and take notes simultaneously on all of them, was totally unhinged by the stern gaze of this handsome cowboy. She wiped damp palms on her jeans, hoping he wouldn't notice.

But he did. His gaze moved upward, taking in the loose jeans, the wrinkled blouse, his expression intense and slightly mocking. "Oh. My new student," he said with barely concealed distaste.

"I…well, I did sign up for lessons." She knew how stupid she must sound, how gauche and unsophisticated.

He continued to look her over, not bothering to hide his disdain. She knew she appeared mousy and unappealing, and worst of all, he was the cowboy she had marked for her own, and his first and perhaps lasting impression of her was of an unremarkable woman who shrank into the shadows and appeared less than confident in herself.

She almost turned and ran, but something made her hold her ground. Maybe it was because she had never run from a confrontation in her career, and maybe it was because she refused to show this man, her ideal man, that he intimidated her.

"You're on line for a private lesson tomorrow at five in the afternoon," he said none too cheerfully.

Her head tilted upward a notch even as her heart began pounding. "Yes. I'll see you then," she said coolly before pivoting and walking smartly out of the stable.

She thought she felt his gaze on her inconsiderable backside as she retreated toward the Big House, but then she decided it must be her imagination.

This cowboy, this Hank who was Justine's brother, clearly found nothing to catch his interest in either her looks or comportment. He didn't welcome the addition of her lesson to what he considered a too-busy schedule. She was an annoyance, a responsibility, a bother. And he had made it clear that he found her downright unattractive.

Disappointment prickled behind her eyes like unshed tears; the man was not what she'd expected in a cowboy, *her* cowboy. The realization was almost, but not enough, to send her skedaddling back to New York without a makeover. Without her dignity. And without a man.

But that would not do. She was going to live out her fantasy at Rancho Encantado. She was going to have a fling with her cowboy if it was the last thing she did. And there was no doubt in her mind that it would be this cowboy and no other, if only because she was not in the habit of giving in to defeat.

AFTER HER RETREAT, Hank ran a hand across the back of his neck as he was prone to do in exasperating times. "Doesn't look to me like this Erica Strong is going to be a whole lot of fun," he said to his favorite mount, Whip, who nuzzled his chest in hopes of finding a sugar cube.

Hank produced the sugar from the pocket of his jeans and stood stroking Whip's neck for a moment. It amused him that his new riding student had been so nervous in his presence. She'd looked as if she were about to jump out of her skin when he first spoke to her, and although she'd recovered in the end, she'd put distance between them as soon as she could. He didn't need another riding student, and he didn't think they were going to get along, but he quickly reminded himself that if it wasn't for people like her, he wouldn't have a job here.

Well, he had another job. That is, if he wanted to return to it. But he and Justine had decided that losing her mother had been upheaval enough in Kaylie's life and that having to part so soon from her familiar surroundings would only cause problems. It would be better, they'd reasoned, for Paloma, her caregiver, to remain a constant in his small daughter's routine until Hank had time to bond with Kaylie, the daughter he'd met only after the tragedy that took his ex-wife's life.

Never mind that Hank's girlfriend kept asking when he planned to return to her and to his real job. Never mind that he and Justine often argued in the perverse way of siblings about things that probably weren't, in the long run, all that important.

Besides, he was enjoying his new life as a cowboy. He liked living in the tradition of his childhood heroes—John Wayne, Gary Cooper, Roy Rogers—all of whom he'd seen over and over again in reruns on TV. It made him laugh to think about how stuffy and insufferable he must have been when he wore a suit to work every day. And to tell the truth, he could hardly recall what Lizette, his girlfriend, looked like. You'd think he would. You'd think that after seven or eight months with her, everything about Lizette would be engraved on his mind. Hair color, eye color—the works.

Were her eyes blue? He couldn't remember. If he

worked up the nerve, maybe he'd ask her the next time he phoned her. Which should be soon, but lately he found that his heart wasn't in those awkward phone calls during which he had to make himself listen to Lizette's prattling on about rebirthing sessions and her job as a life coach and lunches with her friends. He longed to tell her how cute Kaylie was when she laughed and about the way the sunset turned the distant hills to molten gold, and once he had tried to describe how difficult it was to find the right kind of disposable diapers at the local grocery store. Lizette had evinced only scant interest of his frustration over the situation and then had continued talking about whatever it was that she'd been talking about before he'd changed the subject.

"I guess I'm losing my touch with women, huh, old man?" he said to Whip, who eyed him hopefully as if another sugar cube might be forthcoming.

"Well, there's one female who's always glad to have me around," he said, and then he closed the stall door and went to relieve Paloma of her duties. Kaylie, it seemed, was his only love right now, and now that he thought about it, that was okay, too.

As SHE WALKED slowly toward the Big House, Erica reflected that Charmaine hadn't thought much of her longing to look like a cowboy's sweetheart.

"Forget the cowboy," Charmaine had said, chucking shorts and halter tops into her suitcase as she packed for her trip to Aruba. "You need someone as intelligent as you are."

Erica, who had been chugging cold medicine and was feeling woozy as a result, had been sprawled across her sister's bed reading the Rancho Encantado brochure.

"How am I going to find an intelligent man when there aren't any?" she asked, looking up from pictures of tanned blondes reclining around a swimming pool. "All the ones my age are chasing nineteen-year-old table dancers, and how intelligent is that?"

"I told you that you should stop being so opinionated. It's okay to run the show at McNee, Levy and Ashe, but in your personal relationships, you need to let the men call the shots once in a while."

"Aargh! Like I'd want to. Give me a break, Charmaine."

"You haven't met the right guy yet, obviously. When you do, you'll want to nurture. You'll want to defer."

Erica ignored this unlikely pronouncement. "You know, I think I'll take my new digital camera. I used to be a pretty good photographer, and maybe there'll be some good photo ops in the desert. Animals and such. And maybe they don't have table dancers in country-and-western roadhouses. What do you think?"

What Charmaine thought was indicated by the meaningful arch of her eyebrows, which had ended the discussion.

Regarding the question of finding a man, any man, intelligent or otherwise, Erica had long ago given up. When she was younger, of course, she'd always expected that something and someone wonderful and exciting was about to happen any minute. All she'd have to do was go along doing everything right and suddenly the perfect man would appear. Or maybe it was the perfect job, or the perfect pair of panty hose...

These days Erica was older and wiser. She realized that nothing special ever happened in her life, that day after day offered only more irritating sameness, and that was why she'd come to Rancho Encantado.

So what if she'd gotten off on the wrong foot with the right cowboy? There was time to fix it, starting tomorrow after her consultation with a hairstylist and makeup artist. She and Justine could talk about her makeover over dinner, and maybe she'd forget the fact that her cowboy seemed less than enamored of her after their first meeting.

That didn't mean he wouldn't come around eventually. After all, wasn't this Rancho Encantado, where dreams came true? Uh-huh.

Justine answered her knock at the door of the Big House right away, smiling and holding the door open wide. She wore a simple gray dress that hugged her slim figure, showing off her wide shoulders and narrow hips, and she was accompanied by a scruffy tail-wagging yellow dog.

"I hope I'm not too early," Erica said. She indicated the dog. "Who's your friend?"

"That's Murphy. And you're not early," Justine said, giving one last nudge to the vase of hosta daisies standing on the foyer console.

Erica bent to scratch Murphy behind the ears. "The flowers are beautiful."

"I have them shipped in from Mexico every week," Justine said.

"What a sweet dog," Erica murmured as Murphy repositioned himself, the better to be scratched. She liked dogs, and this one had big brown eyes and a wide comical smile.

"Murphy's way too old to chase cattle anymore, so I

took him in,'' Justine replied. "He's a bothersome old
cur, but we suit each other.''

"He's a charmer. Would you mind if I took pictures
of him sometime?''

"Of Murphy? Of course not. He'd be flattered. Come
on, I'll show you around.''

Justine hooked an arm through Erica's and led her into
the living room, which was faced by a gallery holding
shelves of books on two walls. The walls were painted
in cooling colors—sage-green, melon, taupe. Above the
living room, a skylight framed the clear desert sky.
Large Mexican tile gleamed underfoot, and a rock fireplace dominated one wall. A long hall led to three bedrooms, one of which contained a child's crib.

"That's for my niece when she visits," Justine explained, but she didn't elaborate.

After they were seated with Murphy curled at their
feet, Justine wanted to know about Charmaine—what
she was doing, where she was working, the buzz in the
industry. Justine had left the modeling agency after she'd
bought Rancho Encantado with money she'd saved from
her own modeling career, and she still kept up with the
business.

Erica filled Justine in about Charmaine's career, and
then she asked what she could expect as a guest during
the next week.

Justine ticked the activities off on her fingers. "Mud
baths, facials, aromatherapy, yoga, swimming, riding.
Also sunbathing and socializing, if you want. And feel
free to sleep as late as you like.''

"I've always been an early riser.''

Justine smiled. "At Rancho Encantado, people who
ordinarily wake up early, sleep later. Those who eat a

lot go on a diet, and those who don't, stuff themselves with food.''

''What *about* food?''

''You're on the same diet as I am,'' Justine told Erica with a twinkle. ''I'm always trying to gain weight. Don't worry, you won't gain too much,'' she added hastily.

''I wasn't worried about that. It's been all I can do to keep some meat on my bones, considering my schedule,'' Erica admitted.

''Lucky us,'' Justine said, laughing. ''You and I will pig out on the best food our chef has to offer. We'll be the envy of everyone who is trying to lose a few pounds. And we'll have a great time doing it.

''Now,'' Justine went on sympathetically, ''tell me all about yourself. Charmaine has filled me in a lot, but I have a feeling she left out most of the details.''

Erica found herself talking to Justine as if they were old friends. She asked about the riding lessons, the horses and even the stable cat. Justine said blankly, ''You've met the cat?''

Keeping in mind her perception that the gray cat had spoken to her, Erica said, ''Mmm-hmm. I strolled through the stable on the way over for dinner.''

''Oh, well, Mrs. Gray—that's the cat's name—has three kittens that I need to find homes for. I don't suppose you could take one back to New York with you?''

''I'd like that,'' Erica said, surprising herself. ''It would be fun to come home to a pet after being away on business. But I'll have to decline, Justine. I'm too busy to take on the responsibility. And,'' she said, pausing to study Justine's reaction, ''Mrs. Gray doesn't seem exactly, well, normal.''

''Oh, I know. Those eyes and the way she stares. It's

a little uncanny, almost as if she can tell what humans are thinking.'' Justine didn't expand on this, but Erica now suspected what really bothered her about the stable cat. It was her eyes, as Justine said, wide and yellow and unblinking.

Their conversation went on to more conventional topics, such as Erica's makeover, with Justine making a few suggestions about hair and makeup. They soon moved to the dining room, Murphy following, and dinner progressed smoothly with both of them talking and laughing and eating heartily of roast pork, sweet-potato casserole, salad containing hearts of palm, and creamed spinach. And even though she knew her fellow guests were probably partaking of a few shrimp cunningly arranged on a lettuce leaf, Erica did not feel one bit guilty about eating so much rich food. At least not yet.

Because she was going to have the voluptuous figure she'd always wanted. It was a means to an end. A *rear* end that would be softly rounded, maybe even jiggling slightly as she strolled into a roadhouse wearing tight-fitting jeans. And then…*then* Hank, who had looked as if he could barely stand to look at her, would change his tune.

Holding that very pleasant thought, Erica helped herself to another large spoonful of sweet potatoes.

Padre Luis Speaks…

I AM ONLY a humble priest. But *por Dios!* I do my best.

Forgive me if my English is not so good. It is not my native tongue. When I built my school and hospital in this valley, the miners and their families rejoiced. Now they are gone. In the place where my hospital stood, there is a building. It has the inconsequential name of Desert Rose.

I live in my hospital office, or where it once was. Unfortunately this space is in the courtyard of this Desert Rose place. My office is in the midst of a cactus patch. A gardener comes to groom the cactus every week. Whoever heard of grooming a cactus patch? But I cannot feel the spines of the cacti, though I pace among them, to and fro, to and fro.

A woman arrived here today. Her name is Erica. She cannot see me, as I am not as I was. I can only barely see her. She is like a faded picture, indicating an incompleteness of the spirit. Perhaps there is hope for her, if she learns to be real. I will pray for her.

I wanted to speak to her, but no one can hear me. I do not know why. It is my belief that, as I have heard the Anglo settlers say, the cat has got my tongue.

But if the cat has my tongue, why does she not say what I would say? *Por Dios,* there are many things I do not understand.

I am only a humble priest, not worldly and only wishing to be wise. I must pray.

Chapter Three

Hank ignored the blinking light on his answering machine as he stared morosely at the tiny white button in his left hand and the pink-checked pinafore in his right. Actually two buttons had popped off this garment, which was one of his favorites for Kaylie to wear because it was frilly and cute and didn't need ironing. Hank hated ironing. And he had no idea how to go about sewing on a button.

He stuck his head around the corner to check on Kaylie in her alcove. She slept soundly in her crib, her bottom up in the air, her binky in her mouth.

It occurred to him that he could ask Cord McCall, the ranch manager, to be alert for sounds from his small apartment. Cord was a loner, kept mostly to himself, but he lived next door in similar quarters, a door opened between them, and the baby monitor would alert Cord if Kaylie woke.

Although his main purpose in going to the Big House was to ask Justine to show him how to sew on a button, Hank thought it might be a good idea to stop by to see her, maybe apologize for his anger this afternoon. Not only that, but Erica Strong might have heard every word of his argument with Justine, and the last thing he needed if he wanted to repair his relationship with his sister was for Erica to complain.

After Cord agreed to listen for the baby, Hank erased the answering-machine message tape without listening to it. The message was probably from his boss calling one more time for advice on how to snatch the Gillooley communications deal out from under the nose of MacNee, Levy and Ashe, a problem that would have consumed him at one time. But since he couldn't care less about things at Rowbotham-Quigley these days, Hank set off at a fast lope with the two buttons clenched in his fist and the pinafore hanging from his back pocket for lack of any place more suitable to carry it. As usual, Hank walked in the heavy-timbered front door at the Big House without knocking.

But it wasn't his sister who was there to greet him or even the dog. It was Erica Strong, who was leafing through a book from the gallery bookcase.

She blinked at him under the overhead light, her eyes wide and owlish behind her glasses. She seemed alarmed at his precipitous arrival, his bursting through the door without knocking, and he supposed he didn't blame her.

"I'm looking for Justine," he blurted, taken by surprise as he was.

Erica narrowed her eyes. "She's out."

"Out?"

"Justine was on her way out to walk the dog when she was called over to the kitchen. Something to do with someone named Pavel." In that moment, for some reason he pictured her the way she'd been in the stable earlier, when he had confronted her and spoken so gruffly. She had triumphed over her initial uncertainty about his boorishness by drawing an attitude around her like a protective cloak, and despite his annoyance, he'd admired that. Well, since then he'd had time to begin to feel ashamed of the way he acted.

"Oh, Pavel is the chef. He's probably threatening to quit again. And Murphy?"

"Went with Justine. I'll be glad to give her a message if you like," she said. She was a small woman, fine-boned, her eyebrows neatly arched as if she hung constantly on the brink of surprise. Her skin was clear, her eyes bright, and the top of her head came only to his jawline. He had the totally irrelevant thought that if he bent forward, he could kiss her forehead without any trouble at all.

He cleared his throat. "I'll wait for her," he said. "I need a book to read. And by the way, my name's Hank Milling. We haven't met properly."

Her eyes behind the glasses were solemn. "No, I suppose we haven't. But Mr. Milling—"

"Hank," he said.

"Hank, if you really don't want to teach me how to ride, you don't have to."

"I've already factored you into my schedule," Hank said, trying to sound friendly. He was determined to make amends for the way he'd acted earlier.

"I see," she said. She tipped her head slightly to one side, and he found something very arresting about the way she was looking at him. It reminded him of Kaylie, which was ridiculous because Erica was a grown woman and Kaylie was seven months old. Maybe it was that this woman was displaying an interest in him, or that, in her own way, she seemed to be hanging on every word he said. Whatever it was, it made him want to know her better.

He nodded toward the book in her hand. "I hope you found a good book."

She seemed surprised that he had commented about it. "It's a Zane Grey book, *Woman of the Frontier*."

"I've read it. When I was a kid I owned a complete set of his work."

"You did?" She started to smile, seemed to think better of it, and then, as if she was unable to stop it, the smile spread across her face, transforming her completely. He liked the way her eyes sparkled, the curve of her bottom lip, the way she lit up all over.

"My favorite Zane Grey book was *Riders of the Purple Sage*."

"Mine is this one," she said, tapping the book she held with a forefinger. "It's not written to the Western formula like most of Zane Grey's books. It's more a woman's story, and this is the latest edition, which restores pages cut from the original. It was Zane Grey's books, all of them, that got me fascinated by the West."

He grinned down at her, unexpectedly feeling a kinship with her. "You know, maybe I'll reread *Purple Sage*."

"It's over there. Next to the big green one."

When he went to pull the book off the shelf, he dropped one of the pinafore buttons. It rolled under a chair, and he thought he saw where it landed—on the side of the chair near the window.

She asked him what he'd dropped and he told her, then set the book on the table and bent to look for the button. "I know it's under here," he said, groping beneath the chair skirt.

"I think it went slightly to the left," she told him.

"I don't feel it." He felt silly, groveling on the floor.

"Maybe it rolled out at the back of the chair." She went around the chair and said, "Here it is." She handed the button to him.

"It's from my daughter's pinafore." Sheepishly he yanked the garment from his back pocket, realizing that the whole time he'd been talking to Erica Strong, the pink-checked fabric had been waving from his pocket like a flag.

"Oh, you have a daughter," she said, but he couldn't figure out from her tone whether she thought a child was a plus or a minus.

Not that it mattered. But something expanding in his chest, some kind of air forcing out the other negative feelings, made him want to please her. It was a strange urge, and he didn't know what to make of it.

"Yes, her name is Kaylie. She's seven months old. And I don't know anything about sewing on buttons." So help him, he felt his face flushing. Why this should happen, he didn't know. He wasn't embarrassed. Yet something about this woman was causing him to act like a bumbling idiot.

"Well," Erica said briskly, "I can sew on the button for you."

"I couldn't ask you—"

"Don't be ridiculous. Besides, I'll teach you how to do it yourself. You know that old saying—'Give a man a fish, and you feed one man. Teach a man to fish—'"

"'—and you feed a hundred,'" he finished. "Though I sure do hope I don't have to sew buttons on a hundred pinafores."

She looked up at him and smiled. That lit her eyes from within, but in a different way than laughter did.

"The only thing is, you'll need to show me where Justine keeps a needle and thread."

"That's easy. Come with me." He led her through the house to a utility room where there were a washer and dryer and a small closet where his sister stored her sewing machine and supplies.

He dug in a plastic box and produced white thread, a packet of needles and scissors. Then he pulled a small rocking chair closer to a floor lamp so that Erica could sit.

"Watch closely," she said. She threaded the needle and showed him how to knot the thread.

"Then you bring the needle up from the bottom of the fabric," she said, demonstrating. He leaned against the washing machine and watched with his arms folded across his chest as she began sewing on a button, her fingers moving deftly as she plied the needle. She made it look easy.

"Is sewing a hobby of yours?" he asked after a while.

The question seemed to surprise and amuse her. "No, I wouldn't say that. My mother made sure that my sisters and I knew how to sew on buttons and turn up hems before we went away to college."

"How many sisters?"

"Two," she said. "Now watch how I make a knot when the button is secure." She looped the thread and guided the needle through it before snipping off the thread.

"Justine said that Charmaine Strong is your sister," he said.

She shot him a quick look. "Yes."

He shook his head. "I've seen pictures of her. She's beautiful."

Erica tried not to let the admiration in his voice upset her. People had always said how beautiful Charmaine was, and it was true. But sometimes, implied in their comments was the secondary thought *And you're not*.

Most of the time it didn't bother her. She'd grown

immune to people's surprise that she could have such a beautiful sister. Long ago she had decided that those people didn't count and didn't deserve a place in her life. She knew she would never be as beautiful as Char or their older sister, Abby, a former Miss Rhode Island, and that was okay. She was intelligent, was known as the smart sister. She'd decided early on that if she couldn't be gorgeous, she would collect academic degrees and hold a fantastic job that provided lots of perks. So there.

But now, for this cowboy, for *her* cowboy, she wanted nothing so much as to be beautiful. To make him want her. To have him slavering after her with lust in his heart.

"Why don't you try sewing on the next one?" she suggested, holding out the spool and the needle.

She cut the thread and handed him the pinafore, then stood up so that he could sit in the chair.

Hank had heard the expression "all thumbs" for most of his life but had never had it applied to him before. The needle was slippery and the eye so small that he couldn't find it with the end of the thread.

"Need some help?" She had the softest voice, and there was something alluring in the tone of it.

He looked up at her, ashamed to feel so helpless. Who would have thought that sewing on a button could be so hard? Who would have thought, for that matter, that being the sole parent of a baby girl could make a grown man feel so inadequate?

"Here," she said, bending over him, and he caught a whiff of the fragrance of…honeysuckle? Did she really smell like honeysuckle? Every cell of his body went on alert at this whiff of his favorite scent, and he leaned a little closer to her. By that time, however, she had edged nearer to the lamp and was threading the needle with brisk efficiency.

"There you are," she said, handing him the threaded needle. "Now try."

"Yes, ma'am," he found himself saying meekly. He punched the needle into the fabric as he would have through leather, as in repairing a harness or a bridle, sticking his finger in the process. "Ouch!"

"Um, maybe you should do that more gently," Erica said.

He inhaled a breath, blew it out. "All right," he said dutifully. He tried again, feeling a rare sense of accomplishment when he pulled the thread through the fabric. He stuck the button on top and watched as it wobbled down the thread.

"You see?" Erica said. "You can do it."

"'I think I can, I think I can,'" he said, taking his first stitch through the buttonholes.

"'The Little Engine that Could,'" was one of my favorite childhood stories, too," Erica said.

He stared at her. "No kidding. I'm already deciding what storybooks I want to buy for Kaylie. 'The Little Engine that Could' was one of my first choices."

"Oh, there are lots of others. My nephew Todd especially likes a book about a moth. 'Stellaluna,' it's called."

"I didn't know Charmaine had children." He was getting the hang of this button-sewing and found he could talk and sew at the same time.

"Oh, Charmaine doesn't have any kids. Todd belongs to our sister, Abby. She's married to a stockbroker, which seems awfully dull sometimes. I imagine it's much more interesting to be a cowboy."

If she only knew, Hank thought. *If she only knew the*

truth about me. But what he said was, "It must seem that way." He tied the knot neatly and reached for the scissors.

He stood up. "Thank you," he said, wadding the pinafore into a ball before he thought better of stuffing it back in his pocket. "I really appreciate this."

"It was nothing," she said, and all at once he realized that they were standing so close that he could have reached over and brushed a thumb against her cheek. And he smelled honeysuckle again, he was sure of it.

He took a deliberate step backward. "Justine must be having supply problems," he said. "That's why she's not back. It's happened before, the cook's having to adjust the next day's menu because the food hasn't arrived."

"I suppose I might as well take my book and head back to my suite," Erica said. After a moment's hesitation, she turned and led the way through the dim house, her heels clicking on the polished tile floor.

When they reached the bookshelves, she picked up her book from the table, and he tucked *Riders of the Purple Sage* beneath his arm.

"I'll walk you as far as the fork in the path," he said.

Outside, the air had a cool nip to it, and overhead a night bird called. The desert sky was clear, the stars burning hot and bright. As improbable as it might have seemed, a thin mist rose out of that dry desert air, encapsulating them in their own world out there under the stars. Erica walked beside him, and it pleased Hank that she knew enough not to sully the night with words.

When they reached the place where the path divided, he stopped. "This is where I head to my own place. Thanks again, Erica." That she had chosen to help him after so disastrous a first meeting bespoke a good heart and generous nature.

There it was again, that sideways tilt of her head. And he liked the stillness that he sensed inside her, the quietness that few women exhibited. He much preferred it to the constant talk, talk, talk that most women found necessary when in his presence.

"You're welcome, Hank," she said, and the words could have sounded stiff and uncomfortable if it hadn't been for her voice, which was soft and warm and pleasant.

He felt an improbable affinity with her, which seemed absurd after only two encounters.

"Look," he said uneasily, not knowing he was going to say anything but goodbye until the word was out of his mouth. "We got off on the wrong foot today. I hope it won't affect the way you think of me."

She seemed to consider this. "Really, it's okay."

He wasn't entirely sure that it was, but he knew her smile meant that she'd forgiven him and that they were now on a new footing.

"Well," he said, his spirits lifting, "I'll see you tomorrow for your lesson."

"Yes. For my lesson." Behind her glasses, her eyes shone large and luminous in the darkness, and in that moment he saw how pretty she was.

To hide his confusion, he spared her only a curt nod. He watched her as she went, his buoyant feeling fading as she disappeared around the corner of one of the buildings.

He liked her. He found being around her easy, comfortable. He didn't know why he felt that way, but he did.

HER COWBOY had a baby.

Erica had not considered the possibility that he would be encumbered. Oh, she'd thought he might be married, in which case she would have backed off in a hurry. She didn't need the pain and anguish of being the Other Woman. But it had never occurred to her that he would have children.

She smiled to herself at his determination to complete the task of sewing on the button. He had hunched over the tiny pink pinafore, her cowboy, looking sorely out of his element and all the more attractive for making the effort. Clearly he was raising his daughter alone, and that made him interesting to her. It took a real man to take on the burden of child-rearing all by himself.

She booted up her laptop computer, which she hadn't intended to bring along at first. Then Charmaine had insisted that Erica pack it.

"How will we keep in touch if I'm in Aruba and you're in California and you don't have e-mail?" Charmaine had wailed, and seeing the sense of this, Erica had brought the laptop along.

YOU'VE GOT MAIL!

Hi Erica
How's it going? Tell, tell! I want to hear all about Rancho Encantado. There are mosquitoes in Aruba and the climate is muggy. Wish I could have come with you!
Love, Char

Char
I met the perfect guy. He's a cowboy who is going to teach me to ride. And it's not muggy.
Love, E.

THE NEXT MORNING, Erica had her first makeover appointment. The hairdresser and makeup artist, Tico, was a small man, stocky and squat and sporting a waxed handlebar mustache. After an analysis of her skin type, he prescribed a foundation mixed for her exact skin tone and instructed her in the use of blush, eye shadow and concealer.

"A darker lipstick is what you need! No pale tones for you," he said busily as he set upon her with lip liner and tubes and gloss.

Despite his admonition to be still, she got in a few words between the lip liner and gloss. "Are you sure this stuff isn't too dark? I don't want to look like a vampire."

This made him laugh heartily. "A vampire! Of course you will not look like a vampire. What a funny lady you are."

When he was finished, she had to admit that he was on the right track. Who would have guessed that lipstick the exact shade of red geraniums would bring out the color in her cheeks and make her lips look full and lush? Who would have known that a few dabs of concealer on the shadows under her eyes could perk up the sallowness of her skin?

"Ah, but you have such wonderful hair," Tico said, draping strands of it around his fingers and letting them fall into place.

"I never did before," Erica said.

He winked. "But this is Rancho Encantado. Anything can happen here."

"Even a talking cat?"

"I beg your pardon?"

His astonishment warned her not to pursue the subject.

"Oh, nothing. Tell me, what changes would you recommend for me?" she replied cautiously.

"A lighter hair color, of course. As for the eyebrows, we will dye them today!"

"How about my eyelashes?" Hers were virtually colorless.

"Dye! Dye!" He was startling in his intensity, and Erica hoped no one would mistake his meaning. Several clients peered around the door in alarm, withdrawing their heads when they realized that her situation was not dire.

"Back to my hair—how light do you intend it to be?"

"Only a little lightening here and there, we will give it a bit of a trim, and voilà! Rancho Encantado has worked its magic."

"I've never wanted to bleach my hair because it would be too hard to keep up."

Tico produced a sampler of pale hair colors and fanned them out before her. "Lowlights do not require so much maintenance, and I would do a lot of them. Look, we have so many shades to choose from—Butter Cream, Moonlight Madness, Winter Frost—"

"Never mind," Erica said hastily, dizzied by the possibilities. "Choose one. Whatever you think would look best."

"Perhaps I should tell you a blonde joke? It is the last time you will hear one as a brownette."

"I don't think so. I'd rather get started."

"Oh, you will look *fantastico!*" Tico said, clapping his hands together, which brought two assistants running.

As they attacked with hair color and foil, shears and razor, comb and curling iron, Erica hid her face in a magazine. She had no intention of looking in the mirror until Tico and company were through.

BACK IN HER ROOM after her hair appointment, when she finally stopped admiring her reflection in the mirror, Erica booted up her laptop and found a message from Charmaine.

YOU'VE GOT MAIL!

Dear Sis
You already know how to ride. What's up?
Love, Char

Erica, still sneaking peeks at the mirror, immediately replied.

Char
My hair is streaked Palomino Blond. The manicurist gave me acrylic fingernails!!! My cowboy has a baby. And I'm letting him teach me to ride because I want to be with him as much as possible.
Love, E.

THAT AFTERNOON in preparation for Erica's riding lesson, Hank saddled up Melba, the mare who was best suited to beginners. He had decided on this particular horse on the basis of the form that Justine had filled out at Erica's behest. Some of their guests had been riding most of their lives, and others had a smidgen of experience. Erica had been identified as the latter.

When he'd finished saddling Melba, he led her into the ring and leaned against the fence, waiting. Mrs. Gray appeared with her three latest offspring, and she supervised them from a relatively safe position outside the ring as they chased and pounced. The kittens would be okay as long as they stayed out from underfoot, he figured.

Idly he watched a petite woman walking briskly along the lane, which was flanked by rows of eucalyptus trees. The sun picked out golden streaks in her hair, and she looked slightly familiar. He stood straighter, his attention drawn to her face, which was hidden behind big sunglasses.

Melba whinnied and bumped his shoulder, and by the time he'd patted her on the neck and assured her that an apple was forthcoming soon, the woman had disappeared into the stable.

"She must be going to see Paloma," he said out loud, since the baby-sitter often asked friends to drop by; they were helping her to plan her wedding.

Shows what you know, said Mrs. Gray, which caused Hank to wheel around in amazement. The cat's unwavering gaze scalded him, and he reminded himself that cats don't talk. Still, he narrowed his eyes at her, but all she did was cuff one of her kittens as it came too close to the gate.

"Hank," said Erica's voice behind him, and he whirled around, expecting to see her approaching.

But it wasn't Erica who strode toward him, this woman with shiny hair rippling in the breeze, lips full and red. It was someone who looked very like his dream woman, the one he rescued from rattlesnakes, the one who warmed his lonely bed at night.

The woman pulled off the sunglasses, and he was astonished to realize that it was indeed Erica. Her wide eyes, framed by long lashes, were a complex mix of brown and green, the arched brows brushed upward.

"All ready for our lesson?" she asked.

"I...well, I thought you were going to be late."

"I wouldn't miss my lesson for the world," she said. She raised both hands to fluff her hair back from her face, and he noted that her fingernails were long and lacquered shell-pink.

He felt a line unreel somewhere in the vicinity of his heart. It seemed to flow out from him and twirl around her, lassoing her neatly and pulling her toward him. He blinked and it went away. If it had ever been there.

He introduced Erica to Melba and handed her an apple to feed the mare. Erica grinned when Melba left a thread of slobber on her hands. He half expected her to go "Eeuuw!" but all she did was wipe her hand on her jeans. Too-big jeans, he saw now, remembering that she'd worn them last night. He wondered what they concealed. A derriere too large? Bony hips? No curves at all? He couldn't tell, but he thought that the jeans were a sensible choice. Too many women showed up for their lessons wearing skin-tight pants that allowed no freedom of movement.

He spent more than half an hour expounding on the basics, such as how to hold the reins, how to direct the horse, that sort of thing. Erica listened attentively, her eyes seldom leaving his face, her hands folded demurely in front of her.

"Now you're going to ride a horse. Come here to the left side of her," he instructed, walking around. Erica followed him and stood looking at him quizzically, waiting.

"The way you'll do this," Hank began, "is to stand by the horse's left shoulder." He handed her the reins. "Hold these in your left hand and grip her mane. Go ahead."

She took the reins from him, her brief touch engendering a little *brrrrip!* of sensation. The desert air, he thought. It's dry, and static electricity will develop under such conditions, that was all it was.

"In your right hand, grasp the cantle." He pointed to it. "That's what we call the back of the saddle."

Erica did that, too. "Now I'm going to give you a leg up," he said. He formed his hands into a stirrup. "Your left foot goes here."

She looked at him for a long moment, those eyes wide and bright. He realized that she wasn't wearing her usual glasses. As if she'd read his mind, she took her sunglasses out of her pocket and shoved them on. Then she placed her booted foot into his cupped hands and he lifted her up until she'd swung her other leg over the horse. He got a quick glimpse of the fabric pulled tightly over her derriere and realized that those baggy jeans didn't hide any figure fault at all. In fact, she appeared nicely rounded and firm.

"I think I'll need a stirrup adjustment," she said, and he realized that he had almost forgotten he was working.

He notched the stirrups up on each side, noticing that her feet were in the correct stirrup position with the heels pointed down. Most beginners didn't know to do that.

"Good heel position," he said, but she relaxed her feet so that the heels assumed their natural position. She looked guilty, then crooked the heels again until they were correctly placed.

"Settle your weight backward," he instructed, watching until her bottom slid backward to the dip in the saddle. "And now squeeze your legs against Melba's sides to start her going."

He had a vision of Erica's legs squeezing *him*, before he yanked himself back to the moment and to Erica. She followed his direction, causing Melba to begin walking sedately around the ring.

"Keep your heels away from the horse's sides," he warned. "And look where you're going, not down at the horse."

When Melba had made one circle of the ring, he called to Erica, "Take her around again. You're looking good. Have you had lessons before?"

"It was a long time ago."

He watched her as Melba, a sweet-natured hack who was accustomed to new riders, plodded patiently around the corral. He instructed Erica to shift her weight back in the saddle when she pulled on the reins to stop the horse, to move forward when the horse went forward.

He liked the way Erica sat the saddle. She looked relaxed, her back straight but not stiff. He thought she had the bearing of a natural horsewoman, rare to see in beginners.

After several more circuits of the ring, Erica reined Melba in. "Isn't my hour up?"

He glanced at his watch, and sure enough, it almost was. "You have a couple of minutes left on the clock." He couldn't believe how fast time had passed. He couldn't believe he had enjoyed this basic lesson so much.

Horse and rider made one more complete and very sedate circle before stopping beside him. He smiled up at Erica. "You look comfortable on horseback," he said.

"The lesson wasn't very hard." She reached forward and patted Melba on the neck.

"Here, let me help you down." As she prepared to dismount, he started to give her a hand, then abruptly changed his mind. Instead, as Erica swung down from the saddle, he wrapped his hands around her waist. She slid down against him, her body brushing his, so that he felt her breasts moving down his chest, her flat abdomen brushing his belt buckle. Her breasts weren't as small as he'd thought, nor was she as heavy. In fact, she felt featherlight in his arms. She felt as if she could float to earth without any help from him.

"Thank you," she said, her voice high and breathy. He looked down at her then, and her face was only inches from his. Her lips were slightly parted, looking ripe as strawberries and moist. He was mesmerized by those lips and was even more enchanted to see the pink tip of her tongue appear and enticingly lick her lower lip.

He swallowed, hard. In that moment Melba, the stable, the riding ring disappeared, and all that was left was Erica and him and the sky, which was a wide delirious blue. He was peripherally aware of the cat and her kittens, and he thought the cat said, *Kiss her!*

Or maybe Mrs. Gray was merely hissing at the kitten who had pounced on her tail. Whatever, he thought that the advice to kiss Erica was excellent. Why wouldn't he, with her staring up at him out of those wide eyes, with her hands on his upper arms where she could feel muscles made strong from riding, with her hair a golden aureole around her bewitching face?

He closed his eyes, opened them, half expecting Erica to disappear like the horse and the stable. She didn't. She appeared as caught up in the spell of this as he was. Slowly he bent his head; slowly he angled it into position. As for Erica, he didn't think she had breathed even once since she'd come down off the horse. Maybe he hadn't, either. Maybe you didn't need to breathe when you did this.

His lips opened slightly, and he dipped them closer to

hers. He was startled to find out that she was breathing, after all, and her breath fell like petals on his cheeks. He drifted along with the petals, smelling honeysuckle, his favorite scent, inhaling it, along with the fragrance of her sun-washed skin. She yearned toward him, her eyes closed, the lashes casting exquisitely curved shadows beneath. His lips closed in, touching hers, and he knew then that he would crush her in his arms, would overpower her with his strength until she—

"Hank? Hank!"

Startled out of the mood, surprised by the interruption, his head jerked backward. Erica pulled away in that instant, too, putting space between them.

Paloma was waving from the door of a stable that had somehow reappeared. "Excuse me, Hank, but I really must leave Kaylie with you now. I have an appointment in town."

Melba, also restored to being, stamped her feet, probably eager to get to the feed trough. Erica brushed a fly away with apparent annoyance, and Hank became aware of the whine of a jet high above them. Responsibility settled heavily over him like a mantle of lead, pushing him into the ground, letting him know that pleasures such as other men might enjoy were not to be his.

"I'll be right there." Hank turned back to Erica, but she had backed so far away that she was out of his reach.

"I'll be here for the lesson tomorrow," she said in a rush, and then she was gone, walking swiftly out of the ring toward the guest quarters.

He watched her go as he led Melba into the stable. Erica was gone, much like his fantasies, the ones that got him through all the lonely days and nights.

But unlike those fantasies, he knew that Erica was real.

More real than he was, probably. Because he wasn't really a cowboy, but nobody knew that except his sister. And he wasn't about to tell. At least not yet.

IT WAS A GOOD THING she hadn't been required to ride Melba anywhere but around the ring, Erica reflected as she hurried back to her room, because without her glasses she'd been as blind as a bat. After her delight over her new hair color and the cut that made her hair bouncy and the teasing on top that gave her some height, she had been way too vain to wear her glasses. She'd settled on the sunglasses, which were made to her prescription, but they were for distance, and they blurred things close up. When she was fortunate enough to get that close to Hank, she wanted to see everything she could—the little scar on his chin (maybe he'd gotten it when he was thrown from a bronco), the freckle next to his left eye (too much sun) and the bump on the bridge of his nose (another bronco, or maybe a roadhouse brawl). Cowboys often led rough lives, which led to their having imperfections, and Erica wanted to know every one of Hank's.

When she reached her room, she turned on her laptop. Charmaine's e-mail reply was waiting for her.

YOU'VE GOT MAIL!

Erica
HE HAS A BABY? How did that happen?
Charmaine

Erica smiled and tapped out her reply.

Charmaine
I believe it happened the way all babies happen.
Love, E.

For the moment it was nice to contemplate what it would be like to engage, with her cowboy, in the activity that made babies. Nice to contemplate, nice to fantasize.

Which she would do for the next few minutes. And then she'd go to dinner and hope that Hank would stop by to see Justine and maybe bring his baby.

Padre Luis Speaks...

OH, THAT CAT! *Kiss her,* she says to the cowboy. Would I ever say a thing like that? *Por supresto que no!* Of course not.

This Erica, she is still not real. She wants the cowboy. She thinks he is perfect. But her cowboy is not really a cowboy. And the cowboy wants her, but not the real her. It is a confounding thing, this. Why do they not see that until they become real to each other, they will not find love?

I think that they do not know they seek love. They believe they are looking for something else. Sex, perhaps, or... Hmmph. When will these two people learn that love is the only thing that matters? By Jesus, Joseph and the Blessed Mother, I pray that they may triumph over their confusion.

I am spending more and more time on my knees lately. I am glad that I cannot feel the cactus spines when I kneel to pray. Often in my previous existence I wondered why our Lord's garden of earthly delights had to include such a hurtful plant as the cactus. Now I see that it does not matter. Truly the Lord is beneficent.

Still, He seems to ignore my pleadings concerning the cat. If that cat comes around, why, it is apparently up to me to tell her what I think about her stealing my voice.

Not that she will hear me. No one hears me now except God, who sometimes does not answer.

For I am only a humble priest, after all. But I try, I try.

Chapter Four

"You look, well, different," Justine marveled when Erica arrived at the Big House for dinner. "I like you with sassy hair."

"Your Tico is a wonder," Erica told her. "He has released my hair from its brown boringness, and I'm never going to change the color." She all but pirouetted, basking in the attention.

Justine only smiled. "Not to diminish what Tico has done, but the low humidity here is great. You'll need to use more moisturizer on your skin, though."

Erica followed Justine into the kitchen, where a pot was bubbling on the stove. "What's that?"

"The chef sent over chicken and tarragon dumplings, which should help us put on the pounds. Would you mind handing me that dish?"

Erica busied herself spooning fattening hollandaise sauce over asparagus spears and carrying it to the table, which was set with earthenware pottery and chunky candlesticks. Justine brought the main dish to the table and said with a slight laugh, "The table looks so lonely with only the two of us. Sometimes I ask Hank to join me, but these days he doesn't like to take time away from Kaylie."

"That's his daughter?" Erica tried not to appear too curious, but her ears perked up at the mention of Hank's name.

"Yes, and he's new to the job of being a daddy. Poor Hank—he's had a hard time of it."

Erica spooned chicken and dumplings onto her plate, keeping her eyes lowered so that Justine wouldn't suspect her interest. "A hard time—how do you mean?"

"Oh, I forgot. You wouldn't know. Hank took over Kaylie's care when his ex-wife died in an accident a few months ago. Anne-Marie was adamant about not letting him be part of their lives, so he'd only seen Kaylie a couple of times and didn't have a clue about how to take care of her. Divorce is a sad business."

"And so is losing your mother when you're only a baby. Poor Kaylie. How is she doing?"

"Quite well. All of us at the ranch were upset by Anne-Marie's death. She was a fitness instructor here and one of my dearest friends." Justine looked pensive for a moment. "She was a fine person and a do-gooder to boot. Nothing I could say would stop her from riding over the state line to Nevada to that old ranch...but I'm running on, aren't I? Please excuse me, Erica. Would you care for more beans?"

Erica accepted the plate of beans, but her interest had been piqued. "I'd like to hear what happened to Anne-Marie, Justine."

Justine breathed a deep sigh. "Well, we had an elderly seamstress working here when Anne-Marie first arrived. Mattie was half Shoshone Indian, and she'd worked at one of the big hotels in Las Vegas before she came here. She was an excellent wardrobe person, but her arthritis finally made it necessary for her to retire to a ranch just over the Nevada state line. Anne-Marie took Mattie un-

der her wing, was always running soup or cookies or
something out to her at the ranch.''

"But Anne-Marie had a baby, right? Wasn't it difficult for her to get away, even to do good works?''

"No. We have this wonderful baby-sitter, Paloma,
who is happy to be here whenever she can, and I've been
crazy about my niece since the day she was born. I was
a willing sitter whenever I was available. I wish…but
there's no point in wishing. I could have kept Anne-
Marie from going that night. If only I'd said I couldn't
baby-sit, she would have stayed home. I was taking care
of Kaylie that night. A big storm came out of nowhere
when Anne-Marie was on her way back to Rancho
Encantado. She lost control of her car and hit a boulder.
She died instantly.''

Erica's heart went out to Justine, who, judging from
her expression, still held herself responsible for her
friend's death. She reached across the table and touched
Justine's hand.

"It wasn't your fault,'' she said.

Justine bit her lip. "I keep telling myself that. I don't
believe it, though.'' She seemed to pull herself together
with great effort. "Well, enough of that. I need to stop
dwelling on it. Tell me about your day, Erica.''

Erica would rather have heard more about Hank, but
she didn't feel comfortable fishing for information. At
least now she knew how he happened to be a single
father. Knowing that his life had been touched by tragedy, she felt extremely sympathetic toward him. And not
any less attracted.

However, her wish that he would drop by tonight
while she was at the Big House for dinner was probably
a futile one. Nevertheless, she found herself wishing,
anyway.

Justine brought out huge slabs of chocolate cake topped with Rocky Road ice cream, and Erica thought she should wish for something she could actually have. Like a second scoop of ice cream, which Justine was happy to provide.

HANK, WORN-OUT from work, wanted nothing so much as a steaming hot shower and an ice-cold beer.

After feeding Kaylie and eating his own solitary dinner, neither option was in the offing. Instead, at the moment he was picking up after Kaylie as she tossed her toys around the small living room, her favorite after-dinner activity.

Both the beer and the shower would have to wait until Kaylie was in bed, and that could be a while, considering her present energy and insistence that he play with her. He tossed the blue plush duckie into the playpen and jotted himself a mental note to tell Paloma to cut out Kaylie's morning nap.

"Babababa?" Kaylie said.

Hank snatched his daughter up from the blanket on the floor where she played, smooching her at the curve of her neck and making her laugh. "When are you going to learn to say 'Dada,' huh? Isn't it about time you did something more than babble cute nothings?"

"Babababa!"

"Okay, so I'll have to wait for you to talk. That's fine, Kay-Kay. I'm a patient man."

He sat down on the couch with his daughter in his lap, thinking how great it was going to be when he got that beer. Beer and then bed, and the next day he would start the whole routine over again. This was not the life he had lived until three months ago, that was for sure.

Before Anne-Marie's death he had been footloose and fancy-free in New York.

He saw Mrs. Gray standing on her hind legs and peering in through the screen door leading into the stable. Kaylie noticed her, too.

"Babababa?"

"No, Kaylie, that's a cat. Kitty cat." His words were punctuated by a meow from the cat.

"All right, all right. I know better than to deny two females what they want." Carrying Kaylie, he got up and went to the kitchen door. Mrs. Gray zoomed inside when he opened the door a crack. There was no sign of her kittens, who, he supposed, were old enough to get around on their own these days.

Using the one hand that was free, he dumped a sizable portion of dry cat food into the dish beside the stove. Mrs. Gray didn't even twitch her whiskers in that direction. Instead, she sat down and stared at him.

"Come on, Kaylie, let's get those toys put back in the playpen," he said just as the phone rang.

When he answered it, Lizette said brightly, "Hi, Henry. How's my lovey bunny?"

Hank didn't consider himself anyone's lovey bunny, much less hers, but he managed to suppress his annoyance. "I'm fine, Lizette. I'm really busy right now. May I call you back?"

He crunched the phone between his shoulder and his neck and went into the living room, where he deposited Kaylie in the playpen.

"Why don't you ever answer your e-mails?" Lizette wanted to know. "I've sent you a whole bunch."

"Like I said, I've been busy."

"I miss my lovey bunny. E-mail could make me feel

so much more connected to you. When will you be back?''

"Not for a while."

"You could bring the baby back to New York. Don't you think it's time?"

"Not yet," he said. "She's crazy about her baby-sitter. I can't take her away from Paloma."

"I know of a good day-care center right around the corner from my place."

"Day care? Not yet. The situation here is ideal. Paloma is wonderful, and Justine likes to fill in when she can. Kaylie's doing fine with the present circumstances, Lizette."

"The trouble is, Henry, I'm not. I miss you. I want us to be together."

He thought that he would like to know what color her eyes were, but this didn't seem like the right time to inquire. He did remember her nose, for whatever it was worth. Or at least he remembered the nose she'd had when he'd left. Lizette was on her fourth nose and, in the spirit of treating others with total honesty, delighted in proclaiming this fact to everyone. She'd had her first nose job at age fourteen and two more since then.

Kaylie was trying to push a star through the round opening in her plastic ball, and distractedly he reached down and turned the ball so that the star-shaped opening was on top. She poked the star through it and gurgled with delight.

"Henry? Henry! Did you hear what I said?" Lizette was beginning to sound shrill.

"I heard." He made himself consider ever so momentarily day care for Kaylie. He imagined rushing her there in the morning, rushing back to pick her up on the way home to his apartment. Or maybe to Lizette's apartment. She was sounding perilously close to making the "Let's live together" suggestion, and he couldn't imagine living with Lizette while at the same time trying to be a father to Kaylie.

"I have a good mind to come down there and drag you back to New York," Lizette said playfully.

He'd better do what he could to salvage this conversation, which had now gone from bad to worse. It occurred to him that there was probably no salvaging the relationship itself, and the thought didn't make him unhappy.

"Well, Lizette, I know how you must feel, but I don't think that your coming to Rancho Encantado is such a good idea, and I can't leave now. I've got my work cut out for me here."

"How can you say you know how I feel? You aren't the one who was left behind." Lizette sounded perilously near tears.

He raked a hand through his hair. For some reason Erica Strong's face popped into his mind, looking the way it had this afternoon when he'd held her in his arms—flushed, eyes wide, lower lip tremulous. He swallowed and pushed the image to the far reaches of his consciousness.

"I suppose I can't know exactly how you felt when I came to Rancho Encantado to look after Kaylie," he allowed. "I know you must have been disappointed. You've been understanding, Lizette, but I'm not ready to take our relationship to a new level right now."

Silence on the other end of the phone and what might have been a sniff.

"You're a wonderful woman," he added hastily. "We've had a great time. I hope that when I'm ready for something serious, you'll still be available." But did he? He'd met Lizette right after moving from Chicago to New York and was in the throes of his divorce. She'd been kind and understanding. But that was then. This was now.

An audible sniff this time. "I see," she said.

"I'd better go now, Lizette. It's almost time to put Kaylie to bed."

"Kaylie, Kaylie, everything is Kaylie. You act like you're married to that child."

This angered him, but it would serve no purpose to show it. "I'm sorry, Lizette" was all he said, and he clicked off the phone.

"Babababa?"

"Yeah yeah yeah yeah." He heaved a giant sigh and began to scoop toys up off the floor.

"Here's your dolly and here's your jingle ball and here's…" He stopped talking in midsentence. Mrs. Gray was sitting beside the playpen, staring at him again in that uncanny—*uncatty*—way of hers.

"What do you want?" he said not unkindly. The cat only stared with eyes both knowing and luminous.

While he was paying attention to the cat, Kaylie started lobbing the toys out of the playpen again, one by one. Which made him impatient. He couldn't be angry with her, though, because she did it so winsomely.

I don't know why you don't pop over to the Big House for a while and let Kaylie burn off some of her energy playing with Justine.

He whirled around, thinking that someone must be standing at the screen door and speaking to him, but there was no one. He could have sworn…

Cats did not talk. He knew this for a fact. People who thought that cats could talk were not right in the head.

Still, it wasn't a bad idea to pay a visit to the Big

House. Justine would play with Kaylie while he sat and drank his beer. Then he would bring Kaylie back here and they could both go to bed.

He swung Kaylie up out of the playpen and was rewarded by her happy chortle.

"What do you say we go over and see your aunt Justine for a while?" A visit might get the bad taste of the conversation with Lizette out of his mouth, too.

"Babababa!"

The cat did not say anything, Hank was relieved to note.

ERICA AND JUSTINE finished clearing the table, and while Justine was finishing up in the kitchen, Erica wandered into the living room and ran her fingers across the keys of the piano there.

"I didn't know you played," Justine called from the kitchen.

"I haven't for a long time." She sat down and experimented with a few chords.

A sheet of music was propped on the music stand, and after pushing her glasses higher on her nose, Erica played the first bar. She had taken lessons when she was a child and had actually enjoyed them, but she didn't own a piano now and thought she'd forgotten almost everything she'd learned about playing. She hummed along with the music; she used to sing, too, in her high-school choir and in a college glee club.

The thud of boots on the porch interrupted her reverie, and the front door opened suddenly. She stopped humming abruptly and whirled around.

"Keep playing," said Hank. "It sounded great." He stood there in the same T-shirt and jeans he'd worn earlier, and he was carrying a baby that must be Kaylie.

Wishing she'd changed clothes after her riding lesson, she stood and clasped her hands behind her back in embarrassment. "I'm out of practice."

"Hank?" Justine called from the kitchen. "I'll be out in a minute. Right now I'm up to my elbows in dishwater."

Erica's mouth went dry at seeing Hank again after this afternoon when they'd almost... But maybe it had been her imagination that they'd almost kissed. Right now it seemed as if she'd never seen him before, and how could that be when she'd held an image of her ideal cowboy in her heart for as long as she could remember?

Aware of her pounding heart, she wiped damp palms on her thighs. "Um, won't you sit down?" The baby was staring at her with frank interest, breaking into a drooly grin when Erica smiled at her. Kaylie had Hank's blue eyes, deep-fringed and round, pale blond curls and soft pink skin.

"Bababababa?"

Hank smiled. "No, Kaylie. That's Erica." And to Erica, "I used to think that 'bababababa' was her name for me. I know better now, though. Everything is 'bababab.'"

It was all Erica could do not to extend her hand for a handshake, the way she was accustomed to doing in business situations. What did you do when you met a baby? Erica had no idea, so she stood mutely, feeling awkward.

"Would you like to hold her?" Hank said. He couldn't imagine why he offered this, other than knowing that most women seemed to enjoy holding babies.

Erica eyed the baby askance. Kaylie was a beautiful child, but everyone knew she didn't do babies. Anyway, when had she last held a baby? At the moment she couldn't recall, but she had an idea that it would be bad form to refuse, and how could she with this baby looking so cute?

"I'd love to," she said, hoping that she didn't sound as uncertain as she felt, and when she held her arms out, Kaylie went right to her, perching on her hip as though accustomed to being there.

Justine came bustling out of the kitchen, drying her hands on a towel. "Hi, Hank. You should have come over earlier and eaten chicken and dumplings with us. Are you hungry? I could throw a plate together."

"Kaylie and I have both eaten. I could use a beer if you've got one."

"Top shelf of the fridge. Help yourself while we girls visit."

"Can I get anyone else something to drink?"

Both Erica and Justine shook their heads, and Hank started for the kitchen. He found a beer, popped the top and rejoined them in the living room. Erica was sitting on the couch, still holding Kaylie and looking uncertain as to what she was about. He almost laughed at the way she was holding the baby—gingerly, as if she'd break. Well, he himself hadn't known what to do when he first held his daughter, but he'd learned fast.

Justine was sitting on the couch, too, dangling her charm bracelet in front of a fascinated Kaylie. Hank flung himself into the big leather armchair he favored when visiting and took a long pull on the beer. It slid down easily, cool and refreshing. It had been a long day, and it suddenly occurred to him that the best part of it had been the hour he'd given Erica a riding lesson.

He didn't know what made him say it, but the words tumbled out of his mouth before he could stop them. "I was thinking," he said to Erica. "Tomorrow I don't have any lessons in the afternoon besides yours. If you're available earlier, we could take an easy trail ride, instead of your regular lesson.''

Erica shot him a startled look over Kaylie's head. ''I'd like that,'' she said.

Justine, though she appeared surprised at the offer, spoke up quickly. ''If Paloma could drop Kaylie off with me before she goes home tomorrow, you and Erica could take your time while you're out on the trail.''

''Well, sure,'' Hank said. Kaylie hadn't spent much time here lately, mostly because Justine was busy with ranch matters twenty-four hours a day.

Justine looked pleased. ''I'll have Pavel prepare a trail meal for you so you won't miss supper.''

Kaylie erupted in a stream of syllables and held her arms out toward Justine. Erica, looking relieved, let Justine take her. Justine began bouncing Kaylie on her knee.

Hank felt a stab of annoyance seeing Erica's relief at relinquishing Kaylie, though he couldn't have said why. He'd let the woman hold his precious baby, and much to his surprise she hadn't seemed at all grateful or captivated as most women were. He had no idea why he cared about this, but he did. As silly as it sounded even in his own mind, everyone should be grateful for the opportunity to be part of Kaylie's life. He didn't like even a *hint* that she might be a nuisance to anyone.

He wished now that he hadn't asked Erica to go on the trail ride tomorrow. ''Of course, if you'd rather have a regular lesson, that would be fine,'' he said, despite the fact that they'd already left the subject. Justine shot him a narrow-eyed glance, but Erica furrowed her forehead in distress. ''Well—''

Justine wasted no time in expressing her opinion. ''Nonsense, you've already decided on the trail ride, and

I'm looking forward to a long visit with my niece," she said, driving home the point that he'd better live up to his promise.

Erica, sensing the tension between brother and sister, stood up. "I think I'll have a beer myself," she said. She started toward the kitchen.

"Good idea," Justine said. "Drink a couple of those a day and you'll gain weight."

As Erica disappeared down the hall, Justine shot daggers at Hank, the look in her eyes warning him not to make problems. Inwardly he cursed himself for his own stupidity. If he hadn't brought up the idea of the trail ride, it would never have been mentioned and Erica's riding lesson would have gone on as planned. He should have had more sense.

Suddenly he couldn't sit still, mostly because he hated the way Justine was always trying to impose her will on him. He got up and, not knowing what he was going to do when he got there, followed Erica into the kitchen.

He surprised Erica in the process of pulling a beer out of the far reaches of the refrigerator.

"I could use another," he said, holding up his empty bottle though he'd previously had no intention of drinking a second.

Erica moved out of the way so he could reach into the refrigerator.

"Your Kaylie is darling," she said, surprising him. She sounded as though she meant it.

"Thanks." Instead of going back to the living room, Erica leaned back against the kitchen counter and twisted the top off her beer bottle. "I...well, babies are so little," she said. "I wasn't sure I was holding her right."

"Neither was I when I first held her. She was a lot smaller then, too."

Erica brought the bottle up to her mouth and drank, and he couldn't help noticing her long neck and how it swept up into her jawline, which ended at her ear, barely visible under the curtain of hair falling back from her face. He looked away, wondering how it was that he could come undone by merely looking at a portion of her anatomy, and not a portion that usually had sexual connotations, either.

"At first I thought you didn't like Kaylie," he blurted, thinking how stupid he was to set himself up for her denial.

She surprised him. She regarded him levelly, not denying anything. "Actually, when I started to hold her, I didn't know if I did or not, although I thought she was beautiful. She has her own little personality, doesn't she?"

Erica couldn't have replied in a way that would have satisfied him more. Before he knew it, he was replying with enthusiasm. "Kaylie is unique, and it seems like they all start out that way. Before I had a baby of my own, I thought, 'Oh, a baby,' when I saw one and left it at that. I figured they all behaved pretty much the same."

"Don't they?"

"Hardly. For instance, the ranch foreman's baby is as different from Kaylie as night is from day."

"How so?"

He shrugged and relaxed. "The foreman and his wife invited Kaylie and me to their house for dinner, and their baby is exactly the same age. Kaylie has never met a stranger, and she flirted with Dusty, the foreman, and cooed to his wife, Tanya, and smiled at their baby,

Emma. By contrast, Emma didn't seem to enjoy having strangers around. She cried when I tried to pick her up, and they told me that she rarely sleeps through the night. Kaylie was sleeping through the night by the time she was a couple of months old.''

Justine called from the living room, sounding every bit the solicitous aunt. ''Erica, Hank, bring a towel when you come back, will you? Kaylie's drooling a lot.''

''She's starting to cut her first tooth, I think,'' Hank called back. He strode across the kitchen and rummaged in a drawer. ''It's amazing,'' he said over his shoulder to Erica. ''When a baby enters your life, everything starts to revolve around it. Around her.''

''So it seems,'' Erica murmured.

''I'd better deliver this wiper to Justine.'' He walked past her, the towel in one hand, a beer in the other.

Erica followed him, and this time, instead of sitting beside Justine and Kaylie, who had taken over most of the couch, she sat down on the piano bench. From this position she could admire the chestnut highlights in Hank's wavy hair, the rippling abs under his tight-fitting T-shirt. He caught her looking at him, and she quickly cut her eyes to the music. To her embarrassment, a flush began to creep upward from her neck, and she chastised herself for acting like a teenager with a crush.

''Go ahead, play something,'' urged Justine.

''I'll try,'' she murmured. ''Let me look the music over for a moment.''

Hank and Justine went on talking about buying shoes for Kaylie while she studied the piece of music, and when she attempted to play a few notes, they didn't comment.

She began to move haltingly through the music, a light waltz. By the time she reached the end, the others had stopped talking and Justine was tentatively humming along.

Erica paused for a sip of beer.

"Please play something else," Hank said.

"There's more music in the piano bench," Justine added.

Erica rummaged in the bench until she found a book of old standards, and she treated them to a rousing rendition of "Turkey in the Straw."

"This house could use some livening up," Justine said. "I hope you'll play again sometime."

"Perhaps," Erica said.

"If you like, you can take the sheet music back to your room and study it before you tackle it."

"I'd like that."

Hank spoke up. "Kaylie's yawning. I'd better get her home and to bed."

"You can walk Erica back," Justine said.

This surprised Hank. He hadn't expected such an assignment. Erica, to give her credit, had the good grace to appear startled. Without being a total dork, he could hardly refuse, so he made himself smile and say, "Sure."

A flurry of goodbyes followed, and then they were outside in the cool, sweet-scented desert air, Kaylie pressed against his shoulder and Erica walking alongside him, a folder of sheet music tucked under her arm.

Across the way, a group of guests hurried across the open space toward their quarters. As they dispersed to their rooms, they called out cheerful good-nights to one another.

"I hope you don't mind about the longer trail ride tomorrow," he said.

Erica concentrated on putting one foot in front of the

other. Mind? Why would she mind? It was like the answer to a prayer—more time with her cowboy, more time to make an impression on him. Although if the way he was looking at her now was any indication, she was impressing him right this minute.

Erica wondered how much longer she'd be able to act as if she had little riding experience. In fact, she'd learned to ride at age ten, competed in regional gymkhanas throughout her high-school years and still rode whenever she could.

"Whatever you think," she murmured, aghast at herself for sounding so wimpy. Erica Strong never let someone else make her decisions for her; Erica Strong always had opinions; Erica Strong was a leader, not a follower.

Of course, Erica Strong had never met a handsome, virile cowboy in the flesh, the kind of guy who'd been the stuff of dreams since she was a little girl.

And now that she had, she looked at things a lot differently. She smiled to herself, thinking that Charmaine wouldn't believe her sister's good fortune. After all, Erica didn't quite believe it herself.

Chapter Five

"Breathe in. Breathe out. And feel pe-e-e-eace."

Erica, seated cross-legged on a mat underneath a spreading oak, breathed in. She breathed out. And she opened one eye so she could better observe the group that was at that moment riding out from the stable in the distance. It consisted of twelve riders and a leader, Hank. She almost wished she'd signed up for group riding lessons, instead of private ones. If she had, she would be with Hank right now, instead of merely breathing.

The instructor, a tiny dark-haired woman named Ananda, rang a small chime. The resulting notes fairly shimmered in the air. "That's the end of our meditation session for today."

Along with the other participants in the session, Erica returned her mat to the nearby wooden outbuilding and started walking back toward the cluster of buildings that made up the main part of the ranch. It was time for her appointment with her personal shopper.

The shopper's name was Sue, and she was a redhaired bundle of energy. "You need to tell me what kind of clothes you like to wear," she said, sitting down on a couch and patting the cushion beside her.

Erica described her collection of power suits in navy

and charcoal, her numerous little black dresses that could go from cocktail parties to dinners with little or no modification, and her collection of expensive but sensible shoes that were as suitable for chasing taxis as they were for board meetings.

"Well," said Sue, studying her carefully, "what would you like to change about your wardrobe?"

"Everything," Erica declared. "I hate the way I look. I hate navy and charcoal and low-heeled shoes. I want to—" and here she swallowed audibly "—I want to look like someone a cowboy could fall in love with. I want to be cute and charming and curvy. I want—"

"We can take care of the cute and curvy. It's up to you to be charming."

"I will be, so help me," Erica said.

"Stand up."

Erica stood.

"Turn around."

Erica turned.

"You have small bones, and that's to the good. I see on your chart that you want to gain weight, not lose it. That's excellent. Hips, fine. Bust, needs a bit of oomph, no problem there."

"Pardon?"

"They have bras for that. To spiff up your usual wardrobe, I'll order you some blouses in bright colors. I'll find a jumpsuit to show off your petite figure, scarves to spark a bit of color in your face. And you'd look great in short dresses that emphasize your legs."

Erica always wore her skirts long, but she had come here for a makeover, and made over she was determined to be. "All right," she said.

Sue made notations on a color chart. "I can make a few phone calls and have some clothes delivered here today. In the meantime, let's pay a visit to the ranch's gift shop. You'll want to look your best for the dance tonight.''

"No one told me anything about a dance!"

"Your invitation was in the packet of materials you received at registration."

"Oops! Maybe I should have read all that stuff."

"Don't worry, I'll fill you in as we walk over there."

She and Erica started across the grounds toward the gift shop. "Justine hired a country-and-western band to come from Carson City every Friday night," Sue told her. "All guests are invited, and all the employees are required to go."

So Hank would be there!

When she and Sue arrived at the gift shop, Sue immediately led Erica to a rack of square-dance clothes. And after several trips to and from the fitting room, Erica had to admit that the new clothes did something for her. The puffy sleeves of the peasant blouse made her arms look plump and round, the bodice showed her breasts to be especially curvaceous, and as for her hips…well, the bandanna fabric of the skirt moved alluringly when she experimentally swung her hips from side to side. She pulled the elastic neckline low enough to reveal cleavage, and due to a bra that Sue had provided, there *was* cleavage.

Sue grinned. "Well? If you want to look cute and curvy, these are the clothes."

"I'll take all of them," Erica decided in a fit of recklessness.

"Good," Sue said with a nod of approval, and she went off to charge the outfits to Erica's tab.

After promising to have Erica's new clothes pressed and hung in her closet within hours after they arrived,

Sue left her in front of the rec hall, and Erica walked back to Desert Rose pondering this makeover business. By now she knew she looked different. She thought she looked better. But she felt like the same Erica inside.

Two women from one of the other suites in Desert Rose hailed her as she opened her own door. "We're going for a mud wrap. Want to come with us?"

She recognized both of them from yoga class. Natalie was tiny and pert, Shannon was tall and busty. Both wore big smiles and seemed eager for company.

As unappealing as a mud wrap sounded, Erica figured she might as well sample as many Rancho Encantado activities as possible and agreed to meet them in the courtyard in a few minutes.

After she changed into her robe, she hurried back outside. As she waited beneath the Joshua tree, she spotted the group of student riders as they headed back toward the stable. Hank rode at the front of the group, his red shirt making him easily distinguishable.

"I see you noticed Hunk," Shannon said when she and Natalie joined her.

In response to Erica's blank expression, Natalie laughed. "His name's Hank, but we think Hunk suits him better."

It was all Erica could do to suppress a smile. Finally she gave up and grinned. "The name fits," she admitted "Do you know him?"

"Not very well," Natalie said. "He's very business-like and hardly ever cracks a smile."

"We tried to cheer him up. Lordy, how we tried." The two exchanged a look and laughed.

Erica supposed she could have brought up the tragedy that had changed Hank's life, but it didn't seem appropriate to discuss it. Certainly she wasn't surprised that

Hank was attractive to other women; hadn't Justine said that she fielded questions about him all the time?

The three of them learned when they arrived at the spa that the mud-wrap procedure would take two hours. A week ago Erica would have bemoaned a full two hours wasted on something she considered trivial, but now it didn't matter. She didn't have to be anywhere, do anything or be useful to anyone. Willingly she turned herself over to the receptionist, who conducted her into the depths of the Rancho Encantado spa where people went to be massaged, immersed, floated, rolfed and wrapped.

Erica found her skin being exfoliated with loofah mitts and sea salt to the accompaniment of soothing music. When her skin was burnished to a tingle, mud was applied to her entire body, although the stolid attendant was merciful enough to spare her face. Then Erica was wrapped in permeable plastic to "cocoon" for twenty minutes during which she was told to relax. Minutes later, beginning to succumb to the warm sensation of the mud and the wrap, Erica closed her eyes.

She was on the porch outside the recreation hall wearing her new low-necked white peasant blouse and the red bandanna skirt. Her breasts were full and partially exposed; they shone pale in the moonlight that spilled like molten silver over the scene.

Hank, standing on the step below her, glanced at her, his heavy-lidded eyes smoldering with desire. "Erica, let's slip away together. Let's find a place where we can be alone."

From inside the hall came the lively music of a fiddle. Suddenly the music tempo changed, becoming a slow and dreamy waltz.

Erica slid a look back through the open door, where

couples were gliding beneath crepe-paper streamers hung overhead. "We'll be missed."

Hank ran a bold hand up the inside of her leg. "We can be back before anyone notices. Let's—"

"Your time is up," said the white-garbed attendant as she yanked aside the curtain. Erica had to pull herself out of this pleasant daydream to the present time and place, where she was divested of her plastic wrapper, which she had begun to appreciate in the last few minutes.

Still covered in mud, she was led to a multijet Swiss shower and instructed how to position herself so that the attendant could spray her with a high-pressure hose. Then she was treated to a thorough massage. Finally, when she felt as limp as a noodle, she rejoined Natalie and Shannon in the lounge, where they collapsed into contoured chairs, guzzled fruity drinks and laughed together about the experience.

After lunch, Erica kept her appointment with an optometrist, hired by Justine to come to the ranch once a week to help with makeovers.

"I've never been able to wear contact lenses before," Erica said doubtfully when the exam was over. "I've never been able to get a good correction."

Dr. Levin looked up from her notes. "The ones I've prescribed shouldn't pose a problem. You can start to wear them right away, and you should call me if you have any trouble. You'll need to decide what color you want to order."

"They come in colors? That's amazing."

"Sure. You can order hazel, dark brown, light brown, blue with violet centers, deep blue, green—"

"I get the idea," Erica said hastily. "One pair in every color, please."

The doctor raised her eyebrows in amusement but did not comment.

At least, Erica thought, she would have a pair of contact lenses to match every one of her new outfits. She couldn't wait to tell Charmaine. Her sister would probably laugh her head off at Erica's new look, but Erica didn't care. She was having fun for once in her life, and she wasn't about to quit now.

ERICA REPORTED to the stable early for her trail ride and found Hank saddling Melba, who swiveled her head and regarded Erica with mild interest. Erica blinked, astonished that her new contact lenses—the blue ones—didn't blur her vision. If anything, she could see better, which, when looking at Hank, was a plus.

He still wore the long-sleeved red shirt, Western-style, from the morning. He also wore a big smile, aimed at her.

"How's it going?" he said.

She adopted his laconic manner of speech. "Can't complain."

He tightened the saddle cinch, and Erica reacquainted herself with Melba. Now that her eyes were adjusting to being inside the cool shadowy stable, she could see some of the names of the other horses on their stalls. Tango, said one. Sebastian, said another, and right next to that, Dimity. There were also stalls for Stilts and Twiggy and Shawnee.

The horse named Sebastian was in his stall, and because she recalled Hank's telling Justine that Sebastian was the bane of his existence, she moved closer for a better look. He was a handsome horse, square-jawed and maybe fifteen and a half hands high.

"What a gorgeous animal," she murmured almost to

herself. Sebastian had a glossy coat and a long black mane. His only marking was a diamond-shaped white patch that was almost covered by his forelock.

"He's a four-year-old stallion and a lot to handle," Hank said.

Taking note of the way Sebastian nosed over the top of his stall toward Hank, Erica said, "He seems to like you."

"He was trained correctly early on, but for some reason, now he bites. He bucks and even tries to scrape me off under low-hanging tree branches. But we're getting along pretty well." Hank stroked Sebastian's velvet nose.

"I'm glad someone gets along with that fool horse."

Erica turned as a rangy dark-haired man strode into the stable. He was wearing dusty jeans and worn boots, and his hat was pushed back on his head.

"Erica, this is Cord McCall, the ranch manager. Cord, Erica is Justine's friend."

Steady eyes met hers. "Glad to meet you. I hope you're enjoying your stay."

"I've only been here a couple of days, but so far, it's great."

"Good. Hank, I'll be away tonight. I'd appreciate it if you'd make sure to tell the hands to ride out and check on those broodmares tomorrow morning if I'm not back in time."

"Sure thing."

Cord afforded Hank an abrupt nod, said, "Glad to meet you, ma'am," and hurried out of the stable toward the ranch pickup.

"Broodmares? You breed horses here?"

"Some. That's why Justine keeps Sebastian around. She thinks he's good breeding stock." Hank shrugged.

"Cord doesn't seem too friendly," Erica said as they watched the pickup disappear down the road pulling a cloud of dust.

"He wasn't hired to be friendly to guests. He was hired to run the working end of the ranch and has a lot on his mind. Come on, if we're going for a ride, we'd better be on our way, since Justine may tire of baby-sitting Kaylie earlier than she thinks."

She moved away from Sebastian's stall and approached Melba. Hank cupped his hands for her foot, preparing to take her weight for as long as it took her to swing her other leg up and over the saddle. She inserted her foot in the place he had made for it, but before she could boost herself up into the saddle, Hank looked deep into her eyes. She had momentarily forgotten that she wore her new blue contact lenses, and she was unprepared for the expression of confusion that flitted across Hank's strong features.

When she was mounted and looked back down at him, he was staring at her openmouthed.

"You look so...different," he said.

She had carefully contoured her eyes with shadow and eyeliner the way Tico had shown her. The subtle use of blush emphasized her cheekbones and gave her chin a more rounded look. She smiled, trying to pass the comment off as lightheartedly as she could. "That," she said, "is the idea of a makeover, isn't it?"

He continued to look thoughtful. "I guess so," he said, and then he went to tighten the girth on his own horse, a roan gelding that patiently waited near the opening to the corral. The horse shied a little when Hank started to mount him.

"Steady, Whip," Hank said, reining the horse around so that he could see her. "Give Melba a little nudge with your heels and a slight slap with the reins. That's right. Now remember all you learned yesterday, and let's just amble along out of the corral.'' Hank looked brutally handsome in that moment.

As he bent down to undo the gate latch, Erica admired the athletic precision of his movement, the sinewy hands, his concentration on his task. She was painfully aware that he had said she looked different. Not better. Only different.

She certainly *felt* different. She felt…noticeable. And this time, she felt noticeable for her looks, not her brains. And she liked not wearing glasses. It was good not to have to keep pushing them higher on her nose. Without glasses to hide behind, she felt right out there with other people. With Hank.

''The scenery around here is unexpected,'' she said, taking in the purple hills, the snowcapped mountains beyond and the burnished blue sky overhead.

''Unexpected?''

''Remarkable.''

''I suppose that's a good way to describe it.''

She wondered what he would have thought if he could read her mind, what his reaction would be if he knew she had set her sights on him from the time she'd first set eyes on him. She shot him a cautious look out of the corners of her eye, finding it odd that her vision was no longer partially obscured by the frames of her glasses.

''I thought we'd edge along the outside of the ranch property,'' he said as they passed between the rock pillars marking the entrance to Rancho Encantado. Above the pillars stretched a sign: RANCHO ENCANTADO, WHERE DREAMS COME TRUE.

Do they? Erica wondered, then was distracted as they crossed a dirt road that led to an equipment barn, as well as employee quarters, holding pens and loading chutes necessary for a large working ranch. "That's the original hacienda over there," Hank said, angling his head in the direction of an old adobe structure in the distance. "We'll stop by there on the way back so I can check on some things."

"Great. Where will we go now?"

"We'll be taking the path down to the wash, a little stream called Padre's Creek. The priest lived near there when this was church land."

Erica wished that Melba would hurry up a bit, instead of ambling along with so little spirit. It would be more fun to trot along with the wind blowing in her newly coiffed hair. Melba, however, was placid and calm, determined to give her an easy ride.

Hank continued to direct Erica with pointers about her riding, noting that she seemed to know instinctively how to handle the horse. Not, he admitted to himself, that Melba was that much of a horse. She was elderly and not inclined to be skittish even when ridden by the most nervous of new riders.

They passed a hill and the abandoned borax mine, the remnants of its buildings overgrown with mesquite. After they had traversed the hill, a wide trail led them through a grove of cottonwoods, the land sloping gently down to a creek. In the branches overhead, a bird chattered, sounding very loud in the silence.

"It's been so long since I've paid any attention to nature," Erica said in answer to Hank's quizzical look. "In New York I never even go to the park."

"I see that you brought your camera."

"Yes, it's a digital and I'm still learning how to use it. I used to be a pretty good nature photographer with my old camera, but this one's so new I'm still in the experimental stages.''

"Maybe I can help you get some good shots" was all he said. Later he took care to point out a hawk to her as it circled lazily overhead. She snapped its picture, checked it in the preview lens and liked what she saw.

They heard the purling of the stream before they saw it. As they came around the two large boulders that hid it from view, Erica almost gasped. The little creek was beautiful and unspoiled, curving down from the golden hills and disappearing into a gorge in the distance. This stretch was shallow, with little pools in the rocks that lined the bank.

Hank dismounted and so did she. Erica immediately regretted her haste, considering how much more pleasant it would have been to feel his arms circling her as she had yesterday.

"I was going to help you down," he said, a frown marring his features.

"No need," she said, giving a little laugh that sounded so false she was sure it wouldn't fool him. Before he could comment, she tossed Melba's reins into his outstretched hands and brushed past him, heading for the water. Her precipitous flight was one way to hide her confusion, to find privacy in which she could curse her own stupidity and regain her equilibrium.

The path skirted the ruins of a building, its crumbled stone foundation overgrown with straggly weeds. Beside the path was a bronze plaque, and she stopped to read it.

ON THIS SITE LIVED PADRE LUIS REYES DE SANTIAGO, WHO BUILT A SCHOOL AND A HOSPITAL IN THIS VALLEY IN 1876. FRIEND TO ALL, BENEFACTOR OF MANY, SERVANT OF GOD.

"That's all that's left of his house," Hank said as he came up behind her. "The timber from it was salvaged long ago."

"How about the school and the hospital?"

"Gone. The hospital stood where the guest quarters are, probably very close to Desert Rose. The school was near the Big House."

Erica ran a finger across the raised bronze letters of the plaque. "It's sad to think that there's nothing left of this man's life work when he was apparently important to a lot of people."

She heard a rustle of wind among the tree branches, and a shiver rippled up her spine. It was disconcerting, that shiver, because the sun was warm today. Perhaps Hank felt it, too, because he looked around as if he expected to see someone behind him. But no one was there.

If Hank thought anything was amiss, he gave no sign. "I know of a large flat rock where we can spread the food," he said before continuing down the path.

Erica followed him as she massaged the gooseflesh on her arms, still wondering about that shiver. When she joined Hank at the edge of the creek, he was sitting on a boulder and pulling containers of food out of a saddlebag.

She sat down beside him on rocks warm with sunshine. As the gooseflesh faded, it seemed to her that the rocks throbbed with the beat of the earth—its heart perhaps? A silly notion, but she reminded herself that this place was supposed to be a vortex, a site where the earth's energy was said to activate and energize.

"Hungry?" Hank asked.

"Sure."

He set out a pile of sandwiches, fresh fruit and a plastic container labeled "dessert." "This looks better than my usual fare. I usually make do with something from the freezer so I can spend more time with Kaylie."

This was a safe topic, one Erica felt she could pursue without betraying her tendency to have an out-of-body experience when she was around him. "Kaylie—what does she eat?"

"Horrible-looking stuff out of a jar." He laughed ruefully. "She laps it up, though."

"Does she feed herself?"

He stared at her for a moment. His eyes were bracingly blue in the sunlight of late afternoon. "Well, no. She's only seven months old. She can eat finger foods, like cookies, but she has to be fed."

"As in spoonful by spoonful?" Erica asked with a wry smile.

"Exactly."

"That must take a lot of time."

"It does." He handed her a sandwich. He could recall the days when he hadn't realized how much work a baby was, but now that his days and nights were filled with baby this, baby that, he sometimes forgot that not everyone had this specialized knowledge. Even he, with his multiple college degrees in business and finance, had found the baby-care learning curve difficult.

"I guess you know that I don't know much about babies," she said, unwrapping her sandwich. As she did so, her hair fell slightly forward over her face, softening her features, and he saw for the first time that her nose turned up pertly at the end. He hadn't noticed that when she wore glasses.

He leaned back against a rock. "There sure is a lot to

learn," he allowed before biting into a hearty ham-and-jalapeño cheese sandwich on sourdough bread.

"I heard about what happened to Kaylie's mother," Erica ventured. "I'm sorry."

"How much do you know about the accident?" he asked abruptly.

Erica looked him straight in the eye. He liked that, too.

"That your ex-wife was coming home late and had an automobile accident. That she was on the way home from helping someone."

"That's true. She was." He paused for a moment, not knowing whether to pursue the topic, not sure Erica would be interested. She was gazing at him with interest, so he plunged ahead.

"We'd been divorced for the better part of a year at the time. She worked here with Justine, who'd offered her a job when we split. Anne-Marie was a good person, but we couldn't live together. I guess that was my fault."

"Usually it's the fault of both people if a relationship doesn't work out," Erica said carefully.

He grunted, knowing she was right. But it would be ungentlemanly, he thought, not to shoulder the blame for the failure of his marriage. The truth was, he and Anne-Marie never should have gotten married. It had taken only a matter of months for them to discover that they had little in common, and they'd both felt relief when they'd separated. And then, out of a misbegotten sense of obligation, they had decided to give the marriage one more try. It had been a fateful decision, but he didn't regret it. For the first time he felt the need to explain his feelings to someone. To Erica, who was looking at him with a serious expression, one that encouraged him to open up.

He drew a deep breath. "Kaylie is the result of an attempted reconciliation between Anne-Marie and me. Neither one of us expected to make a baby, and...well, I can't say I was happy to learn Anne-Marie was pregnant. But when I saw my daughter for the first time, I was out-and-out crazy about her." He'd been overwhelmed with emotion the first time he'd seen Kaylie's chubby little cheeks, her fuzz of pale hair. He considered his daughter the best thing that had ever happened to him, despite all the huge changes she'd brought to his life.

"She's a darling baby." Erica didn't want to pry, but she hoped Hank would go on talking. His face lit up when he spoke of his daughter, and he looked younger, more carefree. She wondered how old he was. Thirty-four? Thirty-five?

He pushed an apple in her direction, and she caught it before it rolled off the rock. "I can't imagine life without Kaylie," he said truthfully. "She makes everything worthwhile."

"Working so hard, you mean?" She was studying him, her eyes so deep and solemn he could hardly glance away.

His reminder to himself that the work he did now was not his normal job caught him up short. He couldn't imagine how he was going to manage when he returned to his old life.

"That and other things," he said.

"It must be lonely being a single father."

It was, but he'd never admitted it to anyone except himself. He shrugged, embarrassed.

She looked away. "I'm sorry," she said. "It's only that I've been questioning my own life since I've been here where things are so different from New York. When you're caught up in a hectic whirlwind of activity, you don't take time to think that there are options.'' She bit into the apple, a pensive expression settling over her features.

He would have liked to pursue the topic further. There were few people in the world with whom he felt comfortable talking about private matters, but this woman had quickly put him at ease with her disarming and total interest, as well as her quiet acceptance. He wanted to know more about her.

"Do you like living in New York, Erica?"

"It's okay. I grew up in Rhode Island."

"The ranch is a real change for you then, isn't it?" He could imagine her in the city somehow. She had a big-city polish, a big-city attitude.

"The change is a welcome one. I'm glad I came here."

"How long are you staying?"

"A week," she said.

"A week," he repeated thoughtfully.

As he reached for another sandwich, he spotted a quick movement along the bank of the creek.

"Look," he whispered, putting a hand on Erica's arm to draw her attention to where he was pointing. A coyote stood at attention on the opposite bank. Something upstream seemed to have caught his attention, and he seemed oblivious to the two of them. He stood with his ears up, his tail down, in a posture of alertness.

"He's come for water," Hank said.

Erica fumbled for her camera, then focused on the coyote. She snapped a picture, hoping the beep of the camera wouldn't startle him. The coyote's ears still stood at attention, but he didn't run. After a minute or so, he lowered his head and loped out of sight.

Erica sighed, "He was beautiful." Hank's hand still rested on her arm, and he didn't want to move it. She wore a long-sleeved shirt, and her skin felt warm beneath it, warm and solid and real. He thought about how good it would feel to have her warmth pressed against him, enveloping him. He thought about the way her breasts swelled against the front of her shirt. He thought he would have liked to touch his finger to the shadow beneath the curve of her jaw, and he wondered if the skin there would be warm or cool, whether he'd be able to feel the throb of her pulse. He didn't think he could bear it if he never found out.

"I've never seen a live coyote," Erica said. "His coat, the amber and buff, is exactly the color I would have liked Tico to make my hair."

He studied her hair, which was shiny and made him long to run his fingers through it. "Your color," he said judiciously, "is not so far off."

She laughed, and he laughed, too. He discovered that it felt good to be laughing with someone, to feel such camaraderie.

She hit the preview button on the camera, and the picture of the coyote popped up. She zoomed in on it so that the animal's image filled the whole frame and held it toward Hank. "Take a look."

In order to see the tiny screen, he had to slide closer to her and soon he was so close their thighs touched.

"Very nice," he said, but he wasn't talking about the coyote. As he studied the picture, in which the coyote was looking straight into the lens and appeared to be laughing at them, the coyote winked.

Winked? He couldn't have. This was a digital camera, not a video camera. And coyotes didn't wink at people.

Still, he could have sworn that the coyote had winked

at him, and strangest of all, he had the idea that if the animal could have spoken, he would have made one of those comments guys sometimes made to each other when one of them was hot on the chase. Something like "Good luck, pardner."

Which he didn't really need. He was lucky already just to have met someone like Erica Strong.

Padre Luis Speaks...

MADRE DE DIOS! What is taking so long? Erica and Hank went to the site of my house, and I can still see it standing, though they cannot. It is a blessed place.

Perhaps that is why they are making progress. And although I can almost see the outline of Erica when she walks through our courtyard now, she is still hoping for the wrong thing. A "fling!" What is this "fling"? I am beside myself trying to understand these people.

Oh, if these two would only surrender themselves to the inner transformation that awaits them in this spiritual place! Instead, this Erica, she wants to change her hair, change her eyes, change the whole outside of her, which I cannot see, anyway. I can see her spirit, however. It is the color gray. That is not the color of a healthy spirit.

I am beside myself, I tell you! Beside myself!

I need my voice. I must speak to Erica. Where is that cat? When I see her, I will push her into the cactus. No, I won't. God forgive me, I am not a cruel man. But I must make the cat understand that if I do not have my voice, I will have to reveal myself to Erica, and that might make her afraid.

God, I stand before You, Your humble servant. Tell me what to do. Show me what to do. Send me that cat. Help me get back my voice before these mortals do themselves serious harm.

Chapter Six

The battered, hacienda-style house, its adobe walls bleached the color of parchment by the sun, was partially hidden behind a windbreak of tamarisks. Hank had been working to refurbish the old house when time permitted, and he was there now to make a list of needed supplies.

"Is this place the source of the Rancho Encantado ghost?" Erica asked as they drew the horses to a stop at the end of the wooden veranda in front.

"If so, I wish he'd take more of an interest in the hacienda's upkeep. I could use another pair of hands around here." His tone was ruefully amused.

"Want me to wait while you go inside?"

"No, I'll show you around. It's interesting to see how the people lived, ghost or no ghost."

As Hank helped her dismount, he told her that the Iversons, Dan and Betsy, were a young couple when they had homesteaded here around 1910.

"They wanted to farm but couldn't make a go of it. Cattle and sheep had been brought in by miners in the 1860s, and they'd break through the farmers' fences and destroy their crops. After several years of drought, the farmers mostly went to work in the mines. Finally there were full-fledged range wars, farmers fighting the ranchers, ranchers hating the farmers. The ranchers won, and soon the Iversons moved away.''

''That's too bad.''

Hank looped the horses' reins over the old hitching post. ''You could say that. On the other hand, Dan went to work at a tungsten mine and in his spare time managed to uncover a rich silver vein in a nearby mountain. He became a wealthy man, one of the pillars of Carson City. He sometimes said that the best thing that ever happened to him was *not* succeeding as a farmer.''

Erica, while listening to Hank speak, noticed that the front door to the adobe house hung open. ''Don't you lock the door?'' she wanted to know.

He chuckled. ''This isn't the city, Erica. No one bothers this place.''

Inside, a wide arched fireplace, its odor reminiscent of long-ago fires, occupied one wall of the large front room. The walls wore a coat of fresh white paint, and empty paint cans sat in one corner.

Hank pushed his hat back and cocked his hands on his hips as he surveyed the paint job, the narrow metal cot in one corner covered with a colorful serape, the handhewn wood of the table beside the door.

''Who uses this house?''

''I used to come here when I wanted to be alone. That's how I became interested in refurbishing it for Justine.''

''It's primitive now, but it could be beautiful.''

He smiled in agreement. ''It has potential.''

While Hank hauled empty paint cans out to the garbage heap out back, Erica wandered into the kitchen, which contained an old wood-burning stove, a sandstone sink and a massive oak table. While she was studying the cobwebs in the overhead beams, Hank reappeared in the doorway. "Come with me. I want to show you what's in one of the back rooms."

She followed Hank down a hall to a series of rooms that had probably been used as bedrooms when the house was inhabited.

"Justine piled old furnishings here when she let some construction workers live here last summer while they built an addition on the Big House," he told her. "Look, there's an antique pine bedstead, and there are three or four humpbacked trunks. There's crockery, too, in that beatup crate."

The crate had been pried open, the cover tossed nearby. When she looked she saw that the dishes inside were of various patterns—blue willow, one with a border of daisies, some with a heavy green glaze. Erica wondered about the people who had once lived here. These dishes would have been part of their daily lives.

While she tried without success to pry open the lid of one of the old trunks, Hank disappeared into the next room. She heard him opening and closing a window as he whistled to himself. The light and shadow that the late-afternoon light streaming through the window cast on the jumble of furnishings would make an interesting still life, she thought, so she readied her camera and photographed the scene from several different angles.

When Hank returned, he was making notations on a pad of paper. "The windows in this place are in bad shape," he said.

Erica slid her camera back in its case. "How often do you come here?"

"On weekends usually." He tucked the notepad into his pocket.

Erica was mindful of the weekend coming up. Somehow the image of a cowboy repairing a run-down build-

ing on his time off did not seem appropriate; shouldn't
he be frequenting the local watering holes and chatting
up cowgirls?

"It relaxes me to work with my hands," he said, apparently feeling some need for explanation.

A wind sprang up outside in a whirl of dust and tumbleweed, pushing back the door of the front room to gain
admittance, funneling off toward the kitchen in a merry
whoosh and becoming no more than a caress on Erica's
skin by the time it reached the back bedroom where she
and Hank stood. She felt the caress in the same breath
that Hank mentioned working with his hands, and the
wind whispered as it spiraled past the little whorls in her
ear, *You could find him something more personal to do
with his hands.* She saw those hands as they would be
if he reached out and curved them around her breasts,
and for a moment it seemed as if she could feel their
heat and their strength. Her nipples firmed beneath her
new yellow flannel shirt at the thought, and the wind,
having accomplished its mission, settled down at her feet
with a contented sigh.

"Better close these windows," Hank said, moving to
do so while Erica agitatedly hurried into the living room
to do absolutely nothing but shiver in what she thought
was anticipation. But anticipation for what? Even though
she was sure he had almost kissed her yesterday after
her riding lesson, he had shown no sign of being physically attracted to her today. She was imagining things.
She was making things up. She was so accustomed to
having her brain brim full of things to do, was always
rushing from one place to another, that when there was
extra time to be filled, she filled it by daydreaming about
things that weren't happening. Could never happen. In
a million years.

Now Hank was sauntering out of the bedroom, and he was stark naked.

Omigosh.

And then her eyes refocused, and she saw that he was fully clothed. He wasn't anywhere near naked. This was another figment of her imagination, and she'd better put a stop to it. But how? She had been imagining her perfect cowboy all of her adult life, and now that she'd found him, who could blame her for giving her imagination full rein?

She turned away, but he reached out and stopped her by casually resting a hand on her shoulder. When she thought about what she'd just imagined that hand could do, she felt a blush creep up the sides of her neck, the warmth of it staining her cheeks.

He did not seem to notice. "Let's go out back for a minute."

He didn't say why, and she didn't question. It was enough to know that he was enjoying her company enough to want to spend extra time with her.

In the back of the house was a tumbledown wooden shed. "This was where the Iversons kept their farm animals," he said. To one side a trickle of water dribbled from a pipe into a basin made of a hollowed-out rock. A tin cup on a chain dangled from the pipe. "You can taste the water if you like," he said.

She held the cup under the water until she had collected enough to drink. The water was surprisingly cool. "Tastes a little salty," she said after a sip.

"It is," Hank agreed. "But okay to drink."

While Hank stacked flowerpots in the old shed, she took a few pictures of the light and shadow playing across its weatherbeaten boards. By the time the sun tinged the snowy mountain peaks pink in the distance, they were ready to leave.

She remained quiet on the way back to the ranch. The square dance was tonight, and Hank hadn't mentioned it. As they rode into the stable yard, she was mulling over whether she should ask him if she'd see him there, but before she decided, Cord McCall strode out of the feed room.

"Hank, where you been?"

"We've just come from the Iverson place. It's time to fix those windows." Hank swung down from Whip's back, but before he could reach Erica to help her dismount, Cord had reached for Melba's bridle.

Erica dismounted on her own. Cord gave her a curt nod and led Melba into her stall. Not knowing what else to do, Erica tagged along.

"Hank, I'll help you rub the horses down, and then you and me need to sit down and figure out our purchasing requirements for the stable," Cord said.

"I'll need to make sure Justine isn't tired of looking after Kaylie," Hank said. "I was planning to go over to the Big House."

Cord looked disgruntled. "I've only got a few minutes until I have to be on the road," he said. "I was hoping we could settle things before I go."

"I'll check with Justine about Kaylie," Erica said. "If you like."

Hank seemed to notice her for the first time since they'd ridden in. "Would you? I'd be grateful. Tell Justine I'll be there as soon as we finish up here."

Erica set off for the Big House, not minding the errand. Since she had her camera with her, she'd use this opportunity to snap some shots of Murphy. If Kaylie was available, she'd take some photos of her, as well.

But she wouldn't ask Justine if Hank was going to the dance. Her pride wouldn't let her.

AN HOUR OR SO after he arrived back at the ranch, Justine was fixing Hank with a no-nonsense glare. "What do you mean you don't want to go to the dance tonight?"

Hank shifted his weight to his other foot. "I want to take Kaylie off your hands."

"Don't be silly, Hank. We have a whole lot of women who are going to need partners tonight, pardner."

Hank unwrapped a fresh cookie from its cellophane wrap and handed it to his daughter, whose eyes lit up as she grabbed it. "The last job I had, they didn't expect me to work all day and dance all night," he said glumly. Still, he'd bet Erica was going to be at the square dance.

"The last job you had didn't provide free babysitting," Justine said tartly. "Anyway, was it really work to take a leisurely trail ride with Erica today?"

"Not exactly," he admitted. "Hey, did she put you up to this?"

"To what?"

"To insisting I go to the dance."

"No. She delivered the message that you'd be here soon and took Murphy for a run so she could take some pictures of him. We did not discuss you. You like her, don't you?" Justine's sideways glance was mischievous.

"I didn't say that," Hank said, but he couldn't stop a grin from spreading across his face. He quickly quelled it.

"I saw that smile," Justine said. She poked him in the ribs. "You're ready to rejoin the dating scene at last, I'd say."

"Did I mention anything about dating?" he said, dancing out of her reach.

"No, but that doesn't mean much."

"So what if I do indulge in a minor flirtation?"

Justine sobered up at that. "Don't go breaking hearts, Hank. It's not good for business. It's not good for anyone. If you and Erica want to enjoy yourselves in any and every way, it isn't any business of mine, but..."

He nailed her with a meaningful look. "You've got that right. It isn't any of your business. So let's not talk about it, okay?"

"Erica's a nice person. I've been hearing about her from Charmaine for years, and Char's worried about her. She says she's too uptight and she needs this vacation. She doesn't need a broken heart."

"I'm not planning on breaking any hearts."

"Go easy on Erica. That's all I'm asking."

"I get the message. You don't mind keeping Kaylie here all night?"

Justine swept Kaylie up into her arms, gummy cookie and all. Kaylie giggled and Justine grinned. "Do I mind? I'd love it!"

Justine had been good to him and to his family. Hell, she was good to everyone.

"All right, I guess I'll go get my dancing shoes on."

"You'd better show up in full cowboy regalia."

"You've almost convinced me that I'm a real cowboy," he said, handing Kaylie her bottle of juice.

"You are, you are," said Justine. "By the way, there's a stack of mail for you on the hall table."

"I'll grab it on my way out."

The mail was all junk except for a white envelope bearing the logo of Rowbotham-Quigley. He picked it up and turned it over, hesitating for a few seconds before he stuffed it deep in his back pocket.

Wouldn't you know that just when he was beginning to feel like a real cowboy, his firm would remind him that he wasn't? Well, he was a cowboy for the moment, anyway. He might as well enjoy it to the hilt.

AS SHE DRESSED for the dance, Erica realized that the necklace that Charmaine had given her, the gold disk engraved with her initials, was missing. She looked around her suite, hoping to find it on the floor, but it wasn't there. She tried to think of when she'd worn it, and to the best of her recollection, she'd felt it swinging at her throat as she repositioned the still life of discarded items in the hacienda earlier. Perhaps she'd lost it there, in which case she would go back and look for it as soon as the opportunity presented itself.

The blue light on the phone blinked, signifying a call. It was Natalie, phoning to see if she was ready to leave for the dance. "Want to walk over with us?" she asked.

"Sure, meet you in the courtyard." Erica flung a sweater around her shoulders and stepped outside.

The cactus garden in the middle of the courtyard was brightly illuminated tonight by the full moon, and since Natalie and Shannon had not emerged yet, she sat down to wait on the bench facing it. The cacti were beautiful in a strange, unearthly way, bathed as they were in moonlight. You could almost imagine that they were people, giant arms outstretched above their... *Was* that a man standing among the cacti? A portly man with his arms extended in an attitude of benediction?

Surely not. Erica blinked, sure that her contact lenses were distorting her vision. But no. It really *was* a man among the cacti, a man wearing a robe like a monk's.

He wore a benevolent smile and opened his mouth as if to speak. She stared, unable to look away, and waited to see what he was going to say.

"Erica? Are you sure that sweater will keep you warm enough?"

She leaped to her feet and whirled around, but it was only Natalie approaching from the direction of her room. Shannon was close behind her.

"Goodness, Erica, you look as if you've seen a ghost! Is anything wrong?"

Erica looked back at the empty cactus garden and then at Natalie and Shannon. She was too astonished to speak. She was sure there'd been a man standing in the middle of the cactus garden. But who would take up occupancy of a cactus garden in any circumstance? It was bound to be uncomfortable. Unless he really was a ghost. Uneasily, she thought of Padre Luis.

"Don't mind me," Erica managed to say. "I was lost in thought, I guess."

"Well, you can stop thinking. The nightlife here isn't exactly Planet Hollywood, but we're going to have a great time."

Still shaken, and with one last backward look, Erica left with them, unwilling to believe that the ghostly image among the cacti had been anything but one of her flights of fancy. She resolutely put the episode out of her mind and made herself focus on the evening ahead.

When they arrived at the recreation hall, they found that it had been adorned with fluttering multicolored strips of crepe paper. A bar along the side was decorated with Rancho Encantado memorabilia, and an old-time jukebox lit up one corner. Colored bulbs aimed at a revolving mirrored ball above the dance floor sent bright flashes of light arcing around the room.

Shannon seemed to have the scoop on all the cowboys in attendance and was more than willing to dish. "See the tall guy with the scar on his chin? That's Cord McCall, the ranch manager."

"I've met him. He seems grumpy."

Shannon lowered her voice. "The scuttlebutt is that Justine is frantic to replace him. Cord saved the working operation of this ranch from going down the tubes, but he might quit at any time. He's unhappy with his job."

"I know the feeling," Erica replied, realizing guiltily that she hadn't worried once about the Gillooley deal since she'd been here.

"Also, Cord McCall keeps taking off for Nevada, and everybody thinks he's hanging out at Miss Kitti-Kat's Teahouse, which isn't really a teahouse, if you know what I mean." Shannon laughed.

"Who is the guy standing next to Cord?"

"He's called Stumpy, we can only guess why."

Shannon went on naming names until Erica was ready to ask her to cease and desist, but she didn't mention the one that Erica was most eager to hear. Finally Shannon said wryly, "As for Hunk, he's off being hunky somewhere else, I guess. I don't see him here."

Despite telling herself all along that Hank probably wouldn't show up, Erica was swept with disappointment. Well, what had she expected? Hank had been away from Kaylie all day. As much as she longed to see him, to dance with him tonight, it pleased Erica that her cowboy was a conscientious father. It was something else to admire about him.

People began to form up squares, and one cowboy, Vernon, asked Erica to join a square where Tony, the van driver, and Sue, the personal shopper, were the lead couple. Vernon was good-humored and knew his allemande lefts from his do-si-dos. To his credit, he didn't step on her toes once, even though she wasn't giving the dance her full attention, glancing frequently at the door.

She had been there an hour or more before finally Hank walked in. She melted immediately at the sight of his lean body lounging against a pillar as he surveyed the scene. When he caught her eye, his face broke out in a smile. It was all she needed, that smile, to feel an emotional electricity jump across the wide space that separated them, sizzling her sensitive nerve endings and making her want to— Well! He linked his thumbs in his belt loops, spared her a brief nod and headed toward the bar.

Chuck, her partner, chose that moment to make a clever remark, but Erica couldn't have repeated it even if someone had offered her a million dollars. She merely smiled and craned her neck for a better view of Hank.

The band decided to take a break, and Chuck returned her to the table where Shannon and Natalie were sitting with Sal, who was amusing onlookers by ripping beer bottle tops off with his teeth. Hank had disappeared from the bar. Had he left? Erica hadn't been watching the door, but there were several exits, the nearest one leading out onto the long porch ranging along the back of the building.

I hope he hasn't left, she told herself. *If he has, I wish he'd come back.*

No sooner had her thoughts shaped themselves into a wish than Hank materialized at her elbow, almost as if she'd conjured him up.

"May I get you something to drink?"

She shook her head. Shannon and Natalie sat with their mouths hanging open, seemingly astonished that the man they called Hunk had, apparently of his own free will, chosen to talk to Erica.

He pulled a chair alongside Erica and straddled it, resting his arms along the back. "Having a good time?"

She was of half a mind to say that she was having a much better time now that he was there, but the other half of her mind came up with "Yes, I am. I thought you'd be home with Kaylie tonight."

He shrugged and took another swig of beer. "I couldn't pry her loose from her devoted aunt. She's keeping her for the night."

"They seem to like each other."

"That's true." The band filed back onto the bandstand and picked up their instruments. "Would you like to dance?" he asked.

Would she like to dance? Did a horse have four legs? Were the mountains high, was water wet? She nodded and he took her hand.

The mirrored ball overhead sent rainbow refractions of light across the walls, floor and ceiling, and the large rec hall was transformed into a dream world of light and color. She turned to face Hank and rested her hand on his shoulder, embarrassed that her right palm was sweaty and hoping he wouldn't notice. As the band struck up a waltz, Hank guided her onto the floor, and her feet began to move in predictable patterns. She hadn't waltzed in…oh, it seemed like a million years. When she went to parties in New York, there were often bands, but she usually spent the time with her fingers clamped around the stem of one wet cocktail glass after another, listening earnestly to fat bald men who either pumped her for information or pontificated on some topic for her enlightenment.

She'd always been sure that her perfect cowboy would

know his way around a dance floor, and she was not disappointed. His eyes glinting with pleasure, Hank pulled her closer and she closed her eyes in pure delight. This whole scenario seemed like the answer to many prayers offered up in desperation over the years.

Kaylie would be at Justine's all night long. Hank would not have to put her to bed, get up with her when she cried, change diapers or fill bottles.

What better time to embark on a fling? The only thing left for her to do was to convince Hank that she was the one he wanted.

HANK RESTED his cheek against a cloud of honey-blond hair that happened to be attached to the woman he had so recently begun to admire in spite of himself.

Erica Strong, he said to himself. *Erica Strong.* He even liked the sound of her name. He liked her forthrightness, her serious and wholehearted way of listening to what he had to say, the funny little line between her eyes when she was thinking something over. She was so different from Lizette and the other women he knew in New York. They were all, without exception, trendy and flippant and into themselves. They talked about their analysts, their jobs, their girlfriends. They made it clear that they didn't need a man, although they certainly seemed to want one.

Erica never mentioned her neuroses, her work or friends. Unlike the women he knew back in the city, she seemed unfailingly sweet and sympathetic. He could imagine rescuing her from the path of a steaming locomotive. She seemed like someone who would welcome his help and protection. Still, he thought he should perhaps try to find out if she was like all those other women.

"What kind of work do you do?" he asked her.

She jumped slightly as if startled. "I work for McNee, Levy and Ashe. Investment bankers."

He knew the company. Erica, he figured, might be an administrative assistant or something along those lines. He was prepared to inquire further about her job when the music stopped and the band immediately broke into a rollicking polka. His question forgotten, it took only a few seconds for him to change gears, and then they were circling the floor along with the other couples.

There was little opportunity for talking when the dancing was so energetic, and at the end of the dance, the band segued right into another polka. When that one was over, Erica offered up a scintillating smile. His arms involuntarily tightened around her, and he had the wistful thought that he didn't want to let her go. He couldn't recall when he had ever enjoyed one of these dances so much.

"I'll take you up on that offer to buy me a drink," Erica said, and he laughed. Then, his arm around her waist, he found a table for two in the shadows. He gestured to Paloma, who was working as one of the waitresses tonight. He wasn't surprised to see her here. She was working as much as she could so that she and her fiancé could get married as soon as possible.

Paloma's pencil was poised over her order pad. "Yes, Hank?"

"I'll have another beer, Paloma. What would you like, Erica?"

In her daydreams, Erica always ordered a margarita, so she ordered one now. Paloma smiled at them and disappeared toward the bar.

"That's Kaylie's baby-sitter," Hank told her.

"She works two jobs?"

"Paloma is saving her money so that she and Miguel, her boyfriend since high school, can get married."

"She must be very industrious," Erica said, but she didn't really want to talk about Paloma. She traced a damp circle, left by someone else's glass, on the shiny tabletop. She wished she could work the conversational direction around to Hank again. There were many more things she wanted to know about him—how he had come to work for Rancho Encantado, where he intended to go if he left. She surmised that he planned to leave eventually; she could hardly imagine that he would want to go on working for Justine forever.

"You look very lovely tonight," he said.

"Oh," she said, at a loss. "Sue, my wardrobe consultant, talked me into buying this outfit at the gift shop."

"Erica," he said gently, "don't you know how to take a compliment?"

"I...well, I don't hear too many of them," she admitted, and then she cursed herself silently for telling him that. She didn't want him to think that other men didn't find her desirable. In fact, they did. She had dates, when she found the time. Underlying these thoughts was the knowledge that she was more a convenience to the men she dated than a companion. They called her when they needed something, like a respectable partner for a dinner party or a fill-in when someone else couldn't make it or even when they wanted sex. They didn't call her because they wanted her, Erica, for her very own self.

Unbidden tears sprang to her eyes, and she tried to blink them away before Hank saw them. Too late; her head was angled downward, and one fell smack-dab into the middle of the damp ring on the tabletop.

He noticed. "Erica, is something wrong?"

She shook her head and squeezed her eyes closed, thinking that when she opened them, Hank would be gone like all the other daydreams, like all the past cowboys who were figments of her imagination.

But when her eyes opened, he was still there, and he was looking concerned and caring and perplexed.

At that moment Paloma walked up with the beer and the margarita and set the drinks down in front of them.

Hank felt a little tremor of anxiety at the sight of that single tear. He had thought that she was the kind of woman he had always wanted to meet. Now here was this tear, and it might indicate—in fact, probably *did* indicate—that she had come to the ranch like so many other women to get over a love affair gone wrong.

He didn't need the problems a woman like that could bring to his life. He didn't need problems, period. He would have gotten up and excused himself in as mannerly a way as possible except that he had really developed an affinity to Erica Strong. He liked her. His liking went beyond that to include something more akin to lust, but beginner lust, not a full-blown case of it. Perhaps it wasn't too late to nip this relationship in the bud.

Only how to nip it when he wanted to see it in full bloom? Plus, he didn't want to be the cause of another tear falling on the tabletop. Once started, those tears were hard to stop. He knew all about that.

Whatever the problem, there seemed to be no more tears, only a wistfulness he found most appealing. "Will you dance with me again?" he asked gently, and she nodded.

The band was playing something slow, and a few of the couples on the floor were barely moving at all. This was the time of the evening when people paired up, slipping off two by two toward the guest quarters. What about him? He had never paired off with a guest at one of these dances, though not because there hadn't been the opportunity. He'd always told himself he wasn't interested.

"Hank?" Erica was standing beside him now, her shoulders pale in the dim light, and she held out her hand. When he took her hand in his, he felt the softness of her palm, imagined the warmth of her breasts beneath his cupped hands. A quiver of excitement raced up his spine and down again to a much more relevant part of his anatomy, and to save himself the embarrassment of anyone's noticing, he turned to Erica and took her in his arms.

She gave a long-drawn-out sigh of anticipation. Or was it satisfaction? Her curves—and she *did* have curves—melded to the hard planes of his body, and he slid both arms around her waist. It was as if he had always known how she would feel in his arms, as if she were made to fit. She pressed her face against his shoulder, settling in there, and he buried his face in her fragrant hair. It smelled of honeysuckle, his favorite scent since he was a child, and he imagined what it would be like to wake up to that scent.

When the music ended, they didn't want to break apart. Hank wanted to go on holding her until the room and the noise and the confusion of other people faded away, until it was only the two of them.

"Let's get some air," he said unevenly, leading her out a nearby door to the secluded side porch overlooking the palm grove. The breeze rustled the palm fronds and ruffled her hair. A full moon spilled its light over the scene. Erica gazed up at him, her eyelids half-closed, and he realized with a start that this was the fulfillment of a daydream he'd had more times than he could count.

He was always on the porch outside the recreation hall with a gal who wore a white, low-necked peasant blouse and a short, full red skirt. The skirt was the same skirt Erica wore tonight. Exactly as in the daydream, her breasts were lush and partially exposed; they shone pale in the moonlight.

Standing on the step below her, he glanced up at her, smoldering with desire. "Erica, let's slip away together. Let's find a place where we can be alone."

Again, exactly as in the daydream, Erica slid a look back through the open door, where couples were gliding beneath the crepe-paper streamers. "We'll be missed."

It was his dream come true, down to the smallest detail. He felt a rightness and inevitability about this as he had about nothing else in his life. As he had so many times in his fantasies, Hank ran a bold hand up the inside of her leg. "We can be back before anyone notices. Let's—"

The door behind them opened suddenly and slammed closed. A clatter of footsteps made them both whirl around. A harsh female voice exclaimed, "Well, it took me long enough to find you! Are you glad to see me?"

Hank blinked in disbelief at the woman with the geometrical haircut and high cheekbones. At the same time, his daydream popped like a burst bubble. Erica gaped at the apparition before them.

Unfortunately the apparition was no dream. It was real.

"Hello, Lizette," Hank said with tired resignation. "How in the world do you happen to be at Rancho Encantado?"

Padre Luis Speaks...

AH, ERICA. Now I see you, my child. When you cried, you became real. Despite the different hair, different eyes, different figure, different clothes, you let Hank see the person you really are.

Children, you are on the right track. I know you cannot hear me. I still don't have my voice. But at this moment, it is not so important.

What is important is love. Love! I am only a humble priest, but this is what I know. I hope and pray that you will know it, too.

I wish I could leave my office. It is difficult to be so confined. But do you know, I am getting quite accustomed to the cactus plants. At certain times of the year, they grow beautiful flowers. Who would think that among the sharp thorns, a lovely flower could bloom?

The cactus is like our lives. Thorny, but occasionally blossoming into moments of great beauty. How delightful that I have learned this lesson! Truly, truly God blesses us all.

Chapter Seven

As she watched Hank and Lizette disappear into the palm grove, it was all Erica could do not to burst into tears. In her daydreams, the cowboy never walked off with someone else.

"Hey, little lady, what are you doing out here all by yourself?"

Erica whirled around in time to see Chuck through the screen door behind her. He opened it and stepped outside, affording her an easy grin.

"Just getting some fresh air."

"Looked like you might be frettin'."

"No." She could no longer see Hank and Lizette, and she wondered if they had taken the path to the right, which led to the oasis hot pool, or to the left, which would bring them to the guest quarters. Lizette had said she was a guest at the ranch.

Chuck was assessing Erica with interest. His eyes lingered first on her breasts, then on her lips. At one time she might have responded to him, but now that she'd met the perfect cowboy, she couldn't muster the effort to encourage the *not*-so-perfect cowboy. Not that Chuck was unattractive, far from it. But his pale hair, blue eyes and ruddy complexion weren't nearly as exciting to her as Hank's dark good looks.

Nevertheless, he was smiling expectantly. "Want to dance?"

With Hank's swift apology and retreat still ringing in her ears, she was too numb to think of a way to turn Chuck down without hurting his feelings. And before she knew it, she was being led into a large circle of people and the caller was explaining the dance. She was so distracted that she had trouble focusing, but Chuck was kind and forgiving of her missteps.

She wished she had known that Hank had a girlfriend, but would it have made a difference in how she felt about him? Probably not. She would never have dreamed that Hank would be interested in someone so hard-edged. Someone so much like herself.

But she was different now. She was beginning to feel embarrassed about her former attitude, her brusqueness, her lack of interest in anything but her job. There was a whole world out here, one she had only dreamed about, and she was fitting into it so well that she could hardly recall what she had found so compelling about her way of life.

Chuck held Erica close for a moment after the last dance was over, and she knew that the hug was the prelude to an advance. She immediately pulled away. He accepted her rejection with good humor and moved on to the bar, where he sat down next to someone who seemed to welcome his attentions.

"Come with us," called Shannon, who was on the arm of a cowboy that Erica didn't recognize. Natalie was with Sal, batting adoring eyes up at him.

"Sorry, but I'm going back to my suite."

"Aw, c'mon, we're going to party for a while longer," said Sal.

"I'm not in the mood. See you tomorrow."

Hiding her misery as well as she could, Erica slipped out of the rec hall. From the banter of the people who were leaving the building at the same time, she gathered that some of them were driving over the Nevada border into Sonoco. It was not a jaunt that appealed to her, especially in her present frame of mind.

She pulled her sweater closer around her shoulders and started out alone for Desert Rose, mindful that things could have been so different. On her way through the palm grove, she heard the murmurings of an amorous couple near the oasis hot pool. The woman laughed, a provocative sound, and then there was only silence. Erica veered away, choosing another path toward her quarters. What if that was Hank with Lizette? If that was who it was, she didn't want to know.

As she approached Desert Rose, she realized she couldn't face the empty rooms yet. Earlier she'd been anticipating meeting Hank there, and now that he was out of the picture, she didn't want to be alone. Was she angry with him? Oh, yes. He'd led her on. Still, she had come on strong. Perhaps she'd misread his signals, though she was sure he'd never given her so much as a hint that he had a girlfriend. To his credit, when Lizette showed up, he'd first looked astonished, then annoyed. In the end, however, he had introduced them rapidly and hustled Lizette away with hardly a backward glance.

As she looked toward the Big House and saw no lights in the windows, she thought how good it would be to indulge in a session of girl talk with Justine. But it was too late to go visiting, and since she was mindful of the tension between Justine and Hank, it wouldn't be right to take Justine into her confidence.

Yet she was too restless, too upset to call it a night. There didn't seem to be anyone else who wasn't otherwise occupied on this night when she wanted—no, needed—some company so she wouldn't get more depressed than she already was.

Her thoughts turned to the horses—Melba, Whip, Sebastian and those she didn't know yet. Visiting them would give her something to do. Horses accepted people for who they were. They didn't judge or gossip. And they didn't run off with girlfriends you didn't know they had.

She let herself into her suite, exchanged the red skirt for a pair of jeans and threw a warm jacket over her blouse to ward off the chill. Then she headed for the stable, bringing herself to an abrupt halt when she remembered that Hank's apartment was located at one end of the building. She had no desire to run into him so soon after he'd ditched her.

After she'd thought about it for a few seconds, she shrugged and made herself move forward. Considering the fact that he had walked off with Lizette, Hank probably wouldn't be in his own apartment tonight, anyway.

"I'VE BEEN HOPPING on and off planes all day long to get to this godforsaken place," Lizette said to Hank as she tossed her Gucci bag onto the couch in her suite in Sagebrush, the building right next to Desert Rose. Hank thought longingly of Erica back on the porch and how her eyes had widened in dismay at the sight of Lizette, who'd arrived wearing a black wool turtleneck sweater, a long black skirt and black high-heeled boots—all very New York. Once upon a time in a different life he had considered such a getup sexy. Now Lizette merely looked overheated and uncomfortable.

"I was lucky to get this suite—the previous guest had to rush home to take care of her daughter, who came down with the flu. There's a lot of flu going around these days. Two people in my Life Strategy class were out with it this week." She yawned and tucked the front strands of her sleek, squared-off black bob behind her ears. "Do me a favor, Henry. Pour me a drink from that flask in my tote while I change into something more comfortable."

After Lizette went into the bedroom, Hank found the scotch, opened a bottle of soda from the minibar and mixed Lizette's drink. He also mixed one for himself— a very stiff one.

Hank had already downed most of his drink before Lizette appeared in the doorway.

"Lovey bunny, aren't you glad to see me?"

"I wasn't expecting you," he said more than a tad ungraciously.

She glided over to him in high-heeled mules trimmed with maribou. The negligee she wore was almost transparent.

She accepted her drink from his outstretched hand. "Let's lie down on the bed for a while, shall we? I'm really tired."

Unwillingly he followed her into the bedroom and watched Lizette drape herself dramatically across the bed pillows and pat the comforter beside her. "Right here, Henry. Close enough to kiss." She smiled invitingly, and he realized that he had not kissed her hello. Nor did he want to.

He sat gingerly on the edge of the bed, preparing to extricate himself from this situation. The dance was over, and Erica would be walking home through the palm grove, perhaps alone. He hoped she was alone, though he felt guilty for wishing that. He'd noticed Chuck giving her the eye while they were dancing. Of course, Erica wasn't his woman. She could have been his woman for the night, though. He was fairly confident of that.

"Henry? Aren't you listening?"

He stood. "No, I'm not. Lizette, I'm really tired. Perhaps we should both get some rest and deal with this tomorrow."

She sat straight up. "Deal with *what* tomorrow?"

"With…everything," he said.

Her eyes were a sort of amber color. They would have been pretty if they hadn't been shooting yellow sparks. Lizette was hopping mad.

"I came all the way here to see you and you aren't going to spend the night with me?"

"Lizette—"

She let out a sigh of exasperation. "All right, Henry. I'm tired, too. I'll feel better after I get my beauty sleep."

Feeling a wash of relief, he turned to make tracks for the door.

"Oh, by the way, I'll see you on your trail ride tomorrow afternoon. I signed up when I checked in."

He'd almost forgotten he was supposed to lead that ride tomorrow. He didn't want Lizette on it, not by a long shot. There wasn't much he could do about it, though, if she had already signed up.

"Good night, Lizette." Before she could say anything more, he set his glass firmly on the minibar and let himself out the door. The air outside was fresh and cool, and he inhaled deeply of it. It made him feel hopeful.

He heard her say something from behind the door, but he didn't care what it was. Right now he was thinking about Erica, and the scotch gave him the courage to stop off at Desert Rose. He went directly to Erica's door and knocked.

No answer. He knocked again.

Erica came to the door wearing nothing but a robe.

No, he could come up with a better fantasy than that.

Erica came to the door wearing nothing but a skimpy bath towel. "I've been waiting for you," she said, her voice low and sweet as honey.

"You knew I'd be here."

"Yes." She lowered her eyelids and opened the door wider. "Come in. I've got a surprise for you."

In real life, however, Erica didn't answer his knock, and he had no idea what the surprise might have been if the scene was real. Which, standing out here like a lovelorn fool, he wished it was. "Erica?" he said urgently, keeping his voice low. He heard the sound of distant laughter, of a group chatting among themselves as they headed back to their quarters. He listened for the sound of Erica's voice but didn't hear it.

She still didn't respond to his knock. Perhaps she had already gone to bed. He glanced at his watch, realizing that the dance had been over for only fifteen minutes or so. She couldn't possibly be asleep unless she had left early, and perhaps she had. It wouldn't be easy to forget the disappointment on her face when he'd stammered something inadequate and walked away with Lizette.

He shouldn't have done that. It was wrong and stupid and at the time all he'd wanted was to get Lizette away from her. He'd been embarrassed by the condescending way in which Lizette had smiled when he introduced her to Erica, the proprietary air with which she had grabbed his arm. His interchange with Erica had seemed soiled and profaned by Lizette's intrusion, and the realization that he thought more of Erica than he did Lizette had hit him hard in the gut. Which was why he was standing so forlornly outside Erica's closed door, wishing she'd open it. He wanted to apologize. He wanted to make things right. He wanted…

He wanted Erica, pure and simple. But there was nothing simple about this wanting, nothing at all.

As he walked away from her door, Hank thought briefly of climbing into the ranch pickup and barreling off toward town, where he could get royally drunk. He'd like to forget about the problem posed by Lizette's sudden appearance at Rancho Encantado, not to mention the absence of Erica from her room. Getting drunk was probably what a real cowboy would do.

Yet his encounter with Lizette had reminded him all too painfully that he was still masquerading as someone he wasn't. He was Henry Parrish Milling III of the Wall Street investment-banking firm of Rowbotham-Quigley, and it looked as if Lizette was not about to let him forget it.

ERICA GREETED Melba and Whip and quickly made the acquaintance of Tango, a bay mare, and Stilts, a chestnut gelding whose long legs lived up to his name. Sebastian was not in his stall, but she found him in the enclosure adjacent to the corral where someone had left him, perhaps to stretch his legs a bit. He regarded her warily as she approached.

"I wish Hank had let me ride you today," she told him. "I would have loved the excitement, and you probably could use the exercise." Out of the corner of her eye, she saw the stable cat slink past as if surreptitiously observing the scene. It was Mrs. Gray, the same cat that had seemed to talk to her.

"Cats don't talk," she said to Sebastian, almost as if trying to convince herself. The cat didn't reappear, much to her relief.

Sebastian let her move closer and stroke him gently on the nose. "You know," Erica said conversationally, "I could take you out for a ride tonight while everyone else is busy, and perhaps no one would ever know. We could have fun together, the two of us."

Sebastian tossed his head and rolled his eyes to show he was game. She wondered if it might really be possible to ride Sebastian without anyone's finding out. A glance toward the end of the barn told her that the two apartments where Hank and Cord McCall lived were closed and dark, so probably no one was home. This gave her a stab of pain in the region of her heart, but she tried not to think about Hank and Lizette together, their bodies entwined, their passion unfettered.

She shook away the thought. All she knew right then was that she wanted to ride Sebastian, ride until he was exhausted and so was she, ride until dawn if that was what it took to erase the unwanted image of Hank and Lizette from her mind.

She knew how to saddle a horse. She was a good horsewoman. There was nothing to stop her from striking out on her own, nothing but her own inhibitions, and she was prepared to toss them to the wind.

She marched back into the stable and yanked a bridle off a hook. She spotted a flashlight on a nearby ledge and tucked it into her pocket. "Come on, big boy," she said as she emerged into the corral. "I'm going to give you the ride of your life."

Those were words that she had always wanted to say,

only to a cowboy, not to a horse. Well, sometimes you had to take what you could get in this life, and right now that was Sebastian.

As SOON AS Hank ambled into the stable, his thoughts intent on grabbing a carrot from the refrigerator in his apartment and spending a few minutes of quality time with Whip, he spotted Erica mounting Sebastian outside the stable door.

"Steady, boy," she said softly as Sebastian pranced toward the open gate. Then, to Hank's openmouthed and horrified amazement, the horse treated her to a couple of jarring bucks, but she sat her saddle well.

Erica hung in there as Sebastian skittered sideways, showing his mettle. The horse's ears were pricked forward, but even so, he was flicking them backward as if he expected to hear encouraging words from his rider. And despite his head-shaking and rolling eyes, Erica was speaking to him in a low tone, a soothing tone, as Sebastian, the horse that he and Cord had almost given up on, the horse that none of the ranch hands trusted, suddenly spun about and began to circle the ring in a smoothly controlled trot. Hank watched spellbound as Erica rode him out through the open gate of the corral with an air of calm authority, spurring him on with her knees as they reached open ground. Hank shouted once after he regained his voice, but they were too far away by that time to hear.

"I'll be damned."

As Sebastian's hoofbeats died away in the distance, Hank couldn't believe the formidable display of horsemanship he'd just observed. At first, he couldn't even quite believe that the rider was Erica. At the same time, there was no denying that artfully streaked blond hair and pert derriere, that delicacy of bone and supreme self-possession. She sat the saddle as if she had ridden all her life, and at first he thought that this scenario, improbable as it was, must be another daydream of his own making. But he would never have dreamed that Erica would be on a horse riding *away* from him.

"Oh, hell," he muttered to himself. What did Erica, supposedly a neophyte in the saddle, think she was doing? It was clear to him now that Erica was no rank beginner. But Sebastian was a handful, and as impossible as he thought it might be for Erica to have saddled him by herself, he knew she must have. But for God's sake, why?

One thing Hank knew for sure was that no matter how experienced a rider she might be, Erica Strong must be crazy to take a horse like Sebastian out at night all alone.

AS HE BORE HER away into the night, Sebastian was all that Erica hoped he would be. She thought that his reputation as a difficult horse must be a misunderstanding. After that nonsense when she first mounted, which she recognized as a test of her determination, he had accepted her authority. Best of all, with his long loose stride and his exuberance at going on a late-night ride, he was fun to ride, unlike Melba, whose spirit had been ridden out of her long ago.

With the saddle leather creaking in the chill night air, she turned Sebastian toward the path she had traveled earlier today with Hank. The horse had a sensitive mouth and seemed wary of the bit. He needed only the slightest pressure from her knees to guide him.

The night was silent, quiet and peaceful, fragrant with the scent of sage and the night smell of sun-baked rock cooled to air temperature. Erica loved the silence, loved the peace of it. Being out in the open under a great star-filled sky made her at one with nature and helped to blunt the hurt of watching Hank walk away with another woman.

She gave Sebastian his head after they passed the stream where she and Hank had eaten lunch, and as he moved from a trot to a gallop, her sadness and disappointment at Hank's defection evaporated, giving way to elation and a sense of power and freedom, which she was sure Sebastian felt, as well. The steady pounding of his hooves on rock and sand soothed her ruffled emotions.

Before long, Sebastian slowed his pace and trotted along a curving path that ascended a long easy grade toward the mountains. The snowy caps of the mountain peaks gleamed in moonlight that slivered the tips of the leaves on the native sage and creosote bushes.

This ride would be much more romantic if she was with Hank. She could picture the two of them, their low laughter ringing out over the landscape, perhaps dismounting to kiss and touch, then riding on to the inevitable conclusion of the evening. Which would include a lot more than touching, she was sure.

Once they'd reached the road that connected with the highway, she walked Sebastian briefly so that he could blow for a few minutes, then patted his neck. "Okay, fellow, it's back to the stable for you and to bed for me. Take us home."

What she didn't anticipate was that Sebastian preferred the long way home, not going back the way they'd come. The long way meant passing the adobe hacienda where she and Hank had stopped today.

This gave her a good opportunity to stop off and look for the necklace she thought she'd lost earlier. She pulled

Sebastian around near the stand of tamarisk. He didn't seem to understand her purpose and kept trying to head toward the ranch, but she insisted they stop. He blew out an impatient huff, taking her to the edge of the veranda and eyeing her distrustfully after she dismounted.

"Look," she said as she led him around to the back of the house. "Nice cool water for you and for me."

She drank deeply from the tin cup, wondering how late it really was. She had lost track of time, knew only that the ride had helped purge her of the pain and sadness she'd felt earlier. She looped Sebastian's reins over the hitching rail beside the trough and went into the hacienda through the back kitchen door.

Her flashlight illuminated the big kitchen table and then the front room, but its beam revealed no glimmer of gold, no necklace. She wasn't eager to prolong her stay, so she moved on to the room where she'd photographed the jumble of antiques. Almost immediately she spotted the reflection of light on metal between two boxes. She pushed one aside and picked up the necklace, noting that the catch was broken. Not a problem; it could easily be mended.

Suddenly she heard the swift approach of hoofbeats and, alarmed, she switched off the flashlight and hurried to the front room. She clutched the broken chain in her hand in sudden apprehension, knowing she was vulnerable here.

At first she thought of hiding in the darkness, but that was pointless. Anyone who entered would spot Sebastian out the kitchen window in back and know that someone was in this deserted house.

She heard the thud of boots across the wide wooden floor of the veranda, and the door was flung open wide.

A solid figure blocked the doorway, features indistinguishable. "Erica? What the hell are you doing here?"

It was Hank! Her heart pounding in her chest, she switched on the flashlight beam and focused it on the figure standing there.

Hank's fists were clenched tightly at his sides, and his face was flushed with anger. "What do you think you're doing, taking Sebastian out like this? Don't you realize that he's a lot of horse, too much horse for you? You have no business riding him, none at all."

His tone infuriated her, but her annoyance was overlaid by relief that he wasn't with Lizette. The thought gave her a jubilant feeling that far outweighed her chagrin at being caught in a lie about her experience as a rider.

"I, um, know how to ride pretty well," she allowed, staring at him through the beam of light.

He stared back. He wore a down vest over the blue plaid shirt she recognized from the dance. When he pushed his hat back on his head, she saw that his hair was endearingly mussed, from the wind or from being with a woman, she couldn't tell.

"You're not a beginner rider," he said heavily. "I should have known."

"I'm sorry, Hank, if I upset you by taking Sebastian out. But it had been so long since I'd ridden and I was sure I could handle him and—"

"And you were feeling rebellious after I left you on the porch."

She was surprised at the accuracy of Hank's insight. "Yes," she said softly. "Perhaps I was."

"Don't you realize the danger of what you did? It's nighttime, and you don't know the terrain."

Her chin shot up. "There's a full moon, and Sebastian knows the territory."

"That horse can go along as calmly as you please, and then he'll cut loose in a way you never expected. It's not safe for you to ride him."

"We understand each other, Sebastian and I." She glared at Hank, daring him to challenge her.

He exhaled deeply, shaking his head in consternation. She stuffed the necklace into a pocket and flicked off the flashlight, leaving them standing in a pool of moonlight.

Erica decided to cut to the chase, Her problem was that she'd thought Hank was with another woman tonight, so perhaps she thought she might as well confront him head-on.

"You didn't tell me you had a girlfriend, Hank," she said.

He stiffened and flushed. "Lizette isn't my girlfriend."

"Does she know that?"

"She should by now." He spoke with quiet firmness, which under any other circumstances would probably have convinced her that he spoke the truth.

She felt herself relaxing slightly. "I want to believe you," she said.

"Look, Erica, what happened back on that porch...I didn't expect Lizette to show up. I didn't like the way she spoke to you. I wanted her gone, so I did my best to hustle her away. I went by Desert Rose after I left her, but you weren't there. If you had been, I would have explained. As it was—" he shrugged "—I saw you ride off on Sebastian. Here I am. I'm not with her, and I don't want to be."

All the anger drained out of her when she looked at

him standing there, his face raw with emotion, his manner open and direct. She believed him.

She heaved a giant sigh. "We'd better get back to the stable." It was well after midnight, and she felt drained.

"Not so fast. Let's sit down and relax for a moment."

"I don't know, Hank. It's late."

To her surprise, he took her hand. "It's not too late," he said softly, and she knew he wasn't talking about the time of night. He led her to the cot, and she sat down beside him, keeping a fair distance between them. Their faces and bodies were dappled by the moonlight sifting through the branches of the tamarisk windbreak outside, and all thoughts of Lizette evaporated from her head.

His tone changed to a cajoling one. "There's no need to rush back now that I know you're not in imminent danger of being thrown from a horse. Now that I've explained myself, why don't you tell me how you happen to be able to ride Sebastian so well."

She was grateful that he was keeping his tone light and had changed the subject. She sent a cautious edgewise glance in his direction only to discover that he was staring curiously at her.

"Well?" he said.

"I took lots of riding lessons when I was a kid."

He sighed. "All right. Why did you pretend you had little riding experience?"

Erica considered this. In business situations when her bluff was called, she'd learned that it was better to come clean than attempt to cover up. "I wanted... Oh, hell. I wanted to get to know you."

She avoided his eyes by staring across the width of the room, but he raised a hand to cup her chin and turned her face toward him. His eyes were deep and lustrous, their expression one of extreme interest overlaid with a kind of wry amusement. "You wanted to get to know me? Would that be in the biblical sense or would you place the checkmark under 'other'?"

She tried to wrest her head away, but he only brought his other hand up so that her face was captured between them. She was so close that if he leaned forward only slightly, their lips would touch. She swallowed. What would he think if she told him that in her fantasies, she had made love with him more than once? What if he knew that as far as she was concerned, he was the perfect cowboy, the subject of her daydreams ever since she was a kid?

"Erica, won't you please answer me?"

"It seems as if no matter how I answer, I'll sound like a nutcase. Let's put it this way—I always wanted to know a real cowboy."

He said nothing. She didn't know why. He released her and drew away, bending forward so that his elbows rested on his thighs. "A real cowboy," he repeated heavily after a few seconds. And then, under his breath, "Touché."

He said the word so softly that she thought she might have been mistaken. Anyway, what did he mean?

"Erica," he said, and he was going to tell her the truth until he glanced back over his shoulder and looked deep into her eyes. In their depths he detected a yearning, a longing for connection. He smelled honeysuckle, realized that her lips were moist and slightly parted, her eyes fringed with long dark lashes. In that moment he was overcome with a longing of his own, one more physical than emotional.

He straightened and without saying another word, he slid his arms around her and waited until her face tilted upward. It was a beautiful face, full of wonder and delight as she gazed tremulously at him. He saw her as if through a pure lucent light from far away, his perceptions trembling on the verge of something new and not unwelcome.

"Erica," he said in surprise, a bit more shakily this time, and then his embrace became fiercely possessive as he sought her lips. When he found them, when her mouth blossomed beneath his, he realized how glad he was to have followed her here. He felt himself leaning into the kiss, deepening it, making it last. The whole world was, in those moments, that kiss. He was sure he could go on kissing Erica Strong forever if the fates allowed it.

When he released her, she gasped softly and closed her eyes, resting her forehead lightly against his. "We should do this again sometime," she said with a little laugh.

"Right about now," he agreed, and kissed her again. His arms pressed her to his chest, and he could feel the soft roundness of her breasts, imagine the taut peaks of her nipples beneath his fingertips if he dared to be so bold.

He would have dared, but the fates decided not to allow it, after all. They heard the sound of something tearing loose out back, a thump, and other noises not as identifiable.

They broke apart. "What was that?" Erica yelped as they both leaped off the cot.

He made it across the floor in two strides. She followed, her heart in her mouth.

"I don't know, Erica, but I'm sure it has something to do with that fool horse," Hank said.

Chapter Eight

"Sebastian's gone," Hank said flatly when they reached the doorway.

"I wrapped the reins over the hitching rail." She switched on the flashlight and looked around wildly for some sight of the horse.

"Look, the wood is rotten." Hank bent and picked up the broken rail. She saw that it was full of termite holes.

"It seemed solid enough in the moonlight."

Hank let out an exasperated sigh. "Justine won't take it lightly if we've lost her horse." He tossed the rail onto a nearby rubbish heap.

"I'm sorry."

Hank wheeled and walked around to the front. His horse, Whip, stood silently, ears aimed in the direction of the road.

"Sebastian can't have gone far. He's probably right outside the windbreak." Hank swung up into the saddle. "I'll go have a look and be right back."

Erica watched as Hank disappeared up the narrow track. The sounds of the night seemed to close in upon her—the rustling of creatures in the thick underbrush, the breeze whispering through the tamarisk leaves. She wrapped her arms around herself, thinking she deserved a prize for stupidity. She should have made sure that Sebastian was securely tethered.

But perhaps Hank was right. Maybe Sebastian hadn't gone far, after all.

HANK TROTTED Whip toward the road, keeping a sharp eye out for a horse shape in the shadows of the tamarisks. Nothing. Sebastian would probably have headed back toward the ranch, and while this was a logical assumption, there was nothing logical about Sebastian.

Hank tried not to sound discouraged when he went back for Erica. She waited for him on the front porch, looking pale and concerned. "Any sign of him?"

He shook his head. "He might've gone back to the ranch, but we can't count on that. If he didn't, I suggest we take the truck and go looking for him. The headlights will pick him out a lot faster than the beam of a flashlight."

"I wish I—"

He swung out of the saddle and placed a gentle finger across her lips to silence her. A lazy finger traced the line of her cheek. "*I* wish we hadn't been interrupted by Sebastian's escape."

She couldn't speak, mesmerized as she was by his deep voice and his touch. His finger paused on her chin, swept upward again to her lips. "Where did you learn to kiss like you mean it?" he murmured as if to himself.

Her lips parted under the weight of his finger, and she felt his fingernail graze her teeth. Every cell in her body seemed to be on alert; every nerve ending sparkled with energy. His hand went around to cup the back of her head, pulling her toward him. She went willingly and found herself crushed against him, her curves matching the hard-muscled contours of his body, her mouth opening to his. His lips devoured her, and she was more than willing to submit. Oh, she would have done anything he wanted, anything he liked, with his hands running down her back, pausing at the hollow of her waist, moving up to curve around her breasts, all the while kissing her masterfully and demandingly.

His mouth left hers, left her gasping, and he buried his face in her hair. "Damn you, Erica, for not being more careful with that horse. He'll be fine, no doubt, but will I?"

It took her a moment to register that he was joking, albeit halfheartedly. "Come along, we'd better hotfoot it back to the ranch, and I hope to heaven Sebastian is there. If so, we can lock him in his stall and I can ravish you further." He pulled away and straightened the collar of her blouse. Her heart was pounding so hard that she didn't even move. All she could do was cling to him and marvel at the chemistry that had been unleashed between them.

He boosted her up on the saddle, then mounted Whip behind her. He clucked gently to the horse and turned him toward the ranch.

"Comfortable?" Hank asked as she nestled back against his warm, solid chest. The motion of the horse was soothing; she swayed against Hank with each step.

"Very" was all she said, and then she focused on the stars glittering across the black dome of the sky, a sky that seemed somehow less vast than it had only an hour ago.

THE CLUSTER OF ranch buildings loomed out of the dark, the shadowy shapes growing larger as they approached. Lights shone from windows here and there, and as they approached the stable, Erica craned her neck in hopes of seeing Sebastian waiting under the bright spotlight of the corral. But he wasn't.

She waited while Hank went into his apartment to get the keys to the pickup. He left the apartment door open, and Erica peeked inside, wanting to know what his place looked like. From what she could see, the furnishings were sparse but neat and contained an abundance of baby gear—a high chair, a playpen, a wind-up swing.

He brought her a cup of coffee when he came out. "It's instant. No time to brew the real thing, and I figured we might need it to stay alert."

She took the cup from him, her fingers brushing his for one brief moment. He went around and climbed into the pickup on the driver's side. She boosted herself in beside him and they set off in the direction of the mountains.

"How do you know where to look?" she asked as the truck rattled noisily over a cattle guard.

"Sebastian has done this before. He'll head for a canyon or someplace else where he can't be seen from far off."

Erica settled back into the seat, impressed by the competent way Hank handled the shifting of gears and maneuvered the four-wheel-drive vehicle over the rough terrain. They rode in silence for a time, the pickup bumping over the uneven sage flats before it began the climb up the slope toward the mountains.

She kept a sharp eye peeled for Sebastian, but the landscape appeared deserted. Hank chose a likely place, stopped the pickup, opened his window and called Sebastian's name. He aimed the pickup's headlights toward the buttes, and Erica opened her door and jumped down onto the gravel scree. She scanned the desolate expanse illuminated by the headlights but saw nothing.

"It's going to be hard to see him out here," she said.

"Try these," Hank said, handing her a pair of binoculars.

Erica climbed onto the bed of the pickup, but even with the binoculars, she saw no sign of a horse. Discouraged, she climbed back into the cab.

"There are so many rocks and boulders—he could be hiding behind any one of them. I wish there were some way to coax him out," she said.

"You could make a noise like a sugar cube," Hank said, and she glanced over at him, glad of the attempt at humor.

"Sebastian is playing with us," Hank told her. "We'll find him eventually."

"Sooner rather than later," she said. "I'm keeping you from—"

"You're keeping me from continuing what we started at the hacienda," he said quietly. "But you know what? I'm enjoying this."

"You can't mean that."

He jammed the pickup into gear and turned into a gully that offered more traction than the dusty track. "I don't like it that Sebastian is out here somewhere laughing his head off while we ride around looking for him. I hope we find him before he manages to tangle his foot in the reins or gets too friendly with a wildcat. But it's fun being with you, Erica. I've missed this sort of thing. Companionship, sharing a moment—you know what I mean."

"I'm not sure I do." She was touched by his words.

He shot a glance at her, then returned his attention to driving. The pickup lurched over a couple of rocky outcroppings, then settled into a bone-jarring rattle. "You must have had relationships. You must have friends."

"Friends? They're mostly colleagues from work. Relationships? Not lately." Her last real relationship had been several years ago, and she'd broken it off. Compared to the men who populated her fantasy life, cowboys all, Mark had been downright dull.

"Never been married? Engaged?"

"No."

"Why, Erica?" He sounded puzzled.

"I work a lot."

"Yes, but you should take time for a personal life."

"That's why I'm here." Spoken ruefully with a little chuckle.

"This visit to Rancho Encantado is your attempt at a personal life?"

Suddenly she couldn't bear having him look at her. She bit her lip. "You could call it that."

He didn't reply. When she sneaked a glance at his profile, his lips were set in a grim line. She made herself look out the window, where the moonlight was beginning to fade as the moon slipped down below the mountain ridge.

Hank turned the pickup up a steep bank, and they dodged a stand of junipers to find themselves amid a forest of boulders. He slowed their speed as they entered a narrow canyon, its walls jagged and steep.

"This is Bottle Canyon. It's called that because the entrance is narrow, and after a heavy rain, the gully fills with water and blocks the entrance. If Sebastian is here, we're lucky. He can't get out without our seeing him."

Even with the headlights for illumination, it was hard to see anything in the canyon. Hank rolled down his window and Erica did the same. To their left, the slow trickle of water in the gully lent music to the night; to their right was an outcropping of rock and a steep canyon wall.

"Let's chill here awhile, see if there are any signs of him," Hank said, his voice a low murmur. He cut the lights and turned off the engine.

She nodded and stared out the window on her side as her eyes grew accustomed to the darkness. She was looking for the slightest movement, listening for any sound. Her concentration was broken when Hank's hand found hers where it gripped the edge of the seat. He linked his fingers with hers. It felt entirely natural and right, but she stiffened slightly when he ran his hand up her arm.

"Erica—"

They heard a muffled grating sound to their left near the gully. It was followed by the crunch of gravel and stones.

Hank's hand left hers, and he was out of the truck in an instant. "Sebastian?"

Erica slid slowly and cautiously out of the pickup. The canyon was shrouded in shadow, the moon only a faint glow. Somewhere she heard a coyote howl, a lonely sound.

"Shh," Hank said.

She halted. They heard a rustling behind a large boulder.

"It's Sebastian, I'm sure of it," Hank whispered. "Sebastian," he said in a commanding voice. "Come on out, fella."

Nothing. Only silence.

"He's bound to be hungry. There's not much grass to nibble on up here," Hank said, his voice normal now. "We want him to recognize us, trust us." Hank reached into the bed of the pickup and pulled out a rope.

Erica moved forward, squinting into the darkness. She

could make out shapes, but none of them looked like a horse.

"Sebastian?" she called. "Come on out." Another shuffle, and then movement. "You want to go home, don't you, boy?"

Hank moved up behind her. "Keep talking to him. I'll walk around those rocks and grab him if he tries to cross the gully."

Erica kept saying anything that came into her head. She told Sebastian that he was a good horse, that it was time to go home. She reminded him of their ride in the moonlight and what a good time they'd had. She didn't scold him for interrupting a love scene between her and her perfect cowboy. She figured she could save that for later.

She moved slowly toward Sebastian, keeping him distracted from Hank's whereabouts even though she could tell by the way he flicked his ears in Hank's direction that he knew someone was approaching from behind. Soon she was close enough to see Sebastian's eyes, which seemed to hold a sly gleam of amusement at the plight of these humans whose lives he enjoyed complicating.

Hank came into view over Sebastian's shoulder. He held the rope at the ready, but she didn't think the rope would be necessary. Five more steps, and she'd be able to grab the dragging reins. Four more steps, three. Two.

And then Sebastian tossed his head and stepped forward, entirely docile and submissive. She reached for the reins, raised them triumphantly to the sky and was almost bowled over when Sebastian nudged her shoulder, hard.

Hank laughed, slid the looped rope up over his shoulder and came around to Sebastian's other side. "Good work," he said approvingly to Erica. He rubbed Sebastian's nose. "You old reprobate, you thought you were going to lead us a merry chase, didn't you?"

Erica produced a sugar cube, and Sebastian gobbled it down. When he playfully nuzzled her, looking for more, Hank shoved his nose away and said, "Time to go home, Sebastian. There'll be feed in your trough." Hank led the horse to the truck and handed Erica the reins.

As they headed out of the canyon, dawn was sending pale runners of light up from the eastern horizon, tinting the sky delicate shades of peach and silver. Hank drove slowly with Sebastian trotting along obediently alongside, Erica holding the reins through the open window.

By the time they reached the buildings at the outskirts of the ranch where the hands were housed, they saw men coming in and out of the cookhouse, some of them headed toward the barn, some saddling up. The air was brisk and clear, and Erica's stomach reminded her that it had been hours since she'd eaten.

They took Sebastian directly to the stable, where Cord McCall was using a coffee can to mete out each horse's ration of feed. He looked around and nodded abruptly to them.

"Looks like Sebastian broke out of the corral," he said.

Erica started to speak, prepared to tell him that it was her fault Sebastian got away and that they'd brought him back, but Hank put a restraining hand on her arm. "Let me handle this," he said in a low tone. "You go untie Sebastian and bring him in."

"But…"

Hank's eyes locked with hers for a moment, and she decided to do as he said. It wasn't normal for her to take orders from anyone, and it felt strange to be taking them from Hank now. Still, she did Hank's bidding.

Sebastian's ears twitched when he heard her stomach rumble. "I'm so hungry I could eat a horse," she told him. "Don't worry, though. I don't mean you."

She led Sebastian back to his stall and shut him inside. He lost all interest in her once he saw the brimming feed trough.

She heard Hank and Cord talking to each other in the tack room, their tones casual, their manner light. Apparently Hank was handling the situation well.

"Goodbye, Sebastian. I don't think you'd better count on me to take you for moonlight rides anymore." She waited for some recognition that he'd heard her, but he was too busy scarfing up feed.

Yawning, the lack of sleep catching up with her, she headed for Hank's apartment and was pleased to find the door unlocked. The kitchen was right inside the door, and she immediately spotted a frying pan hanging on a rack over the stove. When she found a spatula in a drawer and eggs in the refrigerator, she knew she was in business.

The only thing she really knew how to cook was eggs. She could make a fantastic western omelette, and she meant to prove it now.

HANK WALKED IN from the stable to find his apartment pleasantly fragrant with the smell of bacon and onions and freshly brewed coffee. His first reaction was one of embarrassment: all those baby toys everywhere, and most of the living room taken up with the playpen, and what if he'd left a dirty diaper in the bathroom?

Erica, her hair pushed behind her ears, looked over

her shoulder as he entered the kitchen. "What did Cord have to say about Sebastian?"

"Not much," he said. He kept walking straight through the living room into the bathroom, made sure there was a clean hand towel on the rack, then checked Kaylie's changing table for dirty diapers. He didn't find any and breathed a sigh of relief. When he recalled his bachelor apartment in New York City, he wanted to laugh. He'd been so uptight in those days, so driven. Now things were more casual, all because of Kaylie. And his life was happier because of Kaylie. He never forgot that.

When he came back to the kitchen, his heart warmed to the sight of Erica sautéeing onions. She looked at ease with her task, focused. He'd have thought that a kitchen would be the last place she'd feel at home.

He edged up close to her, reached around her and snitched a piece of bacon from the plate where it drained. He popped it in his mouth, savoring it.

"You told Cord that I took Sebastian out without permission?"

He swallowed and ripped a paper towel off the roll to wipe his hands. "That wasn't necessary," he said.

Erica poured beaten eggs into the pan. "What did you say?"

"He asked me if Sebastian got out of the enclosure, and I said yes. End of conversation."

She turned to face him, eyebrows raised. "That's all that was said?"

"I think he offered a grunt or two. He's not a big talker."

She swiveled back around. Her face was flushed from the heat of the stove, and she'd rolled up her sleeves.

She wasn't wearing lipstick, and he liked the way she looked without it.

She flipped the omelette over expertly, and he brought out plates and silverware. He had to shove aside one of Kaylie's rattles to make room at the kitchen table for them. Then Erica was sliding half the omelette onto his plate.

He sat down, and after getting them both a glass of water, she joined him. "Is there something you're supposed to be doing?" she asked. "Am I keeping you from it? I feel so guilty for being the reason you were out all night."

"If we had continued what we started at the hacienda, I would have been out all night, anyway."

He enjoyed her flustered look. "I was asking because I know I can go back to my suite and rest. I was wondering if you'll be able to get some sleep, too."

"Maybe." He ate a bit of omelette; it was delicious.

She ate too, voraciously. "I'm starved," she admitted.

He'd noticed that she ate three slices of toast slathered with butter and jelly, plus a number of slices of bacon. It was a welcome relief to see a woman who liked to eat. He was tired of Lizette's constant dieting.

This reminded him that he was due to squire a trail ride in the afternoon and that Lizette would be there. He stood up and took his plate to the counter. "I'll wash up, and then call my sister to see how it's going with Kaylie. I may need to pick her up."

"How will you get any sleep if you're looking after a baby?"

"Good question." He felt as though the insides of his eyelids were made of sandpaper, and he was so tired he almost couldn't think straight.

He dialed the number of the Big House. Erica started

to clear the table, but he covered the mouthpiece and said, "I'll clean up. You cooked."

"I don't mind." But her eyes were red-rimmed and bleary, and he realized that she must feel as tired as he was. Erica began to scrape the leavings on their plates into the garbage can, but he tucked the phone between his shoulder and jaw and inserted himself between her and the sink. "Go," he whispered as Justine picked up the phone.

Erica's inquiring look caused him to point to the living room. "Sit down on the couch for a minute. I'll— Oh, hi, Justine. How's Kaylie?"

Erica went into the living room. She turned on the TV with the remote control and flipped channels until the weather report came on. Hank began to rinse off dishes as Justine rattled off information: Kaylie had eaten all of her breakfast, had mushed up two cookies and spit them all over the kitchen table.

"We're having a wonderful time. Don't you dare come get her," Justine said. "By the way, who were you talking with a moment ago? Lizette?"

"No, it wasn't Lizette. Why didn't you warn me she was going to show up?"

"I didn't take Lizette's reservation. I only saw her name on the list of guests this morning. Kaylie and I have been having so much fun that I've left my usual chores to the people I pay to run this place." Justine sounded slightly prickly.

"Okay, okay. I was taken by surprise, that's all."

"I'd have thought you'd be glad to see her."

He glanced toward the living room, expecting to see Erica sitting on the couch. She wasn't there. Maybe she had gone into the bathroom.

"Look, Justine, I'm kind of tied up right now. If

you're not ready for me to pick Kaylie up and bring her back to the apartment, I'd better hang up.''

"No problem, Hank. We're going to get out some of the clothes I've been saving for her until she grows into them and see if they fit.''

"Okay, maybe we can have a fashion show one of these days.''

After they hung up, Hank wiped off the counter and went into the living room. It was time to get some sleep, because if he didn't, he'd have to ask Cord to lead that trail ride for him later today and he was pretty sure Cord wouldn't be around this afternoon. He seldom was on weekends.

Erica hadn't gone into the bathroom. She'd slid down to the end of the couch and rested her head on the two throw pillows there. Her hands were clasped under her chin, her legs drawn up onto the seat, and she was sound asleep.

Her face seemed more rounded, softer, as she slept, maybe because she was totally relaxed. Her hair fell in wavy tendrils across her cheek, and her breath rose and fell gently. The curve of her breasts beneath her peasant blouse, the cleavage rising above the neckline reminded him of how much he wanted her.

Should he disturb her? Walk her back to her suite? Probably. But it occurred to him that he wanted her here when he woke up.

First he clicked off the TV. Then he pulled an afghan down from the closet shelf, unfolded it and spread it over Erica. She stirred slightly, her mouth puckering for a moment, and he found himself thinking how kissable that mouth was. He knew, too, that he would be kissing it again soon.

But for now, all he did was gently tuck the afghan

around Erica's body and hurry into the bedroom, where he fell asleep almost immediately.

Padre Luis Speaks...

AY DE MI! What now?

Erica saw me in the cactus patch last night. She was not afraid. She is not afraid of anything, this woman. Then, though I waited to show myself to her again, Erica did not return home last night. She was with the cowboy all night long. *Madre de Dios,* why do I care? What does it matter?

I pace the confines of my office in the cactus, wringing my hands at their folly. It is odd that, despite being restricted to this space, I know where these people are and what they are thinking. I can only explain it by saying God works in mysterious ways.

Speaking of mysteries, that cat trotted through the courtyard today, widely avoiding the cactus. With her were her three kittens. I thought them quite attractive.

But I digress. I tried to attract the attention of the cat, but she would not look my way. I think she knows that it is my voice she is using and does not care to return it to me.

Por Dios, it is difficult to be a humble priest. But if it is God's will that my voice is to be used by a mere cat, who am I to question? I pray for divine revelation, but it has so far been denied me.

When Erica comes back, perhaps I will be able to see her clearly. I hope mostly that it is God's will for her to be together with Hank. But if not, I will not question. I am a humble priest and also an obedient one.

At least, I pray that I am.

Chapter Nine

When Erica woke up, her muscles felt stiff, and at first she wasn't sure where she was. This definitely wasn't her New York apartment or her suite. She sat up gingerly, took in the baby toys, the windup swing, the box of disposable diapers visible on the changing table in the alcove.

It all came back to her—her wild ride, then Hank, and the night spent chasing Sebastian, eating breakfast together and falling asleep on the couch. Where she still was. Where she was trying to get her bearings.

She heard a gentle snoring from the room beyond and pushed herself into a sitting position. Her contact lenses felt itchy, and she didn't have any wetting solution with her. Perhaps Hank kept some in his medicine cabinet.

Blurry-eyed, she stumbled toward the bathroom door. Her foot smacked against something—the windup swing? the edge of the playpen?—and the snoring stopped. Since the door wasn't closed, she peeked through the bedroom doorway. Her vision wasn't so blurry that she couldn't see that Hank was lying on top of the sheet in all his nude glory. And he was quite glorious.

Quickly she glanced away, then sneaked another look

in midstep. Her foot came down on a squeaky toy, which went *EEEeeekk*. Hank was up from the bed in an instant.

"Wha— Oh, Erica, it's you."

"I'm sorry, I was only going in the bathroom for a minute, it's my contact lenses, I thought maybe you might have some wetting solution, eyedrops. Uh, wow." Totally flustered, she stood helplessly as Hank yanked a towel off the chair beside the bed and wrapped it around himself.

"No harm done. That's how I like to sleep. What time is it, do you know?"

"Past noon. Excuse me," and she went into the bathroom and shut the door.

"You'll find contact lens supplies in the drawer on your left—take what you need," he called through the door as Erica collapsed against it. She'd seen nude men before, but never one like this. He was perfect. But hadn't she known that when she'd decided he was the perfect cowboy?

She lubricated her contact lenses, washed her face and ran her fingers through her hair. When she went back into the living room, the afghan was folded neatly at the end of the couch and Hank was talking on the phone.

"I'll come pick her up after the trail ride. Give her a kiss, okay?"

"I'd better go," Erica said. "I didn't mean to camp out on your couch."

"It's okay. What are you going to do this afternoon?"

"Catch a few more z's. How about you?"

"I'm taking a group on a trail ride. Don't worry, I can get by on a few hours' sleep." He paused, seemed to assess her mood. "I know it's not much, but would you like to drop over for supper tonight? Kaylie will be here, but I could throw some burgers on the grill. I mean, if you don't mind.''

Mind? Of course she didn't mind. She was happy to be invited. She beamed at him, but at that moment she happened to glance out the window and saw Lizette trudging along toward the stables, a determined look on her face. Hank caught sight of her at the same time.

''Are you sure you won't have something else to do?'' Erica asked pointedly as Lizette disappeared from sight.

''Positive,'' Hank said, and his voice had a hard edge to it.

ERICA SLEPT that afternoon, and when she woke up, she looked over her new clothes and tried to figure out what to wear for her date with Hank tonight. Or was it a date? She wasn't sure.

And then there was the matter of ogling his nude body. Worse, he'd caught her doing it. What guy wouldn't invite her over in hopes of getting lucky? But, she thought musingly, she might get lucky, too.

While she mulled this over, the blue light on the phone blinked, signifying a call. She scooped up the receiver. ''Erica here.''

''Erica, is there anything you want to tell me? Not that you have to, but...'' Charmaine's voice trailed off expectantly.

''Charmaine, there isn't anything to tell. Yet.'' Erica laughed.

''Oh.''

''Except I'm having supper with Hank and his daughter tonight.''

''You don't do babies.'' It was a family joke, initiated by their sister, Abby, who claimed to have inherited the only maternal instinct among the three sisters.

Erica replied thoughtfully, "You know, when I held Kaylie and looked into her pretty blue eyes, all I could think of was that she was Hank's daughter and how much she looks like him. He's such a good father, Char. I admire that."

"I hardly know why. You've often said that you didn't understand why parenthood was such a big deal."

"I'm not sure anymore. I felt a definite stirring of maternalism when Kaylie wrapped her fingers around my thumb."

"What are they feeding you out there? Some kind of hormone-saturated meat?"

"They're feeding me quite well, and have you ever considered, Char, that now that I'm away from the city I'm a new person?" She caught a glimpse of her fluffy hair in the mirror across the room. She smiled at her reflection. She not only looked different, she felt different. She felt voluptuous. She felt sexy. She felt like the kind of person who could pass for a cowboy's sweetheart.

"I'm glad you're having a good time," Charmaine said, sounding slightly envious.

"There *are* a couple of things bothering me," Erica admitted, taking the phone into the sitting room and lying back on the comfortable couch.

"Well, let's hear them."

"For one thing, if he asked me over for hamburgers and his baby is there, is it a real date?"

"Probably, if he seemed eager for your company. Or was the invitation only because he's lonely for adult companionship? Some single fathers find themselves babbling baby talk after a week with the kid, and they tend to glom on to any available woman who can string a couple of coherent sentences together."

This stumped her. Hank had seemed eager for her company, or so she thought. But Charmaine's observation shed doubt on the evening. He had said he'd enjoyed her company. Did he enjoy her for herself or because she was an escape from baby food, baby toys, baby diapers, baby everything?

"I don't know," she said finally. "He seems to like me. We spent the night together—"

"You what?"

"Oh, it wasn't like that. We were out looking for Sebastian—he's this horse who escaped and it was my fault after I left him in back of the old hacienda. Hank came looking for me, it was after midnight, and we—"

"Erica! Stop! My head is spinning. Could you please explain a bit more slowly?"

Erica sighed. "You had to have been there, I guess."

"I hope you'll send me some pictures of this guy. You could upload directly from your camera onto your computer and attach them to an e-mail."

"I haven't taken any pictures of him, Char. We've been too busy for that."

"You know, you're beginning to convince me that Rancho Encantado is a magic place, after all." Charmaine sounded wistful.

"You're probably right. I find the talking cat puzzling, though."

"Talking cat? Did you say 'talking cat'?"

"Uh-huh. Bye, Char. Talk to you later."

Erica was grinning as she returned the phone to its cradle. Now if she could only figure out what to wear tonight. It would have to be something she could slip out of gracefully if things got hot and heavy.

HANK RETURNED from his assigned trail ride in a less-than-cheerful frame of mind. Lizette, who had doggedly followed him into the stable, was tagging after him while he saw to the horses.

"Lizette, I really have work to do," he said, hoping she would take the hint. He saw Mrs. Gray, the cat, jump down off a feed sack and scamper over to Lizette, who ignored her.

"Henry, how about if we duck out for a sophisticated dinner in town, you and me?" Lizette said brightly.

"For one thing, there's no such thing as a sophisticated dinner in Sonoco. The only restaurant is a booth or two in the Lucky Buck Saloon. Besides, I have plans for this evening."

Lizette didn't look her best when she pouted, but she pouted, anyway. "Henry, I'll only be here for a couple of days."

"Thank goodness," he mumbled under his breath.

Lizette froze as Mrs. Gray twined through her ankles. "Get this cat away from me," she said crossly. "I hate cats."

Mrs. Gray, looking wounded, went over to the entrance to the tack room and sat.

"You and I need to talk," Hank said firmly to Lizette as he fastened the door to Melba's stall.

Don't bother, said the cat.

"What?" At first he thought Lizette had spoken, but he gathered from the tears in her eyes that she was unable to speak. He didn't have time to worry about talking cats; he had to do something about Lizette.

"Liz," he began in a conciliatory tone.

"Don't call me that," she said sharply. "You know I hate nicknames."

"Lizette," he began again, "maybe we could go somewhere and talk."

"My suite?" she said, brightening.

He didn't want to be alone with her. "Let's take a walk," he suggested.

He started to follow Lizette out of the stable, but before he emerged into the bright sunshine, he turned and narrowed his eyes at Mrs. Gray. "I don't know what you're up to, but stop it," he said sternly, and at least the cat had the good grace to look surprised.

It was cool in the palm grove, and no one else was around. Hank was bored with Lizette's nattering before they even reached the oasis hot pool.

"As I said, I have learned so much by being a life coach. It's opened my eyes, Henry, to what a person can and should be. Take you, for instance. You have such potential. Why are you wasting it? You really should come back to the city." They came to a bench, and Lizette sat down. "I can tell you exactly how I think you should approach your life at this point."

Hank preferred to remain standing, so he rested one booted foot on the seat of the bench. When she realized that he wasn't going to sit beside her, Lizette made a face at the dusty boot and scooted over a notch so she wouldn't have to sit so close to it. She scowled up at him.

"Lizette," he began, "I don't need you to tell me how to run my life."

"But—"

"No buts, Lizette." He fixed her with a stern glare. "It happens that I like this life. I'm dedicated to giving my daughter the best possible childhood, and she is thriving here. She has her aunt and her baby-sitter and me." He drew a deep breath. "I'm not planning to return to New York anytime soon." He almost added, "If ever,'' but decided against it at the last minute. He'd given Lizette quite enough to digest already.

"You have a job there," she said. "You have a life."

"Do I?" he said musingly. "Is rushing from one place to another a real life? Is flying all over the world on behalf of Rowbotham-Quigley enjoyable? Is my two-room apartment a real home? I don't think so."

Lizette looked bewildered. "You're not the only one who lives like that in the city," she said.

"Other people like it."

"You might like it better if...well, I came here with the idea of suggesting that we move in together."

"You and me and Kaylie?"

Her expression faltered. "You and I need time alone, Henry. Perhaps she could stay here with your sister while we settle in."

He was aghast that she would expect him to give up Kaylie even for a while. "No, Lizette. Kaylie stays with me. And I wish you'd call me Hank."

She sprang to her feet. "I'll never be able to call you Hank. It's a cowboy's name. You're not a cowboy. You're a city dweller and an investment banker, and you have cosmopolitan tastes. Don't tell me you're going to give all that up for...for a little brat!" Her lips quivered in anger, and her fists clenched as though she could hardly refrain from punching someone, most likely him.

"I'm not going to tell you more than I already have," he said quietly. "It's over, Lizette." He whirled and strode away.

She had called his beloved daughter a little brat. That was all the reason he needed to remove Lizette from his life forever.

ERICA TOOK a long, luxurious bath, sprayed herself with a flowery perfume from the atomizer on the vanity, then dressed slowly and with great care. Her outfit was a one-piece navy-blue silk jumpsuit, draped at the hips, slender in the legs so that it showed off her calves. The bodice had a low square neck, curved gently under her breasts. When she studied herself in the mirror and saw that she was all curves and no angles, that her hair was bouncy and her face appeared to be a perfect oval, she couldn't help thrusting her fist in the air and yelling, "Yesss!"

She looked like what she wanted to be. She looked like someone a cowboy would desire.

For fun, she added big dangly earrings and a bunch of jingly silver bracelets she'd bought for herself when she'd selected a necklace for Charmaine in the gift shop earlier.

When Hank opened the door of his apartment, she thought he might greet her with a kiss on the cheek, but instead, he appeared with a baby on his hip and a cloth diaper arrayed across his shoulder. He looked harried but happy to see her.

"Come in," he said, beaming. "Due to circumstances beyond my control, I've barely begun feeding Kaylie."

Kaylie grinned and emitted an unintelligible string of consonants. "I think she's happy to see you," Hank said as she entered.

Erica noticed that the living room was much as it had been earlier, but the kitchen was a mess. A baby-food jar sat open on the counter, and the sink was littered with baby bottles. "Sorry," Hank said, looking apologetic. "I was in the process of cleaning up when Kaylie started to fuss. If you wouldn't mind holding her, I'll have things put away in a jiffy."

Erica tried not to seem flustered when he transferred

Kaylie into her arms, especially when the baby immediately reached for one of her earrings.

"Ow!" she started to say as she pried the little fingers away, managing only at the last minute to change the *Ow!* to an "I'll take Kaylie into the living room so she can show me her toys." If Hank noticed that she'd barely avoided screeching in pain, he gave no sign.

Feeling slightly more at ease with Kaylie this time than last, Erica carried her into the living room. "What do you like to play with?" she asked.

Kaylie said, as usual, "Babababa!"

"Translation—anything you want to give her," Hank said from the kitchen door. He was drying one of Kaylie's bottles with a dish towel, and it seemed incongruous to see him performing such a mundane task dressed as he was in a western-style white shirt with pearl snaps, jeans and boots. Her heart warmed to him, to his whole-hearted attempt at domesticity.

"I'll try the fuzzy koala bear," she decided, swooping down and snagging it from the playpen, and at the motion, Kaylie whooped with glee.

"She liked that," Hank said approvingly.

Erica swooped down again, and Kaylie giggled. Erica found that she quite liked getting a positive reaction from the baby; it gave her a sense of accomplishment that wasn't so different from the times she garnered a positive reaction in, say, a business associate. And it was a lot more fun.

She sat on the edge of the couch with Kaylie in her lap and wound the key on the front of the koala bear. The bear began to play "Waltzing Matilda," and Kaylie at first hid her face in the front of Erica's jumpsuit before venturing a peek.

"Isn't that a nice song?" Erica asked her, and Kaylie, braver now, reached for the koala.

"The koala bear is singing to you, Kaylie."

Kaylie studied the key in the koala's chest, poked at it with a finger, and made a face as the music slowed. In the kitchen, the refrigerator door opened and closed, and Hank said, "I'm going to fire up the grill out back, get those burgers going."

"Fine," Erica said. "Need some help?"

"You're helping by keeping Kaylie occupied," Hank said, appearing briefly in the doorway and favoring them with an easy grin.

Kaylie was crooning to the koala bear, and when Erica looked at her, she realized that Kaylie had drooled on the front of her silk jumpsuit.

"Oh, no," she murmured, low enough so that Hank wouldn't hear. She saw a box of tissues on the coffee table, pulled one out and blotted at the drool marks, which only succeeded in spreading the stain. As Kaylie threw the koala bear on the floor, where it landed with a thump and stopped playing music, Erica realized that all she could do was to let the mark dry and hope it wasn't permanent.

Sighing, she bent over and picked up the koala bear, tossing it back into the playpen. She got up and found a round toy with a dial in the middle that played animal sounds when you twisted an arrow to point to a picture of the animal. That held Kaylie's interest for about two minutes. Then for some reason she decided she didn't like it anymore and began to whimper.

"Don't cry," Erica said, distressed that Kaylie wasn't responding the way she thought she should. "I'll sing you a song. What would you like to hear?" Not that her repertoire was so extensive these days, but she could probably summon up the words to something.

"Babababa!" Kaylie shrieked as she closed her fist around Erica's other earring and tried to put it in her mouth.

This time Erica didn't yelp. This time she anticipated the problem and very gently disentangled Kaylie's fingers. "No, cutie. Definitely no."

Kaylie regarded her with doubt, then reached for the earring again. "No." This time Erica spoke more clearly and had the presence of mind to twirl the dial on the animal-sounds toy so that the sound of an oinking pig diverted Kaylie's attention. She lunged for the toy.

"Listen, let's try the cow." Erica cranked the dial around until the sounds of a cow's mooing filled the air.

Kaylie, a beatific grin on her face, looked enchanted. Erica felt inordinately pleased with herself for learning how to manage a baby, even for so short a period of time. Maybe she could get into babies, after all!

When Hank came in from slapping the burgers on the grill, it was to find Erica and Kaylie together on the couch. Kaylie was lying back in Erica's arms, her binky in her mouth, her eyes growing heavy. Erica was singing to her. It wasn't a lullabye. It was "America, the Beautiful." But Kaylie didn't seem to care.

Hank went over to the couch and gently lifted Kaylie into his arms. "I'll put her in her crib. She'll be asleep in no time."

He took Kaylie into her nursery alcove and laid her carefully in the crib. She sighed, smiled at him around her pacifier and closed her eyes. Erica, watching from the doorway, seemed interested in the proceedings, and when he turned to leave the alcove, she had to move out of the way so he could pass.

In the living room, Erica grinned. "I don't know much in the way of songs that would interest a baby. She seemed to like 'America, the Beautiful,' so I kept singing it over and over."

He laughed, a quiet laugh so as not to wake Kaylie, and slid a companionable arm around Erica's shoulders. "Thanks for looking after her. She can be a handful."

Erica looked thoughtful. "Yes, I see that. Except you know what? I never knew that babies could be so much fun."

He looked at her, really looked at her, to see if she meant what she said. Her eyes were glowing as if she'd made a wonderful discovery.

She slanted a look up at him as they came into the kitchen. "Those hamburgers smell mighty good."

He removed his arm from around her shoulders and crossed to the refrigerator to take out tomatoes, lettuce and onions. "I hope you don't mind cutting these up. You'll find a plate in the cabinet, and I'll be back inside when the meat's done."

He left her cutting up vegetables, and when he returned with the meat and buns, she was humming to herself and had arranged everything on the plate.

"I'm not much of a cook, but I make good hamburgers," he said as he set them on the table.

"I'm not much of a cook, either," she confessed.

"The omelette you whipped up this morning was delicious. I don't know how to make one."

"I'll teach you if you'll show me how to grill hamburgers."

"Deal. So let's eat these before they get cold."

She wiped her hands on a towel, and he saw that she'd lined Kaylie's bottles up neatly on one side of the sink.

She'd also folded a bunch of dish towels and put away the coffeepot, which had been draining next to the sink.

He hadn't pegged her for a homebody, but for some reason it cheered him immeasurably that she was showing signs of being one.

AFTER THEY ATE and cleaned up, Hank invited her to go with him to check on Kaylie. They stood in the alcove looking down at the baby, who was sleeping with her little rump in the air, her pacifier still in her mouth.

"She looks so angelic," Erica said.

He moved closer to her, not touching but almost. She felt the hairs on her arm rise, felt every cell in her body go on alert.

"She can be an angel, but she can also be a problem. Fortunately she's more of the former than the latter."

Erica stood, wondering how long they would go on staring at Kaylie, wondering if she would wake up soon. If she did, Erica would probably make her excuses and go back to her suite. And if Kaylie didn't wake up? What then?

"Let's go back in the living room," Hank said, and there was nothing in his tone to clue her in about what was going to happen next. They turned to go, and her shoulder brushed a wall hanging, which swung on its hook and made a slight rustling sound. Hank held his finger to his mouth and took her hand. His palm felt cool against hers.

In the living room, he turned slowly and slid his arms around her waist. "I don't have anywhere fancy to take you. I can't go back with you to your suite. But I don't want you to leave, Erica."

His chin came to rest on her forehead, and she smelled the clean outdoorsy leathery scent of him. His hand came up and cupped her chin. "You understand what I'm saying?"

"Yes," she breathed, taking in the strong, determined set of his jaw, the sensual curve of his lips, the raw yearning in his eyes.

"Come with me," he said. He led her into the bedroom, and she was touched to see that he had found fresh flowers somewhere and put them in a tiny vase on the bedside table alongside the book she'd helped him choose from Justine's library. He went to the dresser, found a match and lit a small candle, which cast the humble room in a golden glow.

He caught her expression and said sheepishly, "I wanted to make it as nice as I could."

Erica swallowed, unable to look away. "It's very nice."

"Ah, Erica, so are you. I like the way you've taken to Kaylie. I like the way you pitch in when help is needed." He pulled her close and kissed her, a gentle kiss that soon became more forceful. She felt the erratic beat of her heart, the weakening of her knees, as his kiss became wild and hard and demanding.

She was, finally, living her daydreams, the ones that always ended too soon. She curved her body to fit his contours, made it easy for him to touch her. His hands skimmed her ribs and came up to cup her breasts, which surged up out of her low neckline; his mouth feathered kisses down her jawbone. A low moan escaped his throat, and she arched backward so that he would find what he was looking for. He discovered the zipper and yanked it down so that her breasts tumbled out, and she shrugged out of the sleeves while he eased the fabric away to expose the rest of her. It puddled around her feet, and she stepped out of it completely. Hank said shakily, ''Oh, Erica, you're even more beautiful than I imagined.''

In the mirror over the dresser, she saw the two of them, saw the reverent expression on his face as he beheld her, and she thought dreamily that it was like looking at two people in a movie. She could hardly believe that she, Erica Strong, was that blond, sexy woman, or that Hank, a big strong cowboy, handsome enough that he could have any woman he wanted, actually wanted her. She blinked, looked again. They were still the two people in the mirror, and Hank had somehow managed to divest himself of his shirt. He caught her against him so that her breasts were crushed against his chest, and then he swung her up into his arms.

The next thing she knew, she was beside him on the bed, her hands on the buckle of his belt and unzipping his jeans. Soon he was lying on top of her, hard and strong and murmuring her name.

She offered him her lips, but it was her breasts he wanted. His mouth sought her nipples, kissed them each in turn. His tongue traced their contours, creating ripples of pleasure that sizzled right to her core. He drew out each sensation to its utmost, and she found herself moving her hips restlessly against his until he could no longer ignore her. He slid a hand around to cup her buttocks, drawing her closer, and his hardness was hot against her thighs. She wanted him, all of him, but he seemed determined not to rush.

''I—I'm ready,'' she gasped, but he only chuckled deep in his throat.

''You only think you are,'' he said gruffly, and then he proceeded with the most exquisite torture, tantalizing her with deep, heartfelt kisses, returning again to her breasts and then finding her lips again. She trembled beneath him, presented herself to him like a wanton woman, and still he didn't take all of her.

She reveled in the taste of him, in the texture of his hair when she wove her fingers through it, and she felt a certain reckless greed as she moved her hands downward. He poised above her, his mouth moist against her throat, his breath hot and heavy. She shifted her head, caught his breath in a kiss, sighed into it as her blood pounded in her ears. Everything was hot, hot and wet, and her hips arched upward, guided him in.

Fiercely, joyfully, she rose to meet him, mate with him. She cried out, the sound muffled against his chest. She felt herself building to a peak, racing to the end, fighting to get there, all the sensation in her body swirling, merging, coalescing in one spinning, swirling explosion of feeling. And then she felt him convulsing, pouring into her, their bodies the instruments that brought them together at last.

He held her, his breath rough in her ear, his skin damp against hers.

"Oh, Erica," he said helplessly. "Oh, my sweet, my darling."

Her mind was beginning to untangle the words, to make sense of the fact that he had called her his darling, when the baby started to cry.

Chapter Ten

"Oh, no," Hank said. He rolled over and reached for his jeans.

Erica clutched the sheet to her chest, suddenly self-conscious. "Does she usually wake up crying in the middle of the night?"

"Not unless something is wrong." He bent over, his hands on either side of her, and kissed her lingeringly and tenderly. "I'm sorry, Erica."

She sat up as Hank went to see what was wrong with Kaylie. She pulled on his shirt and trailed after him. When she got to the living room, Hank walked out of the alcove with Kaylie against his shoulder. The baby had stopped wailing and was snuffling and rubbing her eyes.

"I think she's cutting her first tooth," Hank said.

Kaylie looked so pathetic that it wrenched Erica's heart to look at her. "What can we do?"

"I keep a couple of teething toys in the freezer door. If you'd bring one, maybe that would help."

Erica padded into the kitchen, found the toy and took it to Hank. He gave it to Kaylie, but she didn't want to relinquish the pacifier.

"All right, Kay-Kay," he said, settling down on the

couch with her. "Let's see what we can do to help you. Do you know anything about teething, Erica?"

Erica wished she'd paid more attention to Abby's talk about Todd when he was a baby, but she'd more or less tuned out all those conversations. She sat down beside Hank, and suddenly a memory came to mind. "My mother used to massage my little sister's gums, and it seemed to help," she said.

"I can try that." Carefully Hank removed Kaylie's pacifier from her mouth, and before she could object, he began to rub the bottom center gum where her two first teeth would erupt. Kaylie relaxed, an absorbed look on her face.

"I think she likes it," Hank said hopefully.

"Why don't I get us a snack?"

"There are chocolate-chip cookies in the pantry."

Erica found the cookies and rejoined him. "I didn't think to ask if Kaylie needs something."

"I suppose I could give her a bottle, but I don't want her to get in the habit of waking at night in hopes of a snack. The book says not to do that."

"You must depend on the baby book a lot."

"I didn't have a clue about taking care of babies when Anne-Marie died. I've had to learn it all from scratch. But we've both survived, haven't we, Kay-Kay?" He kissed the top of her head.

"You're doing a great job, Hank."

"It's fun most of the time, but I wish I'd had the advantage of learning everything right from the start."

"Why didn't Anne-Marie want you to visit Kaylie?"

He kept rubbing Kaylie's gum and helped himself to a cookie with the other hand. "She didn't want me coming in and out of her life. She said that she was the only parent Kaylie would need. I didn't agree with her, but..."

Kaylie wriggled and pushed Hank's hand away. He gave her the pacifier; she threw it on the floor. He handed her the teething toy, which she pitched behind the couch. Then she began to whine fretfully.

"May I hold her?" Erica asked.

Hank looked momentarily disconcerted. "Okay," he said, and Kaylie held her little arms out toward Erica when she reached for her. This made Erica feel surprised and even honored, and when Kaylie clung to her shoulder, she felt downright flattered. She also felt protective, a new emotion for her. In the past the only thing she'd wanted to protect was her position at work.

"She might like it if you'd sing to her," Hank suggested.

"'America, the Beautiful'?"

"Why not?" He gave her an encouraging smile.

She began to sing softly, and Kaylie, whose eyes opened wide at first, curved trustingly against her. Hank went to wash off the pacifier in the sink, and when he handed it to Kaylie, she put it into her mouth with a grateful sigh.

"I wish I knew some other songs," Erica said.

"How about 'Home on the Range'? I'll sing it with you."

"You start."

And then they were singing together, their voices blending until they got to the chorus, where Erica surprised herself by singing harmony. Kaylie's eyelids grew heavier and heavier, and before they'd finished the song for the second time, she was sound asleep.

"I'll put her back to bed," Hank said. He gathered Kaylie into his arms, and Erica relinquished her reluctantly. While he went into the baby's alcove, Erica returned to the bedroom where she began untangling her jumpsuit, shoes and underwear. She took them all into the bathroom and had started to dress when Hank rapped on the door.

"Erica?"

"I'm getting dressed."

"Oh." A few moments' silence, and then he said, "I wish you wouldn't."

She halted in the process of zipping up her jumpsuit.

"I don't want you to go," he added.

Surprised, she opened the bathroom door. "You mean it?"

He drew her into his arms and kissed her cheek. "I want to sleep beside you all night long. I want to wake up later and make love to you all over again."

She swallowed, overwhelmed by the emotion she saw in the depths of his eyes. "Well, hey, cowboy, that sounds good to me, too."

He held her away so that she could see the quirk of his lips as he suppressed a smile. "The only thing is, now I'll have to undress you all over again."

"I'll see what I can do to help," she said as she kicked off her shoes and followed him back to bed.

ERICA WOKE UP early the next morning when she heard voices in the adjacent stable. It was barely dawn, and when Hank stirred beside her, he slid closer and curled his body around hers.

"That was wonderful last night," he murmured close to her ear as his hands found her breasts.

"Mmm. You're a terrific lover, Hank."

A silence, and then he chuckled. "I didn't mean the

sex. I meant the way you sang to Kaylie so that she went back to sleep. The lovemaking was okay, too.''

She knew from the way he said it that he thought it was more than okay. She slid around in his arms to face him. ''How long do we have until Kaylie wakes up? We could try to improve. If you're interested, that is.''

''I'm interested, Ms. Strong. Very interested.'' And he proceeded to show her how interested he was.

Afterward he held her close for a long time. She closed her eyes, listening to their hearts beating in unison. He nuzzled her ear, setting off a chain reaction of sensation all the way from her head to the tips of her toes. She couldn't have imagined how sensitive she would become to his touch; it seemed as if every nerve in her body was primed and ready to go on alert if Hank so much as looked at her.

''How about a shower?''

''Want me to go start the water?''

''Go ahead,'' he said. ''I'll be there in a minute.''

After he went to check on the baby, Erica went into the bathroom and turned on the water. While she was waiting for it to get warm, she caught a glimpse of herself in the mirror over the sink. First of all, she noticed that she had gained weight. Only a few pounds, but they had filled out her spare frame so that she was more curvaceous. Her breasts were high and plump, and her waist nipped in above hips that were admirably slim.

To her embarrassment, Hank caught her at it. ''Looking good,'' was all he said, and even though she felt herself beginning to blush, he pulled her to him and said, ''I like your new look.''

Then, before she could say anything, he dropped his towel, turned on the shower and pulled her under the cascade of spray with him. He took her in his arms.

"Slippery when wet," he murmured into her damp hair. "And oh, so kissable."

She surrendered to his kisses, her skin slick against his, the warm water sluicing down in streams. She thought her heart would overflow with the pleasure of touching him, of skin against skin. Like all the rest of him, his body was perfect and fit hers like no other man's ever had; he made her feel desirable, sexy, womanly. When she was swooning from the steam and the warmth and the steady onslaught of kisses, he reached for the soap and, moving slowly and deliberately, began to lather her arms and her legs and her breasts and her buttocks. She wanted to giggle when he tickled a spot above her navel, and she pressed against his hand when he found the sensitive place at the juncture of her thighs.

"Now you," she said, barely able to speak, and he stood still while she ran the soap across his shoulders, over the muscles in his back, across his wide chest and down his abdomen. She hesitated before going lower.

"Go on," he said, his voice husky with emotion, and she moved her hands lower, clasped them around his hardness.

He caged her against the wall, one hand on each side of her. "I can't resist you," he said, his voice low. "There's something about you that turns me on, Erica. Something…" His voice trailed off as she pressed against him, and then he braced himself against the wall and took her there with the water running down, the soap slicking their bodies as they moved against each other, the steam enveloping them in their own private world.

Erica stopped thinking, began living in the moment, this moment. For it was a moment like no other, and this cowboy was real, not a daydream. She wanted to imprint everything about this experience on her mind, her heart and her soul. Because when it was all over, and it would be over, she wanted to remember. She would hold this memory, the memory of Hank, close to her heart. And instead of a daydream, she would have the memory to comfort and keep her long after she returned to her real life.

FOR HANK, it was a busy day. He led a trail ride and gave his scheduled riding lessons. He briefed Paloma on Kaylie's teething and listened to her complain that if Kaylie was no longer going to take a morning nap, Paloma deserved a raise. He was in such a good mood that he agreed to the raise and suggested that he might call Paloma to baby-sit more often in the evening, to which she eagerly agreed.

"It is easy, taking care of Kaylie at night. I am saving so much money, you wouldn't believe. My wedding, it will be sooner than I think, maybe."

For the first time in a long time, Hank discovered that he didn't feel envious of Paloma's happiness.

He returned a call from Justine, who was disgruntled because Lizette had shown up on her doorstep and wanted to talk about his mental state, which according to Lizette, would improve with therapy.

"The only therapy I need at present is for Lizette to return to New York," Hank informed her through clenched teeth.

"Lizette is a registered guest," Justine shot back.

"Whose fault is that?"

"Well, even if you've broken up with her, I hope you'll be pleasant," Justine said.

Hank was on the brink of telling his sister that he had found someone to be pleasant to, except that he didn't know how Justine would take it if she knew he was sexually involved with Erica, so he hung up.

"Sexually involved" didn't exactly describe the way it was between him and Erica. There was more to it than sex. He couldn't stop thinking about the way she'd held Kaylie last night, her sweet voice as she sang, the sweep of her eyelashes as she gazed down at the drowsy child. And Kaylie liked her. This meant a lot to him. He couldn't, for instance, imagine Kaylie falling asleep in Lizette's arms.

He wanted to see Erica again that evening but hesitated to call her because he had so little to offer. Another night of burgers and beer? Another night of possible interruptions?

Another night of sweet, passionate love. Another night of tenderness and falling asleep with Erica in his arms.

He picked up the phone and dialed her suite.

ERICA TOOK PART in Rancho Encantado's usual activities, which included brunch with Shannon and Natalie in the dining hall, a meditation gathering in the palm grove and an afternoon class on choosing wardrobe colors. When she checked her phone messages, she was elated to find a voice mail from Hank suggesting that they rendezvous at the oasis hot pool after dinner. She called him and left a message that she'd be there.

She also had an e-mail from Charmaine.

Erica—
????????????
Love, Char

Erica only smiled. She didn't reply. She wanted to think over what she was going to say very carefully.

Justine called as soon as Erica logged off her e-mail. She sounded worried. "Erica, how about coming early for dinner? You remember Tony, the van driver who picked you up at the airport when you arrived? He had an 'episode,' and they're keeping him in the hospital overnight for observation. I might want to drive over there tonight and visit him. He's seventy-six years old, and I'm concerned."

"I don't blame you. And of course you should go to see him."

"Do you mind if I invite Hank and Kaylie for dinner, too?"

Would she mind? Hardly!

"That would be fun."

"Good. See you soon."

Erica hung up, wondering what Justine would say if she knew about her and Hank. Should she tell her? Considering the conversation she'd overheard in the stable the first day she was here, perhaps not. Although Justine's attitude seemed to be that Hank should socialize, Erica wasn't sure she meant he should sleep with the guests.

Only, she didn't think Hank made a habit of it. She'd seen no signs of other women around his apartment— no extra toothbrushes, no shower caps, no feminine articles of any kind.

Still, what Justine didn't know wouldn't hurt her. She only hoped that Charmaine wouldn't decide to call her old friend and spill what she knew, thereby creating problems.

WHEN ERICA ARRIVED at the Big House that evening, Hank and Kaylie weren't there yet, and Justine was beside herself with worry.

"I talked with Tony on the phone," she said. "It wasn't reassuring."

"What did he say?" Erica asked as she bent to greet Murphy, who was wagging himself into a joyous dither over her arrival.

"Not much."

Erica, recalling the little man's gift of gab, raised her eyebrows. "I think you'd better go see him."

"I've come to the same conclusion myself. I feel a certain responsibility to Tony. He's been like a fond uncle to me." Justine glanced out the window. "Oh, here's Hank with Kaylie."

Hank came in, all smiles. Erica felt suddenly shy around him, but Kaylie reached for her and she willingly gathered the baby into her arms. She began to jounce her semiexpertly, taking heart that Kaylie seemed to like it.

Hank's smile faded when he saw Justine's face. "What's the matter? Is Pavel the cantankerous chef acting up again?"

Justine shook her head. "No, it's worse than that. Erica, why don't you fill Hank in on the situation with Tony while I see to the roast? Help yourself to the cheese and crackers on the coffee table."

After Justine had departed for the kitchen, Hank leaned close to Erica and planted a kiss on her cheek. "What's the problem with Tony?" he asked. "And don't act so scandalized. Surely you don't mind if I steal one little kiss when I'm going to be ravishing you in the oasis hot pool in—" he consulted his watch "—approximately two hours."

"Hank!" she hissed, taking Kaylie into the living room and easing down in front of the crackling fire in the fireplace with her in her lap. Murphy pattered in and sat down beside Hank to be scratched behind the ears, a service that Hank performed before slipping him a cracker with cheese on it.

"Well?" he said to Erica. "Are you going to tell me about Tony?"

With the glow of the firelight playing across her features, Erica brought Hank up to speed on the situation, and his forehead knotted with concern. "Justine," he called into the kitchen, "I'll be glad to go with you if you don't want to drive all that way alone."

Justine appeared with two glasses of wine. "You need to be back bright and early for your group class in the morning," she said.

"I'd feel better if you'd let me tag along. If you got tired, I could drive."

"No, Hank. In fact, I'm planning to take a small overnight bag in case I have to stay. Thanks, anyway." Justine shot him a brief smile before she hurried back into the kitchen.

Hank glanced toward the door to the kitchen. Justine wasn't in sight, but they could hear her clattering around with pots and pans at the stove. "Justine never wants to be a bother to anyone, always wants to be in control."

"She's very capable."

"I know. I wish she'd let other people take some responsibility, that's all." He stopped talking when Justine began to carry food into the dining room. "I'll go help her. Not a word to her about us, at least not yet. Okay?"

"Okay." She smiled at him, a co-conspirator.

Hank and Justine were still transferring food from kitchen to table when Erica realized that Kaylie was sitting soggy in her diaper.

"Uh-oh," she said. "Someone needs a diaper change."

"I'll do it," Hank said immediately. "As soon as I carve the roast."

"Let me," Erica said. "Tell me where."

"In the guest room with the crib. You'll find disposable diapers and everything else you'll need."

"Come along, Kaylie," Erica said. "We'll have you dry in no time."

"Bababababa," Kaylie said agreeably.

Erica tried to recall if she'd ever changed a diaper before and realized she hadn't. She'd never baby-sat as a teenager, nor had she taken care of her friends' children.

She laid Kaylie back on the changing table and unsnapped the crotch of her playsuit. The wet diaper came off easily enough. Erica wasn't sure if you had to dry the baby's bottom with a towel or merely sprinkle powder on it. She finally blotted it with a spare cloth diaper that was draped over the edge of the table, and then she sprinkled on baby powder for good measure. Kaylie, while this was going on, was minutely inspecting a see-through rattle with small plastic shapes floating inside it.

"Am I going about this the right way?" Erica whispered to her. Kaylie only grinned. If she knew, she wasn't telling.

Next Erica unfolded a clean disposable diaper from the box, slid it under the baby and figured out how the tabs worked. In a matter of minutes she was snapping Kaylie's playsuit up again and picking her up.

"That wasn't so bad, was it? If you can forgive me for fumbling around a lot." As Erica kissed the top of her head, Kaylie made a fist and gave her what she could have sworn was a cheerful thumbs-up.

Justine had set up a high chair for Kaylie in the dining room, and the baby contentedly played with her activity box while the adults ate. Dinner was hurried, though the substantial food was as delicious as usual.

"I'm sorry," Justine apologized. "I'm going to have to run if I'm going to see Tony tonight."

"I'll clean up the kitchen," Erica promised.

Hank slid his chair back. "I'll help. That is, Justine, if you're sure you don't want me to come along."

"I'm sure." Justine hurried to the back of her house and returned carrying her overnight bag. "Oh, Hank, there's something you could do for me—look after Murphy. He'll need to go out tonight and then tomorrow morning."

"No problem."

"And don't forget the banana-split cake in the refrigerator."

After Justine left, Erica got up and started to clear the table. Hank walked Kaylie to the kitchen window to watch the taillights of Justine's SUV disappearing down the winding driveway.

"You seem worried," Erica said.

"I wish Justine wouldn't drive all the way to the Las Vegas hospital alone. If she didn't want me to go, she could have asked a friend to go along. Justine never listens to anyone. You'd think after what happened to Anne-Marie, she'd be more careful."

"Wasn't there a bad storm that night? Isn't that what caused the accident?"

Hank took his time about answering.

"There was a bad storm that night," he said, "but I'm not convinced that's why Anne-Marie hit that boulder."

Something about the way he said it caused Erica to stop rinsing dishes and turn off the water. "What do you mean?'' The words hung in the air, and for the first time she noticed the tension in the fine lines around his eyes.

''I've never talked about Anne-Marie's accident,'' he said. ''I've never wanted to speak of it before this.''

She dried her hands on a towel. ''We can sit down and talk for a while if you'd like.''

''I'll put Kaylie to bed first.''

When Hank came back, Erica had already dished up plates of the banana-split cake and was sitting on one of the stools at the island in the middle of the kitchen. Hank sat down beside her.

''The night Anne-Marie died, I was on the phone with her. We had a big argument. It was about Kaylie.''

''You were already divorced, right?''

''Yes, and Kaylie was only a few months old. Anne-Marie worked for Justine teaching physical fitness here at the ranch. She and Justine always got along fine, and Justine refused to take sides in the divorce. Justine kept Anne-Marie on the payroll even during the advanced stages of her pregnancy, which was a big help.''

''Wasn't it hard for you to see Anne-Marie every day around the ranch? When you were going through a divorce and she was going to have the baby?''

Hank looked momentarily disconcerted. ''I didn't work here then,'' he said. ''I didn't come to work at Rancho Encantado until after the accident.''

Erica tried to hide her surprise. ''I didn't know that.''

For a moment Hank looked as if he might want to say something else, but he plunged ahead. ''Anyway, that night, the night Anne-Marie died, I got very angry. She told me that she didn't want me to be part of our daughter's life. She said that she didn't need my help financially or any other way. I didn't like it that she was so independent. I wanted to know my daughter, and I didn't want her growing up thinking that her father had abandoned her.''

''Of course not,'' Erica said. She knew that daughters who felt abandoned by their fathers seemed to have a hard time in relationships with men later in life. Not that this was her problem; her own father had always been there for her right up until the day he died at forty-five, victim of a stroke.

''I'd been reading up on the subject, and that's one of the arguments I used with Anne-Marie. She became very distressed, said Kaylie didn't need a father figure, said all the psychologists didn't know what they were talking about. She grew up without a father, and she turned out fine, she said. I disputed that. I said we might not be divorced if she'd known how to relate to me in a more rational way when we were married.''

''She probably didn't like that much.''

Hank's forefinger traced one of the tiles in the countertop. ''It was like waving a red flag in front of a bull. Anne-Marie went berserk. She said that I could keep my opinions to myself. She said that she would get a restraining order to keep me from seeing Kaylie. She was angrier than I'd ever known her to be, and then she slammed down the phone. It was only minutes later that she stormed out and got in her car to go somewhere. I'm sure that Anne-Marie's mental state contributed to the accident. I'll always believe it was my fault.''

''What a terrible load of guilt to carry around,'' Erica said softly. She reached over and slid her fingers through his. ''Maybe it wasn't your fault. Did you know that Justine blames herself, too?''

He appeared thunderstruck. ''No, I didn't.''

''She says she could have kept Anne-Marie from going that night if she hadn't agreed to baby-sit.''

"I'm not so sure. My ex-wife's state of mind was such that if Justine hadn't taken care of Kaylie, Anne-Marie might have bundled up the baby and hauled her along with her. Anne-Marie was like that. She'd jump in a car and rush off whenever we had an argument. If Kaylie had been with her...my God. I could have lost my daughter." His face was pale, his eyes haunted.

"You and Justine should talk, Hank. You could comfort each other."

He looked at her, looked away. His hand gripped hers tightly. "I never knew Justine blamed herself. And I need to thank her, Erica. I need to thank my sister for the fact that I still have Kaylie."

Padre Luis Speaks...

MY PRAYERS are being answered, thanks be to God.

Erica is made real by her caring for the child and by her love for Hank. Perhaps it will take time for her to realize this is love.

And Hank has grown in wisdom and understanding through sharing his deepest feelings with Erica. She made him see how much he owes his sister. Without Erica, he never would have learned.

Do they see that love is a great teacher? That love smoothes the path of life, whether it be through desert or oasis, cactus or rose petals? Ah, perhaps I should have been a great poet, instead of a poor humble priest.

Now Erica and Hank must find their path together, which will not be easy. And they are still not completely real to each other. This is because neither has revealed the whole truth about themselves.

Perhaps they will. Soon, I hope. I grow weary of their problems and wish to concern myself with others. Those three kittens, for instance. They need a home. Their mother, running around and talking to people in my voice, scarcely pays any attention to them these days.

Dios mio, I must lie down and nap in my bed among the cactus. Perhaps those kittens will come by for a visit. That would be pleasant for a poor humble priest who needs a diversion from the troubles of the world.

Chapter Eleven

Hank took Murphy back to the apartment with him after he said goodbye to Erica at the fork in the path, telling her he'd meet her at the oasis hot pool as soon as he could. Murphy galloped along beside him, tongue hanging out, ears perked.

"It's good to get out once in a while, isn't it, boy?"

For an answer, Murphy looked over his shoulder at him, and Hank could have sworn that he grinned in agreement.

"Ba?" Kaylie said, her sleepy head resting on his shoulder.

"Doggie, Kaylie. Can you say doggie?"

Kaylie's eyelids drooped as she made an agreeable sound low in her throat.

Paloma's small sedan was parked in the gravel parking area beside the stable. She was thumbing through a magazine when he walked into the apartment with Murphy at his heels.

"Hello, Hank. Let me take Kaylie. Hi, little one, how are you?" Murphy sniffed at her feet, waited for her to pet him, then continued on his self-appointed mission to smell every object in the apartment.

"She's been better than last night. Did she act like her gums hurt today when you were with her?"

Paloma shook her head. "Not at all. It comes and goes, this teething, I know from taking care of my little nephew. Oh, Hank, I made brownies today. They're on top of the microwave if you want some."

"Nope, I had a big dinner and I've got a hot date."

Paloma's eyebrows rose into her hairline. "You have a date? Who is the lucky person?"

"Me," he said, thinking of Erica and how her eyes shone when she looked at him.

"Ah, I see. You are in love. I can tell. It was that way with Miguel and me. We met and *pow!* Instant attraction. Then love. Now, we will soon have enough money for our wedding. We should make it a double wedding, perhaps? With you and your lady friend?"

"You're way ahead of me, Paloma. There's no wedding in the works, okay? And while you get Kaylie ready for bed, I'll take Murphy out for a walk."

"Okay, Hank. Hurry back before Kaylie falls asleep. It looks like it won't be long."

Hank let himself out of the apartment. Murphy seemed overjoyed at this chance to explore the stable and environs. He ran from stall to stall, greeting the horses before prancing back to Hank. Then he caught sight of the cats.

Mrs. Gray and her kittens were perched on top of a stack of boxes higher than Hank's head. The three kittens merely spat and hissed, but Mrs. Gray, after a deprecatory appraisal of Murphy, stretched lazily and hopped down the series of boxes until she landed right in front of the dog. Murphy began to bark, and Mrs. Gray arched her back and hissed. Hank wished he had put Murphy on a leash, but it was too late now. Mrs.

Gray, with what Hank swore was a derisive snort of laughter, took off like a streak of lightning out of the barn and across the corral. Murphy followed in hot pursuit.

"Great," Hank said to Sebastian, who was nosing over the top of his stall door and looking on with interest. Hank glanced at his watch. It was almost nine-thirty, his appointed time to meet Erica.

He suspected that the cat had planned this all along. Sighing, he headed out of the stable, calling and whistling to Murphy in hopes that he'd come back. Sooner rather than later.

THE PALM GROVE was quiet, the way through the trees lit by low lights that cast golden circles on the path. An occasional breeze rustled the palm fronds, and Erica clutched her blue waffle-knit Rancho Encantado robe around her as protection against the chilly night air.

She made her way to the oasis hot pool, its rock-lined depths shadowed in the silvery moonlight. The pool was shaped like a figure eight, the hot water bubbling up naturally from the ground. There was no sign of Hank. She slipped out of the robe and stepped from the edge of the pool onto the underwater ledge that served as a seat.

"I thought you'd never get here," said a throaty voice from the other end of the pool, and Erica blinked in surprise toward its source. Directly in front of her, revealed bit by bit as the diaphanous mists parted, was a female body, nude. Oh, it was nude, all right. The clear water didn't hide a thing. The expanse of skin ended in a curly mop that frizzed outward from the scalp, and Erica realized with a jolt that the face atop the body belonged to Lizette. No more did she sport her sleek squared-off cut, which had certainly been more flattering than the hairdo she had now.

"Hello, Lizette," Erica said, feeling her face freeze in a wary expression.

Lizette lounged at the far side of the pool, her breasts bobbing with the bubbles. She saw Erica glance at the sign that stated that guests were to remain clothed at all times, and she laughed again. "Rules are meant to be broken."

Erica eased down into the water, trying to decide if she should leave. However, if she did, that would mean that Hank would show up for their rendezvous and find only Lizette. Allowing that to happen would be stupid.

"How did you know I'd be here?" Erica said, trying to sound as if Lizette's presence was of no importance to her.

"I didn't. But it may be a good time for a woman-to-woman talk, right?"

"I doubt that we need to talk at all, Lizette." Erica bit the words off sharply.

"You have a crush on him, don't you?"

"A crush?" The words didn't begin to describe her feelings for Hank.

"A crush. As in head over heels. As in can't see the forest for the trees."

"Lizette, I don't want to discuss this with you. Hank and I—"

"Oh, stop calling him Hank. His name is Henry. I've had it up to here with this Hank business." Lizette looked even more petulant than she sounded.

"I'll call him whatever I like. It's no concern of yours."

"Isn't it? When we've been discussing moving in together?"

This stunned Erica so much that at first she couldn't speak. But why should she believe anything Lizette said? She didn't seem like Hank's type, not to mention Hank had assured her that Lizette was history.

"I suppose he's been romancing you," Lizette said, splashing water on her face in an unconcerned way.

Erica blew out a long breath. "You could say that," she said. At the same time she knew she didn't want to discuss anything about her relationship with Hank with this woman.

"He's good at it," Lizette went on. "He's also good at some other things, like what goes on in bed."

Erica wanted to get up and leave, but Hank was due here any moment, and she wasn't about to abdicate her position and leave him to the unclothed Lizette. Still, Lizette made her uncomfortable. Very uncomfortable.

"I suppose you already know how good he is in bed?" Lizette inquired sweetly, her tone goading.

Erica was still trying to figure out if she should respond to this when Hank walked out of the swirling mist. He was wearing bathing trunks and a T-shirt. "So what if she does?" he said angrily. "It's no business of yours, Lizette."

"Henry! I've been wanting to talk to you!"

"We've talked all we need to. You'd better leave, Lizette." Hank shrugged out of his shirt and folded himself down into the pool beside Erica. He rested a hand on her thigh, claiming her.

"I'm a paying guest," Lizette said. "I have a right to go wherever I want."

Hank turned to Erica. "Would you like to leave?"

Her response was immediate. "No." She wouldn't give Lizette the satisfaction.

A few more seconds passed, and Erica could tell that Lizette was wavering.

"Henry, I think I'll book you for a private riding lesson," Lizette said. "I could teach you a few things."

"I could teach *you* some things not connected with riding. Like class, for instance. And respect. And how to give up gracefully when it's over."

"In my Life Experiences class, we've discussed what to do about men who are afraid to commit. We—"

"Men are usually not afraid to commit. When it seems as if that's the case, it means that they don't *want* to commit. To you. But—" Erica thought she felt his fingers squeeze her thigh slightly "—a man might be perfectly ready and willing to commit to someone else." His voice was firm, his manner brusque.

For the first time Lizette looked panicky. "After all we've meant to each other?"

The pool bubbled into the silence, and Erica held her breath.

She supposed that Lizette was taking the only avenue open to her at this point when she stood up, exposing her body to view before she grabbed her robe off a nearby rock. Her hands were shaking as she wrapped it around herself.

"Fine, Henry, but don't come running to me when you've had enough of your little cowgirl there." After treating them to one last view of her breasts, she yanked the robe closed and haughtily flounced off through the mist.

"Well," said Hank, "that's that. And that's enough." He removed his hand from Erica's thigh and slid it around her shoulders.

She scooted over on the stone ledge where they sat,

out of arm's reach. "She told me that the two of you are thinking about living together."

Hank rolled his eyes. "I told her I wasn't going to do that, and besides, I don't like the way she talks about Kaylie. She called her a brat."

"She did?"

"She did. And she's never even seen Kaylie."

He moved closer, reached under the water and took her hand. People walked past on the path, their voices low. When the voices faded, Hank entwined his fingers with hers. "I haven't been able to think about much but you since this morning," he said. "It's like I've been enchanted or something."

"Rancho Encantado," Erica said unevenly. "Where dreams come true."

"Where you can meet the woman you've always dreamed about." His face was close now, and it was all she could do not to move hers a fraction of an inch so that her lips would meet his.

Her mouth was dry, and she'd begun to feel giddy. She swallowed and tried to move away, but he slid his free hand to the nape of her neck and held her there. "Kiss me, Erica. Kiss me the way you did last night and this morning."

His breath was warm on her cheek, and she closed her eyes to shut him from her view. The image of his face was still on the back of her eyelids, as if engraved there. Her lips parted, and his moved slowly, agonizingly slowly, toward hers. Her eyes drifted closed again. And then she was kissing him. Kissing him as every cell in her body yearned for him, called to him, begged for more. Lips, tongue, teeth, creating such delectable sensations, such unparalleled pleasure. And then his arms came around her, pulled her close to his wet chest, his lips still working their magic as they feathered down her throat, kissed the hollow above her breasts and lingered there as his hands slid under her bikini top.

The water in the pool was hot, but her skin was beginning to feel hotter. She was burning from the inside out. She was consumed with wanting him, wanting to feel him close enough to guide him into her. With Hank kissing her and taking his time about it, she could anticipate all that was to happen between them tonight. His lips were skilled and they were sexy, and so was she. She blossomed under his touch, her nipples rose to meet his caressing fingertips, and he responded to her soft moan with a hot surge of need.

His hands went around to unhook her top so that her breasts were crushed against his chest, their skin slick and full of sensation. "These are the only breasts I cared to see tonight," he said, and he dipped his head to kiss one rosy peak and then the other. "Yours is the only body in the world that means anything to me."

She arched her back as he drew one nipple into his mouth and sucked gently, then greedily. Her head fell back, her eyes half-closed, and their surroundings—the palm trees and the rocks and the mist unfurling above the pool—seemed surreal.

Without knowing quite how it happened, she found herself facing him on the ledge, felt his hands move under her bikini bottom to cup her against him. Then he untied the side fastening and it floated away. She gasped, reached for it, but he only smiled at her. It may have been his fingers that undid her swimsuit, but it was that smile that undid her emotions. In that moment, the moment in which his eyes took on a gleam of amusement overlaid by passion, she knew she didn't care who or what was watching. She wanted him now, not later, not in a bed or behind closed doors. This was the stuff of dreams, but her dreams had never before reached a level in which she actually cared about the man so much that she would throw all caution to the wind.

Now her emotions were not merely a mind game that she played with herself for amusement and escape. They were the driving force behind all she wanted, all she did. And what she did was reach for him so that he groaned and settled her closer. "If you're going to touch me like that, lady, you'd better mean business," he said close to her ear.

"Now," she urged. "Now. Before anyone walks by."

His fingers found her center, slid upward and in. Her skin shivered, and her back arched, waiting. She felt herself open to him even as he positioned himself, and then finally, when an instant seemed like an eternity, he drove into her in one long, shuddering stroke.

She gripped his hair, clamped her legs around him and rode. She was prepared for a quick climax, wanted it, but he seemed determined to draw it out, to make it last.

"Hurry!" she whispered.

He threaded his hands through her hair and pulled back her head to expose her throat. "Not a chance," he said between kisses. "Not when I've been waiting for you all day long."

Then, moving excruciatingly slowly, he teased her into delirium, into ecstasy, until she cried out for mercy.

"For someone who doesn't want anyone to know we're here, you sure are making a lot of noise," he said.

"Hank, please," she said, her voice muffled against his shoulder.

"I'll please you, darlin', have no fear," he said. Then, in a ripple of movement, he turned her so that she was lying back on the ledge, the smooth surface firm against her back. He rose above her, almost like a phantom in the mist, and then before she could pull him to her, he plunged into her so that she cried out in surprise.

And then she wondered how she could have lived all of her life without knowing what sex, real sex, was like. It had never been like this. It had never been so passionate, never engaged her body, mind and soul, and it had never been with a rugged cowboy who knew how to bring her to these heights. The planes of his face were pressed to hers, the angles of his body complemented the curves of hers, and their hearts throbbed to the same rhythm.

As they raced together toward the moon, she spun away on the ripples of the pool, was drawn into the ribbons of moonlight, became one with the silvery mist. She became satin, she became silk, she became the moon mirrored in his eyes. She inhaled his breath, rose on its life force to spiral into a place she had never gone before, and she was going there with him, Hank, her perfect cowboy.

She thought she might have cried his name, didn't care if anyone heard, and in that moment she knew she was one with the universe and that Hank was the universe for her now, in this moment.

And then, before she could drift down from that wonderful place, she felt her muscles clamp and convulse, felt his shudder at the core of her being and closed her eyes against the tears that threatened to overflow.

Tears of happiness. And tears of sadness that it had taken her so long to find this man.

ERICA OPENED her laptop. Time to write to her sister.

Hi Char

Did I ever tell you about my fantasies of the perfect cowboy? Well, I've found him.

Love,

Erica

Erica,

A man who already has a baby isn't perfect by any means. A baby takes a lot of time and work. A baby gets in the way of a developing relationship. A baby is, well, a baby. You don't do babies, remember?

It sounds like you've taken leave of your senses. Isn't it time for you to fly back to New York?

Your devoted sister who is beginning to wish that she'd never mentioned Rancho Encantado,

Charmaine

To my devoted sister,

Char, I really like this baby. Also, Kaylie has not stood in the way of our developing relationship. If anything, she has enhanced it by making me notice what a fine person Hank is.

Besides, I've really got the hots for this guy.

But enough talk. I'm going to sleep. It's late, and I'm going to his place to cook breakfast for him early tomorrow morning. I think I can manage fried eggs. Can seven-month-old babies eat fried eggs, do you know?

Love from your grateful sister, who can't imagine never having visited Rancho Encantado,

Erica

Erica

YOU MUST HAVE LOST YOUR ALLEGED MIND! YOU DON'T LIKE BABIES AND YOU HATE TO COOK. FIXING BREAKFAST EARLY IN THE MORNING? SHEESH! I KNOW YOU WENT THERE TO GET A MAKEOVER, BUT THEY WERE SUPPOSED TO LEAVE YOUR BRAIN ALONE.

CALL ME, ERICA. CALL ME RIGHT NOW. I MEAN IT.

Charmaine

Chapter Twelve

Hank woke up the next morning and lay in bed, eyes closed. He could still see, in his mind's eye, moonlight dancing over the smooth curves of Erica's body, casting her breasts in sharp relief. Her face in that magical light had appeared carved in silver and was more memorable than any daydream he'd ever had.

He stepped back into that memory, felt her body so close to his that he longed to touch her, and he shut out the place, which was his own bed, and the present, which would soon get very busy. *He kissed her, long and hard and deep, and he slipped his hand between her legs. She was moist and ready for him, and she urged him closer, sighed when he released her lips, floated up and over him to settle in exactly the right place so that his—*

A dog started barking. At first he thought it was far away and part of his dream, but as the dream burst like a bubble, he realized that the barking was right outside the kitchen door. He sternly requested his anatomy to calm down and threw off the covers.

He pulled on jeans and hurried to the back door. There was Murphy, wagging his whole body and begging to be let in.

"You old nuisance," he said, happy to see Murphy

despite the dog's disappearance last night when he set off in pursuit of the cat.

Murphy pattered around the kitchen, looking for his food dish. He found the food Paloma had left on the floor for Mrs. Gray and gobbled down all of it before Hank could stop him.

"Well, I guess that solves the problem of what to feed you," Hank said as Kaylie began warming up for an early-morning complaint. He went to the refrigerator and took out a baby bottle full of milk.

Kaylie cheered up when she saw Hank with the bottle, and she gave it her best effort while he changed her diaper. Then he lifted her into his arms and took her into the kitchen, where he settled her into her high chair and proceeded to heat up her cereal.

Murphy watched every move. "I wonder if Justine came back last night," Hank said to him, but Murphy looked blank. Hank dialed the number of the Big House, but Justine didn't answer. He'd try again later.

"So, Murphy," he said conversationally as he started to feed Kaylie, "what happened last night? Did Mrs. Gray lead you on a merry chase?"

Murphy looked noncommittal and quite raffish.

"Oh, so you found a lady friend?"

Murphy flopped his tail up and down enthusiastically.

"Well, so did I. And we... Uh-oh, here she is."

Erica spotted him through the window on the door and smiled. She let herself in, wearing a brightly patterned pullover against the early-morning chill; her rosy cheeks made her gray eyes sparkle. He didn't have time to register the fact that her eyes weren't the color they'd been last night, and besides, she looked fantastic. He got up and took her in his arms.

"Mmm," she said, inhaling deeply. "You smell like sleep."

"Mmm," he echoed. "You smell like soap. So will I after I take a shower. I thought maybe you'd like to join me, but you're way ahead of me."

"I woke up early. Couldn't sleep." She opened the refrigerator and took out the eggs and bacon.

He sat back down and started to feed Kaylie again. "Anything wrong?"

Erica looked abashed. "I kept thinking of things I want to know. For instance, does Kaylie eat fried eggs?"

"No, she's not into fried. She'll eat poached and soft-cooked. This is her breakfast this morning."

Erica bent over and sniffed the cereal. "Good heavens," she said under her breath. "Do we all start out eating that stuff?"

"Pretty much."

The phone rang, and Hank got up to answer it. He handed Erica the spoon. "Here, would you mind taking over the feeding duties?" He disappeared into the living room.

Erica looked uncertainly from the spoon to the cereal and then to Kaylie, who was gazing up at her with equal uncertainty. "Well," Erica said with false bravado, "let's proceed as though I know what I'm doing."

For an answer, Kaylie banged the flat of her hand on the high-chair tray. Erica sat down on the chair vacated by Hank and scooped up cereal with the spoon. Tentatively she held it out toward Kaylie, who opened her mouth like a baby bird. Erica had no idea if she was offering too much or not enough, but she held her breath and dumped the contents of the spoon into Kaylie's open mouth. Kaylie promptly spit half of it down her chin.

"Too much," Erica muttered as she wiped Kaylie off with a napkin. "I'll see if I can do better this time."

The next spoonful held only about half the cereal that the last one did, and this time Erica knew to angle the spoon so that Kaylie swallowed most of the contents. What she didn't swallow dribbled down the baby's chin again, only now Erica had a napkin at the ready.

"Tests? What kind of tests?" Hank was saying into the phone in the other room. A silence, and then Hank spoke again. "You should stay as long as you need to. No, I'll take care of Murphy. Don't worry about it." Another pause. "Sure, I have to teach. Right. Why don't I ask Erica if she can help out?"

Erica, distracted by this conversation, heard a little *clink!* on the spoon. At the same time, Kaylie squinched up her face so that Erica looked at her sharply, and when Kaylie opened her mouth for another spoonful of cereal, Erica noticed a speck of white in the middle of Kaylie's bottom gum. She looked closer. A tooth! A tooth was erupting there!

"Hank?" she said unsteadily. "Hank!"

Her tone of voice must have alarmed him because he rushed into the kitchen, phone in hand. "Is something wrong?"

"I think Kaylie has her first tooth!"

He bent quickly to look. "Why, it is!" He raised the phone to his ear again. "Justine, Kaylie has her first tooth. No, Paloma didn't discover it. Erica did."

Erica wiped Kaylie's face, raising her eyebrows at Hank. Now their secret was out. Now Justine would guess what was going on.

Hank rolled his eyes. "Erica is here, yes." A pause while Justine talked. "She was feeding Kaylie her cereal. Yes, I know she's a guest, but you know the policy of Rancho Encantado—if it feels good, do it.'' Another silence, while Erica shook her head violently, willing Hank to be quiet.

"Of course I know that's not the policy here, Justine, but did you ever consider that it should be? Sure, you can talk to her. Just a minute.'' He appropriated the spoon from Erica, motioned for her to get up and sat down to feed Kaylie himself.

Erica took the phone from him and went into the living room.

"You wanted to feed Kaylie?'' Justine said with a large helping of skepticism.

"I, well, yes.'' Erica decided to let it go at that.

"I see,'' Justine said, though she still sounded puzzled. She cleared her throat. "I have a few favors to ask of you. Tony's staying here for tests this morning, and I've decided I'd better stick around. If you wouldn't mind going over to the Big House and dealing with my phone calls for a while, I'd appreciate it more than I can say.''

"Of course,'' Erica murmured, watching Hank feed Kaylie. It was funny the way he made a game out of it, making the spoon fly up into the air like an airplane and down again into Kaylie's mouth.

"A vendor will be calling today, and you'll need to tell him that I'm not interested in serving any more processed foods. Also, Pavel says he wants a vacation, which would be disastrous for us. If you could convince him that he's much appreciated, that might help. Oh, and there's a message from a freelance reporter, Brooke something-or-other, who wants to write a series of articles about Rancho Encantado. It's good free publicity, so I'm inclined to offer her a free makeover if she calls back. That's all I can think of at the moment.''

Erica assured Justine that she didn't mind helping out, and after she hung up, she rejoined Hank and Kaylie in the kitchen. "I think Justine suspects we've got something going," she told him.

"I hope so. I'd hate for her to think that my main attraction is a baby who needs feeding."

"Oh, you," Erica said, pushing at his shoulder.

He caught her hand. "Oh, you. And me."

He pulled her down and kissed her on the mouth, and when he did, Erica couldn't have cared less what Justine thought. Or anyone else, for that matter.

BY NOON, Erica had rebuffed the vendor, soothed the chef and spoken with the reporter, who expressed interest in the makeover and agreed to call back when Justine was available. She was in the process of applying her considerable organizational skills to Justine's desk when a nervous clerk rushed in from the main office.

"We have a problem, and I hope you can help," said the woman, whose name tag identified her as Bridget.

"What is it?" Erica said, moving the tape dispenser to the top of a file cabinet and stashing a stack of receipts in a drawer.

"It is this woman, a guest here," Bridget said, all but wringing her hands. "She is attacking me."

Erica glanced up in alarm. "Attacking you?"

"Oh, not physically, but I told her there was no one to drive her to the airport. We sent out a notice that Tony was sick, and we asked everyone who needed a ride to the airport in Las Vegas to be at the main desk by nine o'clock this morning so that one of the ranch hands could drive them. A number of people showed up, but this Lizette, she did not. She says it's not her fault. She says the staff is lax and unfeeling and—"

Erica interrupted. "Lizette? Are you sure?"

"Yes, and she says she will make trouble for me, for everyone, if she doesn't make her flight in time, and it leaves this afternoon. She booked it this morning apparently, and now she expects us to stop everything and find her a ride. There is no one to take her, no one at all."

"I see." Erica, accustomed to handling more severe crises at MacNee, Levy and Ashe, was sure she could deal with this one. She only wished that it didn't involve Hank's ex-girlfriend.

"Would you come and talk to her? She's very angry."

As happy as she'd be to send Lizette on her way, Erica immediately nixed the idea of talking to her. She racked her brain for some way to get the woman to the airport without creating more problems than she solved.

"Is there a van available?"

"The only van has gone to the airport."

"I'll see what I can do, Bridget," Erica told her nervous visitor after ushering her out of the office. Then, with the woman fidgeting outside the door, she tried to track Justine down in Las Vegas.

First she tried calling the hospital, which entailed a wait while the operator paged Justine.

"She doesn't answer the page," the operator told Erica. "Since she didn't, I have no way of finding her."

Erica asked that Justine be paged again before hanging up. Then she considered the situation.

Certainly she believed Bridget's claim that there was no ranch employee available to drive Lizette anywhere. Erica could drive Lizette to the airport herself, but this wasn't a good idea. She could only imagine how incensed Hank's former girlfriend would be at being cooped up in a car with her for two hours. Perhaps Hank would drive Lizette, but that seemed like another recipe for disaster, and besides, she knew he was teaching all morning. What to do?

A glance at the desk clock told her that it was lunch-time, so she called Hank, hoping to catch him at home. He answered, much to her relief.

"Hank, here's the situation," she said, then launched into an explanation.

When she'd finished, Hank expelled a long breath. "I agree that neither you nor I should drive Lizette any-where." He paused, seeming to think things over. "Pal-oma could take her," he said after a few moments. "I'll ask her."

"Hank, wait! Who would take care of Kaylie if Pal-oma is driving Lizette?"

"You," he said without a moment's hesitation. "If you wouldn't mind."

At one time Erica would have been discomfited by such a request. She didn't do babies. But that wasn't true anymore—she *did* do babies, and maybe she even had a knack for it. She felt pleased that Hank trusted her to look after his daughter.

"Of course," she said warmly. "That's the perfect solution."

"I'll ask Paloma to bring Kaylie over to the Big House." He muffled the phone for a moment. When he spoke again, he was chuckling. "Paloma is nodding her head. She likes to go to Las Vegas. They have lots of wedding shops where she can look for her wedding finery."

Erica heard Paloma laugh in the background, and then Hank hung up.

Bridget was overjoyed to learn that Erica had found a driver. "Thank goodness," she said over and over. "I couldn't face that woman if I went back and told her she would miss her plane.''

Which is the last thing any of us wants, considering that all she's done is stir up trouble, Erica thought, but didn't say.

Paloma, smiling as always, lost no time in bringing Kaylie to her. ''She hasn't yet had her bath, so she'll need one some time today. She will also need an afternoon nap.''

''If she sleeps this afternoon, will she want a later bedtime?''

''No, she will go to bed at the usual time,'' Paloma said, and Erica thought that sounded good. She wanted Kaylie to sleep well. She wanted to spend her remaining evenings at Rancho Encantado enjoying Hank's undivided attention.

This reminded her that she would be leaving before long, leaving her perfect cowboy and everything he represented. The thought made her hold Kaylie even closer because the baby was a little bit of Hank.

Through the window, she saw Lizette climbing into Paloma's sedan, and then the car set off slowly up the driveway to the highway. Erica felt melancholy at the thought that she would soon be the one getting into a car and being driven to the airport. Her return to real life was inevitable, and for the first time, she realized what a wrench it would be to go back to the city and all the city represented.

''Oh, Kaylie,'' she said brokenly. ''I'm going to hate to leave.''

''Bababababa,'' said Kaylie, sounding serious, but Erica knew that the baby's attempt at consolation was really only a sign that she had spotted Murphy lying under Justine's desk and wanted him to come out and play.

PUSHING KAYLIE in her stroller, with Murphy trotting along beside them on his leash, Erica walked over to Desert Rose in the early afternoon to get her camera. Kaylie and Murphy seemed to have a real affection for each other, and she thought she would never have a better chance to take pictures of them together. She thought it was cute the way Kaylie showed her feelings for the dog by squealing with glee whenever he walked into the room, and Murphy showed his for Kaylie by slurping her face with his tongue. Not that Erica approved of this means of showing affection, but Murphy could be persistent and usually struck when her back was turned.

She stopped off at the kitchen for a word with Pavel, who'd seemed to warm to her when she'd talked with him on the phone. He was a highly volatile Russian who considered himself to be a food artiste, not a mere chef, and she found him supervising the creation of low-fat canapés for the evening's wine-tasting party.

"Yes, yes, what do you want?" he demanded irritably when she appeared at the kitchen door.

"A word with you. I'm Erica Strong," she said with some trepidation. Though he had been easily mollified earlier, he was indeed daunting.

He abandoned his truculent attitude and threw the door open with a courtly gesture. "Come in, come in, you and your baby."

Erica felt herself flush with embarrassment. "Kaylie isn't my baby. I'm taking care of her for Hank Milling."

"Ah, Hank," the chef murmured. "Justine's brother."

"Yes, and I've been thinking about making baby food for her. My sister did it for her son, and she said that it was much better for him than the stuff in little jars at the supermarket."

"Oh, yes, that is true. A baby should eat only organically grown food, no preservatives!"

"I'm hoping you'll let me have fresh vegetables from the kitchen," Erica said hopefully as Kaylie beamed at Pavel most charmingly.

"For the baby, no problem. You come to me every day, I will give you the most fresh vegetables." He chucked Kaylie under the chin.

Before they left, he heaped the stroller basket with bags of green beans and peas. "These are on today's menu. Tomorrow, beets! Kale! Broccoli!"

Since Erica liked none of the above herself, she thought privately that she might make do with the beans and peas and skip tomorrow. Pavel told her exactly how to cook the vegetables before puréeing them in the blender.

After bidding Pavel goodbye, they headed toward Desert Rose, where Erica tied Murphy to the bench in the courtyard and instructed him to lie down while she and Kaylie went inside. Murphy obediently bedded down under the bench, his tongue lolling out.

While she checked her e-mail, Kaylie sat in her stroller and chewed on her teething toy, making Erica think that her second tooth might erupt in the not-too-distant future.

"You'll look mighty grown-up with those two front teeth," Erica told her, and Kaylie treated her to a sloppy grin.

It was then that the tiny black-and-white kitten scampered out from under the couch. Erica immediately recognized it as one of Mrs. Gray's offspring and bent to scoop it up.

"How did you get in here?" she asked, charmed by its wide, bluish-gray eyes and air of innocence.

The kitten, not having Mrs. Gray's gift of gab, said nothing, but it did start to purr.

"How sweet," she murmured. "But you can't stay here. You have to go back to the stable."

The kitten went on purring, and reluctantly she set it down on the floor, where it spied a small length of thread and began to stalk it like a panther. While Kaylie chortled in amusement, Erica went to check for places where the kitten might have gained access. Sure enough, she had left the bathroom window open that morning, and there was a ledge where the cat could have climbed in.

"Well," Erica said to the kitten, "since you're so cute, I'll let you hang around until I've checked my e-mail." The kitten rolled over on its back and gave the piece of thread a swift rabbit kick with its back feet, which amused Kaylie even more.

Since the kitten was doing such a good job of entertaining the baby, Erica went and switched on her computer.

YOU'VE GOT MAIL!

Erica, okay, okay, so my last message was way out of line. I admit I was worried, but deep down I know your common sense won't let you go overboard for a mere cowboy, so I apologize.

I guess you're enjoying the oh, so exotic delights of Rancho Encantado? Getting to know Justine and having fun? I hope so.

Let me hear from you soon, unless you're still angry. Again, I'm sorry.

Love,
Char

Hi Charmaine.

No, I'm not mad, just busy.

Today I'm taking care of Kaylie. Right now she's

sitting in her stroller and laughing at the kitten I found in my suite. Did you ever look, really look, at a baby when it laughs? It's pure sunshine. It makes you feel good all over.

The chef is giving me fresh vegetables every day so I can make baby food for Kaylie. It's time for me to get back to the Big House and figure out where Justine keeps her blender.

Love,

E.

As Erica logged off her Internet connection, Murphy started raising a ruckus in the courtyard. Mindful that some people in the other units at Desert Rose might be napping at this hour, she hurried outside to shush him.

"Murphy, quiet! What's the matter with you?"

The dog kept on barking. He had unfurled his leash to its fullest extension and was straining at the end of it as he tried his best to charge into the cactus patch.

Erica tugged at the leash, trying to make him cease and desist. Murphy ignored her and began to growl at the cactus patch, his teeth bared.

"Good grief," Erica muttered, wondering what Murphy could have seen that had incited him to such fury.

She untied the leash and gave it a couple of sharp yanks. After a few more barks, these less frenzied than the last, Murphy allowed himself to be distracted by a dog biscuit Erica found in her pocket.

After he'd eaten it, she bent to scratch him behind the ears. "What happened? Did you spot a rabbit?" Then, recalling that she'd thought she'd seen the faint figure of a man in the cactus garden one night, she narrowed her eyes and peered into it. All she saw was an attractive arrangement of cactus and a lizard sunning himself on one of the rocks.

"A lizard! He can't hurt us, Murphy. I'm surprised at you for making such a fuss." She noticed Mrs. Gray sitting in the shade provided by the roof on the other side of the building. "Or were you barking at the cat?"

Murphy declined to give her any clues. He only begged for another dog biscuit, which Erica couldn't provide.

"We'll go back to the Big House, and I'll feed you as many biscuits as your heart desires. As for you, cat, one of your offspring has made himself welcome in my suite. Wait there, and I'll go get him."

When she came out juggling the kitten, her camera, the stroller with Kaylie in it and Murphy on the end of his leash, Mrs. Gray had disappeared. Murphy spared one more bark for the cactus patch, then turned his curious attention to the kitten.

Erica set the kitten on the ground. "Go find your mama," she said as Murphy sniffed the tiny feline with interest. The kitten capered out of Murphy's reach and gazed up at her so uncertainly that Erica almost relented. "Go on," she said, and to her relief, the kitten finally began to bat a leaf around on the sidewalk.

She figured that the mother cat would return to retrieve her kitten, so she resolutely turned her back on it and started back toward the Big House.

"Babababa?" asked Kaylie.

"We can't take the kitten with us," she explained gently, although halfway to the Big House, Erica began asking herself, *Why not?*

But by that time, they'd gone too far to turn back,

considering that Kaylie needed a diaper change and Murphy was begging for more biscuits.

HANK PHONED as she was spooning puréed peas out of the blender, having successfully completed the home-made baby-food venture.

"Good news, Erica. Tony's going to be okay. Justine says they'll be home this evening. Apparently he didn't eat breakfast before he left on his run to the airport, and he started to feel weak."

"Will they be back in time for dinner?"

"No, but what are we having?"

She warmed to his use of the word *we*. "Pavel said it's his Rancho Encantado beef stew, whatever that means."

"It's stew with fresh artichoke hearts in it, and he puts parmesan cheese biscuits on top. It's wonderful." He paused. "How are you and Kaylie getting along?"

Erica glanced at Kaylie, who was lying on her back in the playpen cooing at a cloth book.

"We're doing fine. She's so much fun. Why, I even gave her a bath."

"You did?" He sounded surprised.

"Yes, Paloma said she hadn't had one yet today. It gave us a chance to play hide the rubber duckie and peekaboo, and I dried her off and dressed her in the cutest little polka-dot outfit, and then I played the piano for her and—"

"Hold on, hold on." Hank was laughing. "You make the afternoon sound as much fun as an amusement park."

"Your daughter is like an amusement park all crammed into one little person."

His voice softened. "I'm glad you feel that way, Erica."

"I'm enjoying her," she said, amazed to realize it was true. She loved watching the light of understanding flare in Kaylie's blue eyes when she learned something, and the way Kaylie gave her her total attention when she was feeding her or diapering her or giving her a bath. That was more than you could say for clients, even when you were making a fantastic presentation.

"I'll be early for dinner, and maybe after we put Kaylie to bed, you'll enjoy taking care of the baby's daddy." Hank's meaning was unmistakable, and Erica laughed.

"Maybe I will," she said, and when they hung up, they were both laughing.

She heard the clink of the mail slot in the front door and went to pick up the envelopes that were scattered on the floor. She was surprised to find one addressed to Hank and bearing the return address of Rowbotham-Quigley, the firm that was competing with her own firm for the important Gillooley account.

Wondering what business Hank might have with a major investment firm in New York, she set it on top of his other mail and left it on the table for him to pick up. Then she went to see if Kaylie found homemade baby food to her liking.

AFTER DINNER, Kaylie, sated with a large portion of puréed peas, fell asleep in her crib in her bedroom at Justine's house. Hank lit a fire, and Erica played the piano for him. When she finished playing, he came up behind the piano bench and rested his hands on her shoulders. He massaged them gently and said, "Let's step outside for a while. It's such a beautiful night."

Erica smiled up at him and pulled on one of Justine's

jackets, following him out into the walled garden off the dining room. The air was faintly scented with the pungent fragrance of creosote, and Erica wrapped her arms around herself to keep warm.

"Cold?" Hank asked.

She nodded.

"I can fix that," he said, pulling her into his arms and resting his chin on the top of her head. She inhaled deeply of his scent, that outdoorsy smell mingled with the faint suggestion of leather. "Warmer now?"

She nodded, dislodging his chin, and she wasn't surprised when he tipped her face up toward his. "I don't suppose I could talk you into extending your stay here," he said, his eyes delving deep into hers.

She bit her lip. "I'm supposed to be back at work on Thursday."

"We've barely begun to learn about each other."

"I know."

"If you could stay a while longer, we'd figure out where we're going with this," he said, and his face was so serious that she caught her breath. She suddenly felt as though she was on the verge of a major discovery, about to step through a mystical gate whose secrets would be hers to explore if only she said some magic word....

Stay, a small voice commanded, and she broke her gaze to look around for the cat. But this was a walled garden, impossible for the cat to enter. But then, she hadn't thought a kitten could enter her room, but he had.

"Erica?"

She told herself not to be distracted. "I'm sorry. For a moment I thought someone was here."

"No one is here but you and me, a fact for which I am profoundly thankful." Hank's lips grazed her temple, and her heart skipped several beats while she tried to center herself, to remember why she couldn't stay. Oh, yes. The Gillooley deal.

"Erica, please listen to what I say. Please take me seriously. I never thought I would be saying these words, least of all to someone I've only known for a short period of time, but…well, I don't know how to say this other than to blurt it out. I'm falling in love with you." He stared down at her, the world in the depths of his eyes.

She felt dizzy. "Hank, I don't know what to say." It crossed her mind that this was supposed to be nothing more than a fling. "I'm not sure what you expect of me," she managed, knowing it was too soon to tell him she was crazy about him, that he fit her notion of what the perfect cowboy should be.

He raised her hand and pressed his lips to the palm. "It's too early to expect you to return my feelings, I know. That's why I was hoping you could stay here for a while."

Possible scenarios crashed through her head, crazy-making scenes of her living here at Rancho Encantado, cooking over the stove in the small apartment. Riding with Hank across the salt flats, her hair blowing in the wind. And in time, Kaylie on her own little pony, giggling as they showed her the peculiar rock formations at the Devil's Picnic Ground, racing to catch up with them as they rode toward Bottle Canyon, calling Hank Daddy, calling her Mommy. It was this last one that really gave her pause. She'd never thought to hear herself called Mommy.

"I know it's sudden, but I've been hoping we could work something out." This last statement was punctuated by the lights of a car swinging across the top of the wall and the car's halt in the parking area beside the garage.

"That's Justine," Hank said. "Let's continue this discussion at my place as soon as possible."

He held her hand as they went back inside, only releasing it when they heard Justine turn the doorknob.

Justine looked pale, but she seemed relieved. "Tony has agreed that he will never again attempt to drive all the way to Las Vegas on an empty stomach. Whew! He had me worried. I was up almost all last night, hardly slept. Which is why I'm going straight to bed." She paused, giving them a keen look. "Is everything okay with you two?"

"Um, yes," Erica said, self-conscious under Justine's scrutiny.

"We're going to collect Kaylie from her crib and be on our way," Hank said.

Justine insisted on looking in on Kaylie, and then she excused herself, yawning widely. "I'll see everyone tomorrow," she said.

"I'll come over in the morning and put the coffee on for you," Hank said.

Justine's eyebrows flew upward. "Why on earth?"

"I'd like to talk to you about something."

"Nothing's wrong, is it?" Justine sounded alarmed.

"No, something's right." Hank smiled at her.

Justine, looking mystified, only said, "You've got me curious, but it'll have to wait. I'm dead on my feet. Good night, all." She walked down the hall to her room and closed the door.

"What was that about?" Erica wanted to know.

"I'm going to tell Justine not to feel guilty about what happened to Anne-Marie."

"Does that mean that *you're* still feeling responsible for the accident?"

"I'm getting over it. I've begun to see that blaming anyone—even Anne-Marie herself—isn't helping matters. The accident happened. It changed our lives. It's time to move on." He looked so contemplative that Erica touched his arm in support.

He rested his hand over hers for a moment. "Let's get Kaylie. I'm ready for some alone time with you."

Kaylie scarcely made a fuss as Hank lifted her into his arms and Erica gathered her diaper bag and toys. Murphy tried to follow them, but Hank made him go back. "Tomorrow, old fellow," he promised, after which Murphy went uncomplainingly to his bed in the kitchen.

"Now," Hank said, "I'd better take my mail along." He went to the hall table, Erica close behind him. "Can you grab it? I'll open it at my place."

Erica scooped up the mail with the Rowbotham-Quigley envelope on top. "About this letter," she said, holding it up for him to see. "Do you have business with them? I deal with R-Q in my job at McNee, Levy and Ashe."

His eyes locked on hers for an overly long instant. "Yes," he said slowly, seeming to gauge her reaction. "I work for them."

"You do?"

"I'll soon make partner if things stay on track."

Erica stared at him, her brain unable to wrap itself around his words. "You mean you're not really a cowboy?"

"No, Erica. I'm really an investment banker." His eyes were steady and sincere.

Her mind reeled with this new information, which she

could not readily compute. She was overcome with a rush of disappointment, and she felt the color drain from her face. She could hardly believe his words. "You mean you're an investment banker? With R-Q? And not a cowboy at all?"

"That's right," he said evenly. "If you love me, it won't make any difference. Or will it?"

Chapter Thirteen

"Why didn't you *tell* me? Why did you let me think you were a cowboy?" Erica was all but wringing her hands as she faced him over the kitchen table in his apartment. She was still numb at his startling revelation. "I thought you really were a cowboy. I saw all the trappings, saw that you knew horses—"

"I never *said* I was a cowboy. I never said I was an investment banker, either. And neither," he said pointedly, "did you. I assumed you were an administrative assistant at McNee, Levy and Ashe."

"You thought I was someone's assistant?" She knew she sounded as indignant as she felt.

"Why wouldn't I? You never told me otherwise."

Erica didn't know what to say.

"If you'll recall," Hank went on, "I didn't make a big deal out of the fact that you weren't a neophyte rider. Face it, Erica. Appearances aren't always what they seem."

"No, they aren't," she said tightly.

"As it turns out, we both do the same thing for a living. What's wrong with that? The way I see it, this gives us much more in common. It's probably why I've felt so comfortable with you from the very beginning."

"You work for Rowbotham-Quigley. I work for McNee, Levy and Ashe. Am I the only one who sees a conflict of interest here?" She stood up and paced to the other side of the kitchen, running a hand through her hair in agitation.

A panorama of expressions flickered over Hank's face, bewilderment only one of them. "To me, it doesn't matter what you do. It only matters who you are, Erica."

She let out a huge sigh of exasperation. "I wanted a fling with a cowboy, nothing more. I never thought I'd end up madly in love with you or that you would fall in love with me or that you'd have a child who would make things difficult."

His expression darkened. "Is that it? You can't accept my daughter? That's too bad, because Kaylie and I are a package deal, Erica. That's the way it is."

She was horrified that he'd mistaken her meaning. "No, no," she said, going to him and kneeling beside his chair. "Kaylie makes things difficult because what I feel for her gets all tangled up in what I feel for you. I can't explain it. I don't know how."

"I can," he said gently. "Come with me into the bedroom and I'll show you what it's all about. It's about love and commitment and caring. It's about the physical expression of those emotions."

"I have to go back to New York," she said unsteadily as he stood up and brought her up with him.

"And I'm supposed to go back there, too. There's a big push to acquire a major client, and your firm is the one we have to beat in order to get his business."

"The Gillooley deal?"

"Yes. How did you know?"

"I'm the leader of the presentation team on that one."

"They want me to come back to work on it. I don't know yet if I can."

"Hank, *you're* my competition on the Gillooley deal? You're their *numero uno* team leader?" She pulled away from him.

He dragged her back. "Looks that way. At this point, I don't know if I can go back to R-Q at all, much less close the deal."

"What's your alternative?"

"Quit the job and stay at Rancho Encantado. I've been thinking more and more that it would be better for Kaylie to grow up here where she has a doting aunt and horses to ride when she's ready and the whole outdoors as a playground. Erica, stay here with us. Don't go back."

Even as his eyes pleaded with her, she knew she couldn't give up her hard-earned position and the power and prestige that went with it.

"You don't understand," she said softly. "My job is all I have. It's what makes me *me*."

He shook his head. "You have me now. And you have Kaylie."

"You don't understand. I couldn't be beautiful like Charmaine and—"

"You are beautiful, Erica. Who ever said you weren't?"

"I always knew it, that's all. Char is the most beautiful sister, Abby's not only a former beauty queen but a great wife and mother, and I was always Erica, the smart one. The loner. I had to excel at school and in my work because that was the only way I *could* excel."

"Please don't put yourself down. You've always been beautiful to me. Oh, when I first saw you in the stable after my argument with Justine, I didn't find anything special about you, but that night after you taught me how to sew on buttons, I saw how pretty you were."

"Pretty? Me?" She trembled on the verge of tears. No one had ever told her she was pretty, much less beautiful. "It's the makeover, Hank. It's what Tico and company did for me."

His hands came up to grip her shoulders. "No, it isn't the makeover. You hadn't even started your makeover that first night. I'm attracted to the person you are inside, the one who listens so carefully, who cares not only about me but about my child. It's *you*, Erica. You. I love you, not your hair or your eyes or... Do you mind if I ask you something?"

She looked at him blankly and nodded.

"What color are your eyes?"

"B-brown."

"They look lavender to me."

She shook her head to clear it. "It's the contact lenses. I have a pair in every color. Blue, green, lavender, turquoise—"

His arms went around her again, and he was chuckling. "Okay, I love you no matter what color eyes you happen to be wearing."

Her tears began in earnest as she absorbed his words, understood that he really meant them, and she couldn't hold back the tears. They coursed, hot and salty, down her cheeks, soaking his shirtfront, dripping on the floor.

"Shh, sweetheart," he whispered soothingly in her ear. "Let's go to bed, and in the morning we'll talk about it."

She clung to him. "You think that will solve everything? That making love will fix what's wrong?"

He kissed away her tears one by one. "Well, I don't know, but for lack of any better ideas, I'd say we might as well try it," he said, and then she was laughing through her tears and allowing herself to be led to the bedroom.

Later, after Hank was asleep, Erica nestled close to him, his heartbeat thrumming in her ear.

She couldn't think about all this if she had to see him every day. She couldn't decide what to do if confronted with adorable Kaylie while she was trying to work things out in her mind.

And so she would go back to New York. On schedule. Then maybe she'd be able to find some perspective.

THE NEXT MORNING Hank, who had not slept much the night before, was true to his word. He had coffee ready for Justine when she emerged from her bedroom in the Big House ready to begin her workday.

When she saw him at the coffeemaker, she tossed her braid behind her shoulder and regarded him with her hands resting on her hips. "I thought I was only imagining things when I heard you say you'd be here bright and early to make coffee. What gives, Hank?"

He handed her a full cup. "I don't know how you take your coffee," he said sheepishly.

"No reason you should," Justine said. She went to the sugar bowl and scooped out a spoonful. "Black with sugar, in case you ever find yourself in this helpful mode again. By the way, you look mighty tired this morning. Is something going on with you I should know about?"

He shook his head. "Not that you should know about. Well, maybe something *is* going on with me. I want to talk to you about Anne-Marie. About the night she died."

Justine slowly went to sit on one of the stools. "Is this a good idea, Hank?"

He sat down beside her and studied her face. "I think so. I need to tell you something." He drew a deep breath before continuing. "The night of her accident, Anne-Marie and I had a terrible argument over the phone. When we hung up, I knew everything wasn't okay. I tried to call her back, but she didn't answer. I think she'd already gone."

"Must you tell me this?" Justine was visibly upset.

"Yes, because I've always thought that the argument was the cause of the accident. I've blamed myself all along."

Justine's eyes widened in horror. "Oh, no, Hank! I didn't realize that."

He nodded, swallowed, closed his eyes for a moment. When he opened them, Justine's expression was one of understanding and sympathy.

"Did you know that I blame myself, too?" she asked gently.

He shook his head. "No."

"But you found out?"

"Yes."

"Erica?"

"I hope you don't mind. She didn't think she was betraying a confidence, I'm sure."

Justine reached for his hand. "Of course I don't mind. I've assumed that you must have heard me say somewhere along the line that I thought the accident was my fault. If I hadn't taken Kaylie that night, Anne-Marie wouldn't have had a baby-sitter and she wouldn't have gone to see Mattie."

"But because of our argument, she would have gone, anyway, don't you see? She was angry with me—she used to always fly out of the house when she got mad."

"Ah, Hank, perhaps neither of us was responsible for

what happened. There's a chance that Anne-Marie was no longer angry about your argument by the time she was driving home. Also, maybe if I hadn't baby-sat Kaylie, Anne-Marie would have gone, anyway, and taken her along."

"That's why I'm here, Justine. If you hadn't kept Kaylie, I'm sure she would have been in the car with Anne-Marie. If you hadn't baby-sat that night, I could have lost Kaylie, and that would have been the worst thing that could have happened to me."

The thought of losing Kaylie was still devastating. He blinked back tears, and before he knew it, Justine had enveloped him in a hug.

When they separated, Justine had tears in her eyes, too. "Well, little brother, we're going to have to communicate more often and on a deeper level, wouldn't you say?"

"Exactly."

"No more blame game?"

"Not for you or for me."

Justine wiped away her tears, and they smiled at each other.

"I noticed you're not having coffee," she said.

"I have to get back to the stable. Maybe I could take a cup with me."

Justine got up and started to pour it, but then she turned back toward Hank. "You know, I don't think I know how you take your coffee, either."

"Black, no sugar."

"I think maybe we're finally getting to know each other better," Justine said as she handed him the cup.

"You know what, Justine? I think it's time for me to rejoin the world of the living and get a life," he said as he swung down off the stool.

"Well, hallelujah," Justine said. "What brings this on?"

He only grinned and tugged at her braid on the way out, the way he used to when they were kids. But he didn't enlighten her. He might be getting to be better friends with this sister of his, but he wasn't yet ready to share the details of his love life.

YOU'VE GOT MAIL!

Erica,
YOU'RE MAKING BABY FOOD? THIS IS WORSE THAN I THOUGHT! ANSWER YOUR PHONE! I'M GOING TO GIVE YOU A GOOD TALKING TO!
Love,
Charmaine

Char,
I'll see you on Thursday. Have plenty of tissues handy, and a big box of chocolate. I'm going to need both.
Erica

ERICA AND HANK made the most of their remaining days together, riding up to Bottle Canyon the next afternoon after Hank's last class and making slow, sweet love on a blanket beside the gully. They came home and cooked steaks on Hank's grill, staying up late and talking about everything except Erica's coming departure. The next morning they cooked breakfast and made love again before Hank left for the stable. Later Erica took Kaylie over to the Big House and let her play with Murphy while Justine worked, forgoing the sybaritic pleasures of the ranch for the bigger pleasure of watching Kaylie's eyes light up when she was happy.

That night, the last night, was the hardest. Erica didn't want Hank to remember her with red-rimmed eyes and stuffy nose, so she didn't cry. But it was hard not to, especially when Kaylie woke up with teething pain in the middle of the night and Hank brought her into bed with them. Kaylie fell asleep in the curve of Hank's body, and Erica spooned herself around Hank. It felt cozy and right to sleep that way, but the trouble was, she really didn't sleep. Instead, she lay awake and stared into the darkness, wondering what it would be like to sleep with Hank every night for the rest of her life. She fell asleep, finally, just before dawn.

When it was time to go, Hank bundled Kaylie into her warm coat and silently walked Erica to the van for the ride to the airport. Erica was the only one with a plane to catch that day because she was leaving in midweek, which was not popular for either arrivals or departures.

Tony idled the engine, steadfastly looking straight ahead while she and Hank said their goodbyes in the pale morning light, and now that their time together was over, she thought of many more things she wanted to tell him. But she felt too constrained by Tony's presence to say them now.

"It's been wonderful," she managed, hoping Hank understood that the words were inadequate to express her true feelings.

"I love you, Erica. I wish you wouldn't go."

At that point Kaylie started to cry and reached out her arms to Erica, but because Tony was now openly consulting his wristwatch, all she could do was give Kaylie's tiny hand a warm squeeze.

Getting into the van was complicated by juggling the cat carrier containing the kitten that Justine had finally persuaded her to take home, the same one she'd found in her suite. The kitten mewed pitifully at being jostled about, and Tony said, "You got everything?" Erica knew she didn't have everything she wanted, she didn't have Hank and Kaylie, but this wasn't something Tony could help.

"Yes," she said, shoving the cat carrier in and preparing to climb in after it. "I've got everything I'm going to take."

In the last moments Hank pulled her to him, and her arms went around his neck. Kaylie was between them, warm and smelling of milk and talcum powder. Erica clung desperately to the two of them, eyes squeezed shut to keep from crying.

"Time to go," Tony called.

"Bye, Hank. Take care."

"Bye, Erica."

Then she was climbing into the van, settling the cat carrier beside her, and Tony was starting the engine. The last sight to fill her field of vision as the van bumped toward the highway was Hank's devastated expression. The last thing she heard was Kaylie's screaming. It was a nightmare scene, worse than she could have possibly anticipated.

They drove under the Rancho Encantado sign, the one that said WHERE DREAMS COME TRUE. Erica buried her face in her hands as they left the property. She had come here for a makeover, but she had never thought that the results would be so painful.

THE DAY AFTER Erica arrived back in New York, Charmaine came breezing through her apartment door.

"Erica, you look great," she said, adding quickly after a look at her red-rimmed eyes, "on second thought, no, you don't. You look awful. You'd better tell me what happened right away." She spotted the kitten peering out from behind the couch and halted in her tracks. "What's that?"

"Justine talked me into bringing one of the stable cat's kittens home with me. She said a pet would be good company."

"Cool," Charmaine said, looking surprised. She held out a box of chocolates and another of tissues and stared curiously at the cat, which disappeared behind an armoire.

Erica accepted Charmaine's offerings and went to sit on the couch. The kitten, named Tux because his black-and-white fur resembled a tuxedo, ventured out from his hiding place and began to wash his face.

"All right, Erica, I can't stand one more moment of suspense. What happened between you and, uh, Hank?"

Erica stared for a moment at the skyline of Manhattan outside the window and sniffed. "Hank's not a cowboy at all," she said.

Charmaine sank down on the chair across from her and, with an air of forbearance, propped her long legs on the ottoman. "Go on. I'm sure there's more."

Erica knew that her sister was refraining from saying how stupid she was for falling in love with Hank in the first place, but she already knew that. What she didn't know was how to explain what had happened without putting either of them in a bad light.

She drew a deep bolstering breath. "My perfect cowboy turned out to be Henry Parrish Milling III. He works for Rowbotham-Quigley, my firm's biggest competitor for the Gillooley account. Gillooley is going to revolutionize the communications industry, and I'm planning to make a presentation next week in hopes of getting their business. R-Q is pestering Hank to come back to work long enough to win Gillooley over, and I'm probably going to see him when I fly to Kansas City for the presentation, and if I do I'll just die.''

Charmaine raised her eyebrows. "Yikes." She paused and studied Erica critically. "I really like those streaks in your hair."

Erica flung her hands out in exasperation. "Char, I open my heart to you, and all you can say is that you like my hair?"

"I thought you might like to know I think it looks great."

Erica tucked the sides behind her ears. "It doesn't look as good as it did at Rancho Encantado."

"So there really is something to the place's reputation? To the vortex and the ghost?"

"I don't know about the vortex and Padre Luis, but if you mean did Rancho Encantado work miracles in my life, the answer is that it did for a while, but after you leave, you're the same as ever. Except for knowing how to apply makeup."

"Oh? You think you're the same as ever after falling in love? No one is the same after falling in love, Erica." Charmaine frowned and tore the wrapper off the chocolate box.

"You can't change who you really are. I found that out."

Charmaine raised her eyebrows. "Maybe you don't want to when who you are is good enough." She paused. "You were in love with Hank, right?"

"*Am* in love with him. Can't ever have him. Wish I were dead," Erica said glumly, reaching over and plucking a chocolate crème out of its nest. She wondered if it was possible to eat a whole box of chocolates in one sitting. Probably, if she wanted to, and she had Charmaine to help her. She took another one, a chocolate-covered cherry this time.

"Why can't you have him?" Charmaine wanted to know. "You were compatible, you liked his kid."

"Loved his kid," Erica said.

"You *loved* the kid?"

"Kaylie is wonderful." For a moment an image of Kaylie flashed across her memory, and she could almost smell the fresh baby-powder scent of her, could almost feel the weight of her cuddled against her breast. She felt her eyes well up and grabbed a clean tissue from the box.

"Oh, I'm sorry! I didn't mean to make you cry." Charmaine sounded aghast.

"Since the moment I left the ranch, anything makes me cry. I miss Hank and I miss Kaylie. He wants me to come back, but how can I? If I go, there's no guarantee that he won't decide to return to the city and work for R-Q."

"That's not so bad, is it?"

"Think about it, Char! If he comes back, we're in direct competition with each other with our work, and it wouldn't be the same. We'd be two people obsessed with making money and getting ahead. Also, what about Kaylie? She'd have to be in day care, and she's so happy with Paloma, and raising a child in the city is a far cry from raising her on a ranch."

"Obstacles, obstacles," Charmaine agreed.

"Plus I have to have my job. I wouldn't be anything without it."

Charmaine stared at her. "Are you joking?"

"No joke. I mean it. Who would I be if I weren't on the fast track to make partner at McNee, Levy and Ashe?"

"Listen to me, Erica. You'd still be the same person we all know and, yes, love."

"But—"

"Don't bore me with denials. Fill me in about why you can't live at the ranch."

"There are too many problems no matter how I look at it," she said, feeling more woebegone by the second.

"How did you leave it with Hank, then?"

"He said he loved me," she said in a whisper.

"Erica, do you love him? Really love him?"

As her eyes blurred with tears, she could only nod yes.

Charmaine's eyes blazed for a moment, and then, barely controlling herself, she lit into her sister. "Erica, you may have multiple degrees from prestigious universities, but you are one stupid person if you don't change your life to accommodate this new relationship. I can't believe you walked away!"

"Well, I did." Erica blew her nose forcefully. Tux looked up at her with a quizzical expression, then jumped on the couch and curled up beside her.

Charmaine stood up precipitously. "Look, Erica, I'd better run before I say something I'll regret."

"I could use some sympathy, Char," Erica reminded her. "I could use some support."

"Nope, no can do. I've given you tissues, chocolates and a willing ear. It's up to you to fix this. I can't support out-and-out idiocy, even though you are my dear sister."

Erica suddenly remembered something. "I almost forgot," she said as she handed Charmaine the silver-wrapped package from the Rancho Encantado gift shop.

Charmaine opened it quickly and lifted out the turquoise-and-silver necklace. "It's lovely," she said. "I can wear it tonight when I go out to dinner. Want to come with us, Erica? I'm going with some of the photographers and models I met in Aruba. You'd like them."

"I don't think so. Not tonight."

They hugged goodbye. "If you want to discuss how to get back together with Hank, *then* call me," Charmaine told her.

"Um, okay. Thanks, Char." She trailed her sister to the door.

"You're welcome." Charmaine's hand was on the doorknob.

"Hey, aren't you going to wish me luck?"

"With what?"

"With the Gillooley account. I leave for Kansas City tomorrow."

"Not a chance. The only thing I wish for you is that you'll find your way back to that cowboy of yours."

Erica closed the door after Charmaine and rested her forehead against it. "He wasn't really a cowboy," she said out loud, but there was no one there to hear but the cat.

ERICA WENT to Kansas City and discovered that Hank wasn't part of the Rowbotham-Quigley presentation team, after all. It was a relief not to see him, or was it? She couldn't help wondering why he hadn't gone back to his job, and how he and Kaylie were getting along, and whether Kaylie missed her, and whether Hank had found someone else. A week went by, then two. She learned that McNee, Levy and Ashe had succeeded in obtaining Gillooley's business, and she should have taken pride in her involvement. But she didn't.

She took Tux to the vet for his shots, and soon he'd settled in at her apartment. She found a retired school-teacher on her floor who would look after him for her when she had to be away. It was nice to have a pet waiting for her when she arrived home after a long, hard day at work. Justine had been right about that.

She pored over the pictures she'd taken at the ranch. Some of Kaylie, some of Murphy, some of scenery. One of the coyote she and Hank had seen at the creek near Padre Luis's house. There were none of Hank. She hadn't taken any.

Sometimes, when she sat in her darkened apartment at night looking out over the lights of the city with Tux purring beside her, she tried to summon one of her fantasies to console her. She didn't know why, but her rich fantasy world was gone. She would have liked to conjure up one of her favorite daydreams, picking up a cowboy at the Last Chance Saloon. Or the one that had actually taken place on the porch of the rec hall, so rudely interrupted by Lizette.

But it was as if those daydreams had never happened, as if she'd never entertained those lovely notions about the perfect cowboy. As the days flew by, she found herself unable to recall the way Hank looked. First she forgot the exact way his hair fell across his forehead, then she couldn't remember exactly what it felt like to rest her head against his broad shoulder. Soon she could only remember his blue, blue eyes, and she thought despairingly that it was only a matter of time before she would no longer be able to remember them, either.

And then one cold rainy day she stepped into the elevator at work and noticed in the mirror there that she was disappearing, too, fading the same way as she had been on the day that she first agreed to go to Rancho Encantado. She blinked at her faint reflection. Suddenly there she was again, her hair lifeless and flattened by the humidity of another rainy day, her makeup inadequate under the fluorescent lights. Most of her lipstick had worn off. Somehow, it didn't seem to matter. As soon as the elevator thumped to a stop, she hurried outside to hail a cab.

Getting a cab in this blustery weather wasn't easy. Eventually the foggy mist parted long enough to reveal an available taxi down the street, and she summoned her flagging energy to wave at it until she caught the driver's eye.

As she stepped back under the portico to get out of the rain, she noticed a tall, handsome cowboy climbing out of another cab a half a block away. He wore a blue shirt, faded jeans and a Stetson hat. For a moment, she thought it was Hank. But then the reality of the scene jerked her into the here and now, and she knew that it wasn't her perfect cowboy at all. It was only another businessman who walked toward her, the edges of his raincoat flapping in the wind, his collar turned up against the chill.

She turned away, a lump in her throat. Despite the fact that she had been stuck in cruel reality ever since she'd come back from Rancho Encantado, this return of fantasy was not as welcome as she'd thought it would be. What if she started seeing Hank everywhere she looked? Tears suddenly stung her eyes and ran down her cheeks, warm but not welcome. She missed him. She missed him so much.

"Erica?"

No. She wouldn't turn and look. She didn't want to

give in to the torment of unbidden fantasies. She wouldn't. She'd think about the meeting she was supposed to attend tomorrow, a meeting that would result in millions of dollars of business for her firm.

"Erica."

A hand touched her arm, and she reflexively jerked away. You had to be careful in the city. There were people who would do you harm. You had to defend yourself, you had to…

That voice. She had to look. It was Hank's voice.

Slowly she turned her head and took in the face of the man who had touched her arm. Despite the tired lines around his eyes, despite his drawn expression, he looked like Hank. He sounded like Hank. Did she dare to trust that it actually was Hank and not a trick of her mind?

The pain in his eyes gave him away. Her own eyes widened in disbelief.

"It…it can't be you," she stammered.

"It's me. Or the person I'm supposed to be," he said, heavy on the irony. "And it looks as if you're the person you're supposed to be. Erica Strong, I believe? May I introduce myself? I'm Henry Parrish Milling III. I'm happy to make your acquaintance."

"Hank," she said faintly. "What are you doing here?" She blinked at him, still unsure that he was not merely a fragment of memory come back to haunt her.

"I came back to see if I could fit in again in New York. To find a day-care center for Kaylie. To resume my real life."

"Oh," she said, unheeding of the rain streaming down her face. "How did you happen to be getting out of a cab only a half a block away?"

"I rode over here to pay a visit to you at McNee, Levy and Ashe, and here you are."

"Yes." Her eyes drank in the way he looked in a business suit. He was still perfect, still Hank.

"Do you think we could step out of the rain?" His eyes, so expressive and so bleak, pleaded with her.

The cab she had hailed braked to a stop in front of her. She ignored it. The driver rolled down the window on the passenger side.

"You want a taxi, lady, or not?"

She looked from the cab to Hank and back again. "Come with me," she said urgently. "We can talk."

"Gladly," he said. He opened the cab door, and she got in.

She turned to him right away, unable to get enough of the rugged lines of his face, the strength of his jaw. He might not be wearing the clothes she was accustomed to seeing him wear, but his city garb couldn't diminish his solid good looks.

"Where's Kaylie?"

"With Justine until I can find a day-care center for her." Judging by Hank's avid study of her features, he liked the way she looked, even with her hair wet and straggling against her cheeks.

"Where you going?" the cabdriver demanded none too cheerfully.

"Just drive around," Hank said before Erica could speak.

"Okay," the driver said. He rammed the car into gear and slipped effortlessly into the stream of traffic. Behind them, another car's horn registered an objection, setting off a cacophony of other horns. The windshield wipers went *swish-swish*, and they could hear the hiss of tires on rain-slick streets. Inside Erica could hear her heart pounding, and her palms grew sweaty. She wiped them on her raincoat so that they only became more damp.

Dear God, she wished that Hank would look at her like this forever.

"Marry me, Erica," he said, his eyes burning holes all the way to her soul. "Marry me."

She couldn't have heard him correctly. "Do what?"

"Let's get married and live at Rancho Encantado. I love you, Erica. I can't let you go."

The cabbie let out a deep sigh and began to tap his fingers impatiently on the armrest, underscoring the absurdity of the situation.

Erica's heart seemed to have leaped to her throat. "I love you, too," she managed to say.

"Kaylie misses you. I can't sing 'America the Beautiful' worth a damn."

Laughter bubbled up in her throat. "I thought you came here to go back to work for Rowbotham-Quigley."

"That was my original intent, but being with you, sitting here beside you, remembering all we had together at the ranch, I know I can't do it. I thought I'd have a better chance with you if I lived in the city, if I could see you on a regular basis, but that's not right for us. We'd be miserable here."

She knew he was right. "Suppose I said yes. What about my job? How could the three of us live in your little apartment at the ranch?"

"First of all, if you say yes, I'll be the happiest man on earth. You can quit your job at McNee, Levy and Ashe and manage Justine's administrative matters. She really needs the help. Paloma can continue as baby-sitter, at least for a while. And we can live in the old hacienda, the three of us."

"Four," she said. "Counting Tux."

"Fine. There's room for more children in that house, Erica. Three or four or however many you want."

"I don't do babies," she said faintly. "Everyone knows that."

"Except Kaylie, who loves you. You're great with her. I don't know how you ever got the idea that you don't do babies."

"In my family," she began slowly, "Charmaine was the beautiful one, Abby was—"

"I know. You were supposed to be the smart one. So if you're so all-fired smart, why did you leave us? We belong together, Erica, you and Kaylie and me."

"You must have been talking with Char. That's something like what she said."

"What," Hank said interestedly, "exactly did she say?"

"I don't know, I can't recall," Erica said. Then the air whooshed out of her lungs as Hank pinned her back against the seat.

"I have ways of finding out," he said. "Like this." He began to tickle her, and she squirmed in an unsuccessful attempt to get away.

"Char—stop it, Hank!—Char said that no one is the same after falling in love and that I was a fool for leaving someone who loves me."

"Your sister is a woman of great good sense." He gave her ribs one last tickle for good measure and backed off, his eyes twinkling with humor. "Would you mind telling me your reply?"

Erica made an attempt to straighten her suit jacket. One button had popped off her blouse, and she groped for it on the floor with the hand that Hank wasn't holding.

"I said that you... Oh, here it is," she said, holding the button up before dropping it in her purse. "I said that I'd found out that you can't change who you really are. Coloring my hair, getting contact lenses, all of that was fun. In the end, though, I'm still me. Still Erica Strong.''

"Thank God for that," Hank said fervently. He brought her hand to his lips and kissed the palm. "Now that we're straight about who you are, let's talk about who you want to be."

She looked at him as if he'd taken leave of his senses.

"Think of it this way. Who you want to be is a promise to yourself," he prompted.

"I wanted to be a cowboy's sweetheart," she said in a low tone. "But you're not a cowboy." She was still having a hard time accepting this.

"You're *my* sweetheart. Does it really matter so much what I do?"

His expression was so compelling she couldn't look away. "Perhaps not," she said faintly.

"Taking this one step further. If who you want to be is a promise to yourself, couldn't who we are together be a promise to each other?"

"Maybe."

"Hey," the cabbie called over his shoulder. "You want me to keep driving around?"

"No, we'll go to her place," Hank said. "Where do you live, Erica?"

She reeled off the address, and the driver went back to driving. "I have a meeting," she said. "It starts in ten minutes."

"You can call and tell them you've been unavoidably delayed," Hank said.

"I have?"

"Yes. First we're going to bed, and then we're ordering dinner in."

"Aren't you being a little overbearing here?"

"I think I'm downright restrained, considering that I haven't seen you in a few weeks. I think I'm remarkably calm." Regarding her with an expression of exasperated tenderness, he swept her into his arms and kissed her resoundingly.

She didn't want him to stop. Ever. And she remembered what Charmaine had said: that when she met the right guy, she'd want to defer to him. She had certainly not been in the habit of deferring to guys or to anyone else, but if she was going to start, Hank might be as good a place as any.

"I think it's your honeysuckle perfume that made me fall in love with you," Hank said when he stopped kissing her.

This caught her off guard. "I never wear perfume."

"But you do. It's my favorite scent."

Erica was about to say that he must be imagining things when she caught a glimpse of the driver's curious expression in the rearview mirror.

"Do you two mind if I ask you a question?"

She and Hank exchanged glances. She shrugged.

"Buddy, how come you're getting married if you don't even know where she lives?"

Hank cleared his throat. "She lives in my heart," he said. "She's always been there, only I didn't know it was her."

"Oh," said the cabdriver with an air of perplexity.

"Is that true?" Erica asked Hank.

"I had these fantasies about the perfect woman. I knew what she looked like, except for her face. That was always a blank. I would save her from runaway locomotives, shoot rattlesnakes so I could save her... Oh, you wouldn't believe my daydreams."

"I might," Erica said softly.

"I didn't know that you were the one until that night on the porch outside the rec hall. I had this enormous sense of déjà vu, as if I'd been there, done that before, but the only place I'd done it was in my fantasies. Suddenly the face of the woman I wanted was no longer blank. It was your face, Erica. And you were wearing the same clothes you'd worn in my fantasy. A white peasant blouse—"

"—and a red bandanna skirt," Erica finished. "In my daydream, you would run your hand up my leg and you'd say—"

"Holy cannoli," growled the cabdriver, "could you spare me the details?"

They both ignored him as realization dawned. "You mean we were having the same fantasies?" Erica gasped.

"It sounds like it. Could that happen?"

"I don't know, but did you ever have the one about the Last Chance Saloon? Where you asked me if you could buy me a drink and I ordered a margarita and you asked me if I was up for a little fun?"

"Yes, and when we got to your place you weren't wearing any underw—"

"Here we are," said the driver, pulling over to the curb.

Hank dug money out of his pocket.

"You can skip the tip," the cabbie said. "This was great entertainment."

Hank gave him a tip anyway, and as they stepped out of the cab, the sky suddenly cleared and the sun came out.

"It's like magic," Erica said, awestruck at the suddenness of the rain's disappearance.

"It *is* magic," Hank said, and he wrapped his arms

around her and kissed her in front of everyone. In that moment, it was as if they had never left the ranch, as if the air in their vicinity went perfectly still as it did in the desert in the hour before dawn, as if Hank was really a cowboy and she was really his girl.

"Marry me? Let's make that promise to each other, Erica," he said close to her ear.

"Yes," she replied unsteadily, "I'll marry you, Hank," and in that moment she saw a cactus garden burgeon in front of the door to her apartment building. As she watched, flowers burst into bloom on the cactus plants, big and bright and beautiful. That wasn't all; amid the spines and flowers of the cacti stood the rotund figure of a priest, who was smiling at them benignly.

Which was perfectly ridiculous, because everyone knew that there couldn't be a cactus garden on a New York City street. And as for the ghost of Padre Luis, well, she wasn't sure if there was a ghost, but she was certain that even a ghost wouldn't give up the beauty of Rancho Encantado to hang out in front of her New York apartment building.

HER PERFECT COWBOY was waiting in the gallery of the Big House at Rancho Encantado as she approached on the arm of her uncle Steve, who had insisted on walking her down the aisle. Hank's expression as they approached was one of expectance and joy, not to mention love.

Somewhere toward the front, Kaylie said, "Baba-baba!" and Justine hushed her gently. Charmaine and Abby, who were her maid of honor and bridesmaid, respectively, wore big smiles as they waited for Erica beside the flower-bedecked bower, and when Uncle Steve placed her hand in Hank's, Hank whispered, "I love you, Erica."

It all seemed like another fantasy. But this wasn't a daydream; it wasn't wishful thinking. The squeeze of Hank's hand, his joy as he slipped the ring on her finger—these were real, as real as Hank himself. As real as their love for each other, as real as their future together, and as real as eternity.

Forever and ever, amen.

As they kissed, Erica could have sworn she heard someone say those words, yet she knew it wasn't the priest who'd just married them. Nor was it Mrs. Gray, whose whereabouts had been unknown for the past few days.

"I love you, wife," said Hank.

"I love you too, husband," she replied softly.

"Mamamama?" said Kaylie.

Hank scooped her up from Justine's arms. "Now you're really talking," he said approvingly, and everyone laughed as the three of them embraced, ready to begin their new lives together.

Padre Luis Speaks...

THANKS BE TO GOD! He is merciful and He is good.

Have my prayers not been answered? Have Erica and Hank not found true love? Has Erica's soul not expanded to a rich, robust red, the exact color of fine wine from the cellars of my friends, the Franciscan brothers? Is Hank not happy to have found a woman capable of loving his child? I ask you further, have I not done an excellent job of the task set before me? I am but a humble priest, but if God chooses me His wonders to perform, I do not question His judgment.

Do you realize that I am speaking to you in my own voice? The cat has run away with a tom who lives up at the old borax mine. She does not need my voice for yowling her pleasure at the tom's attentions. It is love, after all. I approve. The best thing is that before long, there will be more kittens. I am very fond of kittens.

I would have liked to officiate at the marriage of Erica and Hank, but she asked her own parish priest to come to this place and marry them, and that is good. I got in the final words, however. *Forever and ever, amen.* I think Erica might have heard me, too.

Now I am given another problem. A woman has occupied the rooms of Erica, and she is so transparent that I can barely see her. Her name is Brooke. She is troubled. Furthermore, she is with child.

Again I have my work cut out for me in this special place. *Madre de Dios,* is there no rest for a poor humble priest?

* * * * *

Watch for Pamela Browning's next
Harlequin American Romance,
BABY ENCHANTMENT,
available November 2003.

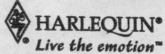

MIRA®

Once you cross that line, there's no turning back....

Judith Arnold

Heart
on the Line

Hip, savvy Loretta DeAngelo and sexy
thirtysomething Josh Kaplan are just friends.

Josh and Loretta are just friends because Josh has a girlfriend, Melanie—
1,200 miles away in Florida. They're just friends when he agrees to become
Loretta's "arranged" blind date for a ratings-boosting show. They're just
friends when he pretends to be her boyfriend to get her marriage-obsessed
family off her back. They're just friends when they fall into bed...and in love.

Now what? Sometimes, if you want something badly enough, you have to put
your heart on the line, even if it means doing something a little crazy....

**"Charming, humorous and loaded with New York references, this
lighthearted tale is satisfying subway reading."**
—Publishers Weekly on *Love in Bloom's*

Available the first week of August 2003 wherever paperbacks are sold!

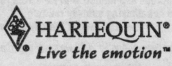

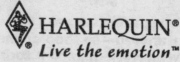

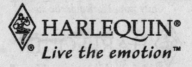

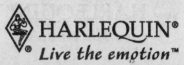